Outcaste

Outcaste

A Novel

Matampu Kunhukuttan

Translated from the Malayalam by
Vasanthi Sankaranarayanan

ALEPH

ALEPH BOOK COMPANY
An independent publishing firm
promoted by **Rupa Publications India**

Published in India in 2019
by Aleph Book Company
7/16 Ansari Road, Daryaganj
New Delhi 110 002

Copyright © Matampu Kunhukuttan 2019
Translation copyright © Vasanthi Sankaranarayanan 2019
The author has asserted his moral rights.

All rights reserved.

This is a work of fiction. Names, characters, places
and incidents are either the product of the author's
imagination or are used fictitiously and any resemblance
to any actual persons, living or dead, events or locales is
entirely coincidental.

No part of this publication may be reproduced,
transmitted, or stored in a retrieval system, in any form or
by any means, without permission in writing from Aleph
Book Company.

ISBN: 978-93-88292-49-8

1 3 5 7 9 10 8 6 4 2

Printed and bound in India by Replika Press Pvt. Ltd.

This book is sold subject to the condition that it shall not,
by way of trade or otherwise, be lent, resold, hired out, or
otherwise circulated without the publisher's prior consent
in any form of binding or cover other than that in which
it is published.

Contents

Author's Note / vii

Outcaste / 1

Afterword:
The Many Incarnations of Kuriyedathu Thatri by Dr J. Devika / 213

Translator's Note to the Current Edition: Twenty Years Later / 223

Translator's Introduction to the First Edition / 225

Appendix / 237

Author's Note

At the time of the events described in my novel, observance of chastity was expected only of women of aristocratic birth, meaning Namboodiri women, or antharjanams. It was not a requirement for women who were not considered to be of honourable birth. They could choose a man of their liking and later discard him as well. Even if they had a man in their lives, they could instal another as husband. This was the accepted social custom in Kerala a hundred years ago. This only pertained to Hindus, however. Christians and Muslims had different customs. Within Hinduism, too, sexual morality as a virtue was expected only of Namboodiri women. So the lords of Brahminism had decreed. The suspicion of adultery was not relevant to other women. The religious trial to cast out a Namboodiri woman suspected of adultery was a ritual created by the Namboodiris themselves.

This novel is based on the 1905 trial of a Namboodiri woman called Kuriyedathu Thatri (or Paptikutty), who had been accused of adultery, a trial which shook Malayali society then. The convulsions are felt even today.

The Namboodiris were a small community, and in order to preserve their knowledge, wealth and power, they established rigid codes of control. In their eyes, the purity of society was vested in the woman alone. A man's chastity was not subject to debate. Although other women, too, were held responsible for preserving the purity of their clan in varying degrees, I will not delve into these aspects of Kerala caste strictures as they are beyond the scope of this introduction and novel.

However, a Namboodiri woman is human. She too has feelings like all living beings. A body's hunger cannot be satiated by filling the stomach alone. Sexuality requires fulfilment. If societal norms do not permit it, loopholes will be found to quench that hunger.

It was not Kuriyedathu Thatri's intention to set right the flaws of creation by unleashing her sexual desires. However, even at a young age, she was sexually very aware. Perhaps, this was because she was being prepared to fulfil some destiny. Perhaps, this destiny was to drag powerful Namboodiris on to the right path. While it is true that there had been earlier instances of Namboodiri women choosing to have relationships with men other than their husbands—and these had resulted in excommunication, with the guilty men having to leave their homes for distant lands in order to absolve themselves of their sins—Thatri's case was unique for a reason.

Even though she was aware of the consequences of her actions and was sure that she would have to face some kind of a trial, she still slept with sixty-four men.

But no one will be able to say with any degree of certainty why Thatri conducted this kind of a manhunt. It was definitely not for sexual fulfilment. If the aim was sexual satiation, one or two physically fit men would have been enough. It was not to earn money either. It is said that she had a youthful yearning for beautiful things. But we can't wholly believe that either. Could revenge have been her motive? To punish the men who desired her body, she used the same body to excommunicate them. But we do not know for sure if she mentioned any of the names with a motive for revenge.

One thing, however, can be stated with certainty. It was inevitable that the Namboodiris who indulged in all manner of excesses because of their wealth and immense pride in their caste would get their comeuppance. Any stone fort can easily be opened from within. The impregnable fort that the Namboodiris built was opened by Thatri from the inside. The strong bolt that couldn't be broken open even by elephants was dragged open by the brass bangle that adorned the hand of that young girl. Any community has its ups and downs. That is decided by fate and history. The heady days of the Namboodiris ended. And Kuriyedathu Thatri was the reason for their downfall.

Matampu Kunhukuttan
Kiraloor 2018

1

Sixty-four arts.[1]
A patron sage for each art.
The sixty-fifth—the lord of all art—Siva.
And in the end, Maya, the Illusion.
Sixty-four men.[2]
All of them sages.
The sixty-fifth, the Lord of all men.
And in the end, Paptikutty.
Goddess of illusion. Beauty of the three worlds.
Brahmins.
Kshatriyas.
Vaisyas.
Sudras.[3]
Sixty-four in all.
And then?
'Enough,' said the King. 'Let's stop.'
Purusha, Prakriti.[4]
Power, illusion.
Paptikutty.
Cheriyedathu Paptikutty.
The embodiment of death.

---

[1] The sixty-four arts are described in Bharata's *Natyashastra*.
[2] The heads of the sixty-four Namboodiri families.
[3] The four castes of ancient India based on social functions: Brahmins—scholars and priests, Kshatriyas—rulers, Vaisyas—traders and Sudras—menial labourers.
[4] Male and female energy represented as human form and nature, respectively.

Dancer in burial grounds.

Did the list spare anyone?

Excluded from the list were the undistinguished: those Namboodiris who stayed home and whiled away their lives, chewing and spitting betel leaves. Excluded were the ordinary overlords, who wore immaculate white clothes and followed the ceremonial sword and shield that led them. No Nair[5] serving in Namboodiri households or crawling from place to place lugging Kathakali costume boxes was on that list.

No, they were not on the list either: the Vaisyas, who made a living by begging and selling from house to house.

All that was affected was the country's glory.

Sixty-four learned men, masters of art, experts in the Vedas and Vedanta, true sages.

And then, the King himself.

'Stop! Enough!'

The trial proceedings were stopped. The Chief Canonical Investigator was bathed in perspiration. The other investigators, masters in philosophical concepts, looked at each other and heaved a sigh of relief. But the country was despoiled.

The descendants of Manu fell on their heads with a crash. The threads of canonical law swung to and fro in a quivering atmosphere.

Time poured water in a purificatory rite of blazing torches placed on the hump of Brahminism, steeped in prosperity and fame.[6] The burning glow of the torches spread in the directions of the blowing winds. Brahminism stretched its limbs and opened its eyes wide to witness the fiery annihilation of the caste system, only to close its eyes again and thrash about helplessly in an epileptic fit.

---

[5] A caste group of wealthy warlords.
[6] A reminder of a similar custom performed on the fourth day after a girl comes of age; an act of purification.

Those sages, composers of the *Rig Veda*, who came away from the land of the five rivers and covered a span of a thousand years, now witnessed, benumbed, the destruction of their future generations. They prayed to their gods.

The King gave his orders.

The trial began.

∽

The trial of the abased woman was conducted briskly. Doubts gave way to clear evidence. Nothing will be left unproved. The King—you know who he is? The very incarnation of Lord Sri Rama![7] The Lord of Dharma! Is it possible to fool him? After imprisoning the Object,[8] whose adultery had been proved, in the outhouse (the place for the polluted), her relatives and other Namboodiris met the King and explained the matter to him.

The order was communicated to the canonical investigators and the temple attendants.

The Special Investigator was also contacted, informed of the King's orders and given the responsibility for conducting the investigation. Soldiers were sent to guard the women's quarters. The country waited with bated breath. How many would be incriminated? What does the Object want?

It seemed that she was not satisfied with five or ten names. The sure signs of Kali! Undoubtedly, the beginning of Kali Yuga.[9]

In the outer yard of the palace, the traditional white cloth atop a black rug was spread to receive the King.

---

[7] Hero of the Ramayana and an incarnation of Mahavishnu.

[8] The individual on trial was not even accorded the status of gender.

[9] According to Hindu cosmology, the last and most evil age; the other three being Krita, Treta and Dwapara.

Just twenty years old! Alluringly beautiful! Urvasi[10] personified, the most beautiful woman in all the three worlds. Paptikutty! The Goddess of Revenge!

The investigators woke up interpreting the *Sankarasmriti*[11] and fell asleep chanting the *Manusmriti*.[12] As they slept, the punishment for impurity, as yet unknown, began to take shape. Those keepers of the cellars of customs woke up with a shudder and looked at each other suspiciously. They argued. Can the age-old customs of a country be ignored? The King's command—can it be opposed?

They sought a way out to atone for their own sins, finding peace by fiddling with their sacred threads.[13] The investigators had lost touch with their natural instincts derived from the wind and the sun, and instead, sought answers in books.

It was time to declare the final order.

The light from the lamps made of wood reached all the way to the upper storey of the palace. As the smoke rose from the castor-oil lamps, the dark faces of the investigators grew hideous. The King was unperturbed.

Where is the Brahmin child to proclaim their pronouncements?

The Chief Canonical Investigator rinsed his hands and stood up.

Midnight, a time when the five elements of nature melt and fuse into one, stood still. The four directions—East, West, North and South—sang in praise of their guardian spirits. Time shivered and stood still within the four walls of the palace. Daylight hesitated

---

[10] One of the four famous dancers in Indra's (Lord of the Devas) court. The others are Rambha, Menaka and Tilotthama, famed for their beauty and seductive charm.

[11] A law book codifying a set of canonical laws, supposed to have been compiled by Adi Sankara, an eighth century teacher-saint.

[12] A law book codifying canonical laws compiled by Manu.

[13] The thread worn by the upper castes, slung across the left shoulder and fastened just above the waist. The wearer is symbolically bound to righteousness and is considered to be reborn spiritually.

to peep in, afraid of the guards.

His Highness the King arrived and sat on the throne. Contentment reigned on his round face. An oil lamp beside him, fashioned from three metals signifying caste, religion and custom—bearing signs of a thousand flaws, patched up a thousand times—flickered and burned.

A Namboodiri wife turning to prostitution! And that too, on purpose!

A maiden confined to the inner quarters, never exposed to sunlight. The daughter of Thazhath House. That beautiful woman, who had mastered poetry and grammar.

How can it be explained? What is to be done? Ethical canons... customs...

What led to this?

Orders? Fear?

The King may be deemed cruel in observing strict justice. He belonged to the clan of Sri Rama, the One who had banished his own dear queen to the forest, suspecting her chastity.

This same King had risen respectfully from his throne to welcome the white-skinned foreigners who had come seeking to establish a factory. On his own, he had made an offer.

The courtiers sang praises of his limitless generosity. He was mindful of his heritage. The scion of the clan of Ikshvaku![14]

I offer you a place to build your forts and bastions.

I sanction the commencement of sea trade.

The presents offered to royalty—the sword and the silk cloth—were preserved. Daily prayers were offered at twilight.

The foreign physicians were given what they wanted in the

---

[14] A king of the Sun-clan who was supposed to be one of the ancestors of Lord Rama.

tradition of Raghu.[15] Those who came from Nazareth[16] were welcomed in the traditional way, with a measure of paddy, and given a place to settle down. The Jain monks were welcomed with the eight auspicious objects.[17] Special prayer halls were constructed from which Mohammed Nabi's sayings reverberated.

Unity—Brotherhood—Secularism.

Even in the preparations concerning his nightly routine before he went to sleep, the King was scrupulous. He visited his wives by turn and blessed and enjoyed them according to their seniority.

The God of Dharma![18] The impartial upholder of justice. His subjects were punished for proven crimes, drowned in the backwaters with weights tied around their waists. He pretended to befriend the visitors, according them a status above the highest caste. He performed his routine duties sincerely for the welfare of the kingdom on which the sun never set. While bowing to gun power, he insisted that his own soldiers use only bows and arrows and wear their long hair in topknots. He instructed the soldiers to leave their weapons in his palace. He slept on an intricately carved sandalwood cot and savoured erotic verses.

The air in the palace was still. The melmundu[19] slipped from the King's shoulders. His emerald chain was bathed in perspiration. His flabby chest heaved.

'You may begin.'

'Let the verdict be spelt out. Where is the Brahmin child?' The

---

[15] The founder of the clan of Lord Rama.

[16] The reference is to the Jews who came to Cochin and settled there.

[17] These are paddy, rice, a mirror, lamp, water, sandalwood paste, the Ramayana and cloth.

[18] The carrying out of personal duties in a righteous manner in order to maintain socio-cosmic harmony. Note the number of sarcastic references to the King's behaviour.

[19] An upper cloth worn across the chest and shoulder.

Chief Canonical Investigator's lips were pursed. His voice hid itself in the pit of his throat.

The total destruction of Parasurama's[20] clan. Can it be borne?

The concept of four castes was made by me.[21]

I made it. For *me*. And for my grandchildren.

Yet a Kshatriya gives the orders. Perhaps he is interested in the welfare of the people. It may not be an act inspired by selfish indulgence, but by true feeling for the people. Perhaps, but so what!

The King became the very instrument of time.

The investigators who represented internal authority dropped their melmundu several times.[22]

The Chief Canonical Investigator repeated the same question several times: 'Do you wish to name anyone else?' He could not show any leniency.

What next?

The symbols of finality: the ritual of water being poured, signifying the severing of relationships, the closing of the gates and offering last rites to the dead, the offering of a feast of atonement to the pure-minded.

Oh my God! Oh!

Never before had rites been performed on such a scale.

Sixty-four people.

'Need I say any more?'

'Enough,' the King ordered. 'Enough. Let's stop.'

---

[20]Parasurama is supposed to have established Brahmins from the North in Kerala. The purpose of this sixth incarnation of Vishnu was to humble the Kshatriyas and protect the Brahmins. After completely vanquishing the Kshatriya clans and distributing their land to Brahmins, he was left with no land to sit in meditation. So he threw his axe into the sea and retrieved a piece of land, which was later known as Kerala. This is the legend of the origin of Kerala.

[21]The Bhagavad Gita, Chapter IV, verse 13.

[22]A symbolic expression of doubt.

Is anything else required to spell out the annihilation of the land of Cochin?

The Brahmin boy dipped himself in the pond sixty-four times and emerged dripping wet. An immersion for every polluted name called aloud.

Just naming a prostitute is a maha-papam, a great sin. And corrupting a pure woman? There can be no atonement for such a crime.

∽

At midnight, when the Chief Canonical Investigator who had referred all night to the canonical law looked up bleary-eyed, some miles away, in the small circle of light around a wooden lamp, a young Namboodiri sat in his house, tearing his hair and agonizing over his dreams of a world that lay beyond the land of the King of Cochin. His imagination wandered into realms beyond the Western Ghats and even the great Himalayas. A world filled with people other than those who wore loincloths and carried palm-leaf umbrellas; people who did not observe the laws of untouchability. They must indeed be the highest of the high castes!

'What did they do on similar occasions? Were they apprehensive? Did they cast out intelligent, able people, exiling them from the land of their birth? Did they, too, shut the doors of the women's quarters and deny them the light from the outside world?'

The twenty-year-old Namboodiri scratched his beard and twisted his long hair and knotted it. He shut his streaming eyes in an attempt to embrace the goddess of sleep. He tried in vain to remember the essential mantra.[23] But he could only call to mind the new.

Change.

---

[23] A special arrangement of words which, if uttered repeatedly, aids concentration and is believed to empower the chanter.

Revolution.

Words that had never been heard before in Kerala, or ever found a place in Malayalam.

Revolution.

The King searched for the Chief Canonical Investigator; his people sought the roots of revolution.

'Not another word,' was the entreaty.

The command of the King, whose very words seemed afraid of him, emerged. He said this from a towering throne. 'Why not?' asked the King.

'Nothing. But I have my doubts, as nothing like this has ever happened before,' said the Investigator, fearing consequences.

'I, too, am uneasy. The erudite people from my court who surround me, I know them. Let Vishnu, the God of the essence of the Trinity,[24] help us.'

'Isn't the Brahmin child there? Isn't he ready?'

The attendant in charge of the procedure sounded the huge tongue-shaped pendulum of the brass bell twelve times, apparently controlling time itself. But he was controlled by the King.

He collapsed at the clangour he had made.

'No more delays!' said the King with feigned anxiety, presiding over the destruction of the Namboodiris. 'Starting tomorrow, let there be an elaborate floral worship of Lord Vishnu. After that do whatever else is required. Did you hear me? Tell the Namboodiri and make him do it. Where is the Chief Accountant?'

The corpulent Chief Accountant, whose every limb reflected slavish respect for the King, arrived.

'Haven't you heard?'

'Yes, Your Excellency.'

---

[24] The Trinity—Brahma, the Creator; Vishnu, the Preserver; and Siva, the Destroyer.

From the outhouse, Paptikutty, waiting for the total annihilation of her five senses, called out imperiously, 'The rest, my aunt will narrate.'

2

Twilight.

Chematiri Otikkan,[25] who had reached the bathing house near the pond for his evening rituals, heard the sound of the lizard[26] calling. He froze. This inauspicious portent so shook this man of action that he forgot the mantra for his evening recital.

'No, it can't happen,' Chematiri Otikkan consoled himself. Not yet. Surely it did not signify his death. He had longer to live. Then why this sign! Otikkan, famed for his intelligence, stood bewildered.

'A girl is born at Thazhath House.'

These words fell like molten lead on Otikkan's ears as he stood with water cupped in his palms, ready to recite the Gayatri Mantra.[27] The water in his palms rippled. The science of astrology drew square patterns[28] in his mind. He, the embodiment of Varahamihira,[29] the astrologer of astrologers, heard the clatter of cowrie shells being

---

[25] One who is proficient in the recital of the Vedas.

[26] The sound of the lizard, depending on the time, place and occasion, is supposed to be an omen—good or bad. There is a whole set of omens based on lizard sounds, described in a text titled *Gowlishastram*.

[27] A sacred verse that celebrates knowledge. Brahmins recite this as many times as possible during the day. Women were not allowed to learn or recite this particular mantra.

[28] Astrologers use squares to calculate the position and influence of the planets on an individual.

[29] One of the famous nine courtiers—known as the Nine Gems (Navaratnas)—in the court of King Vikramaditya of the Gupta dynasty, Varahamihira is considered to be the father of Indian astrology.

placed on the squares.

'Siva! Siva!' Chematiri Otikkan stared at the speaker, opening his palms and letting the water flow away as he closed his eyes in despair.

'What is it, Otikkan, why are you so perturbed?'

'Great news! Didn't you say that a girl is born at Thazhath House?'

'Yes.'

'Her horoscope is indeed outstanding.'

'What—what?'

'Wonder how many will be ensnared. It is the end.'

'Why, is it so bad?'

Chematiri Otikkan completed the ritual the speaker had interrupted. He went into the bathing house reciting the Gayatri Mantra.

Prostitute!

Would it come true? The indications were that the whole clan would be destroyed.

Can I trust my own prediction?

Can the great Varahamihira's calculations fail? What about his own? I can swear on the temple bell. 'My Vedic recitals and astrological predictions cannot fail.'

First born of the Thazhath Namboodiris! Fruit of the first labour pains! Try as he might, Otikkan could not control his thoughts. His mind, a forest in which multiplications and divisions took place continuously and tumultuously. Both the birth star and the time of birth embodied human form before his mind's eye. The exact time took shape and approached him. Everything unfolded and became clear.

No, no more doubts.

'Aum, Bhur Bhuvaswa, Tat Savitur Varenyam.'[30] Otikkan's voice rose.

'Look, Chematiri, I knew I'd find you here. A girl is born in my house. Can you tell me what her horoscope is like?'

Thazhath Namboodiri had been searching for Chematiri Otikkan to ask him what the future had in store for his eldest daughter. What could Chematiri say? If he remained silent, Namboodiri would be unhappy. 'It is a girl, isn't it? You will have no problem finding a bridegroom for her. Her time will come as soon as she turns fifteen. Isn't that enough for now?'

'No, give me all the details and I shall be satisfied.'

'Come on Namboodiri, isn't it a girl? That will do. Why think any further? She has a long life.' Chematiri, immersed in his rituals, said nothing more.

He lingered by the pond, not realizing that it had grown dark. The hourglass filled and emptied, not once, but several times. Chematiri's wife waited at home near the sacrificial pit, chanting, holding the black thread[31] around her neck. What was the matter with him, she wondered. She had never known this to happen before. Should she check what time it was?

Meanwhile, in the outhouse, the younger Namboodiris were reading *Shakuntalam*. The young boys who came from all over the land to learn the recital of the Vedas and the essence of poetry were seated around them.

Why not call her son? Her stomach rumbled with hunger. She tried to remember how long she had been married to Chematiri. She was only ten at that time and Chematiri Otikkan had just completed his spiritual training.

---

[30] A free translation of the Gayatri Mantra is 'Let that brilliance which is worth acquiring, inspire our intellects.'

[31] Namboodiri women wear black threads around their necks after marriage. Every day the woman holds her thread and prays for the welfare of her husband.

What could have happened?

Usually so regular in his habits: no deviation from routine, never ate more or less, not the slightest indiscipline. What could have happened today to change that? She went upto the outer veranda, wanting to send the young boys after Chematiri.

But that also was not done since no one ever had to remind him about anything. 'Are you all there, brothers...children?'

'Pachu, your elder brother hasn't come back. It is very late.'

'I, too, have been wondering. What has happened to elder brother? Shall I go and look for him?'

'Don't call him. Just find out what he is doing. Unni, just go along and take a look. Be careful. Don't startle him.'

'I've been waiting for elder brother to return, to clear a doubt.'

'Who said it, Sankara or Manu? Do you remember, brother Vasu?'

'I cannot remember the whole of *Sankarasmriti*. But I know *this* verse by heart. So it can only be Manu. Not that I have grave doubts. Doesn't it talk about the adultery of housewives?'

The adultery of housewives!

Chematiri Otikkan, returning from the bathing house, heard the words of his brothers and stood thinking on the steps that led to the house. Suddenly it all came together.

'What is happening?'

At the sound of Chematiri Otikkan's voice, all talk from the outhouse ceased.

'Nothing much. We are unable to recollect who said it, Sankara or Manu.'

'Is it Vasu who can't remember? Or Pachu? Anyway, even if you can recollect it, there is no point. We will think of it after eighteen years.'

He stepped into the inner veranda.

This house of the Otikkans, famed for five generations as a

family of erudite people, was where the Vedas and the Shastras had virtually taken residence. Chematiri Otikkan's father was none other than the famous Akkithar, a man who had fasted twice a month for the past thirty-two years, eating only one small ball of rice on the day before the new moon. It was increased to two, three and so on, till on the full moon day, he ate fifteen balls of rice. Again, he gradually reduced one ball every day until the fifteenth day when he would eat only one ball of rice. Such was his discipline in the matter of food. Every day at dawn, one would find him at the temple, and he would return home only after the twilight worship. As soon as he came back, he had his dinner—a small ball of rice—his one meal for the whole day! Only then did he drink a glass of water. To him it was the same—whether he ate one ball of rice or fifteen. Soon after his meal, he went to sleep. He never enquired into the matters of the house and spoke but rarely. When he spoke, it was only to his eldest son, Chematiri. If someone had to say something to him, they had to wait for the time before he left for the temple or after he returned. At other times, he was absorbed in relentless penance. His physique was impressive, his hair and beard were twined and matted into locks. His waist cloth barely covered his knees. He carried a walking stick taller than a man and a round palm-leaf umbrella which seemed to cover the skies.

'Has he retired for the night?' Chematiri enquired.

'We saw him going in that direction.'

'Was it a long while ago?'

'Elder brother, you want to see father? What is the urgency?'

Whatever the urgency, no one woke him.

'Shall we try, Pachu?'

'Vasudevan will be a better choice.' Pachu Otikkan excused himself. 'If it has to be done, our elder brother is the right person.'

'Let me see…' Chematiri got up and went to the inner veranda and peered into the room where his father was sleeping. Akkithar had taken off his waist cloth and spread it beneath him on the bare floor where he lay. Chematiri's eyes misted over when he saw his father lying thus.

I can't wake him. No, this can wait till he is on his way to the temple tomorrow.

'Who is it? What do you want?'

Chematiri was stopped in his tracks by his father's gentle yet awe-inspiring voice. His blood vessels expanded. My father knows, he thought. Was this intrusion a nuisance? Oh, God! Help me.

'It is me, Unni,' mumbled Chematiri.

'What is it? You may ask. Don't hesitate.'

God! Ancestral Deities! Protect me.

'It seems that a girl is born at Thazhath House.'

'Yes.'

'I heard it when I was praying, making an offering of water to the deities.[32] Namboodiri came, requesting me to prepare the horoscope.'

'Yes.'

'I told him he would not have any problems with regard to her marriage.'

'Didn't you also tell him that she would never be a widow?'

Siva! Siva! He knows everything.

'I was very perplexed. I have never seen such signs. I thought that I might have gone wrong in my inferences. It was very upsetting. When I grew thoroughly restless, I came here.'

'All right. Now go to sleep. You haven't made any mistakes. Advise your brothers to be careful for their own good. Have they gone to sleep?'

---

[32]Offerings during prayers are made with different objects—water, flowers, leaves and fruits. Water offering is the most common among them and is used in all forms of worship.

What! Here was a warning that Pachu and Vasu should be careful. So that part of his inference was also correct. Oh, God!

'Is there no remedy?'

'It is very difficult. Still with the power of the Gayatri Mantra…'

Chematiri Otikkan paced to and fro in the front veranda, unmindful of the passage of time. He stepped into the open courtyard and gazed at the stars. He tore a betel leaf and counted its veins,[33] closed his nostrils and concentrated,[34] reciting the canons of astrology. He made mathematical calculations according to the *Leelavathi*[35] and came to the conclusion that it was the fault of the times.

Not the fault of karma.

They had to suffer and endure.

∽

The tribe, which had originated with Angiras, Brihaspati and Kasyapa,[36] generations of which had proudly uttered the names of the heads of their clans and preserved the true sound of the great Vedas uttered by the sages without marring the original tone and rhythm set by those divine beings…

This spiritual realm was now invaded and conquered by secular authority. Ignorance ruled. The King, yearning for brahminical

---

[33]Reading signs and predicting the future is done in many ways. Using cowries and drawing squares is the most scientific form of astrology. But there are less scientific methods of reading signs such as listening to the sounds of lizards, watching the ripples in water mixed with turmeric and lime or doing calculations by studying the veins on a betel leaf.

[34]'Closing the nose and preserving the arrow' is to denote the preservation of energy before the prediction of the future. It is another method of reading astrological signs.

[35]A book of mathematics, believed to have been compiled by Bhaskaracharya.

[36]Names of some of the great sages of ancient India.

qualities, longed to be a sage. The Ruler of the Earth, with all her plenitude, still yearned to be a Brahmin.

A fusion of the two enlightened castes—the Brahmins and the Kshatriyas. The clan of Viswamitra[37] grew. Aeons slept with their eyes shut tight. The descendants of Parasurama, the Brahmin who annihilated kingly power twenty-one times over, were now busy hiding the glory of being Brahmin. Now, the sacrificial pits that used to hold the fires lit by arani[38] burned brightly with the sparks produced from polishing swords. The holy fires in the northern section of the quadrangular houses smouldered and blackened the walls. In the hall of sacrifice, the helpless wail of animals made the Chief Priest squirm as he tasted the flesh from the sacrificial fire. The women's quarters moaned. The seat meant for the wife on the right side of the man who offered sacrifices increased from one to many.

The darbha[39] used to light the sacrificial fires was never long enough. Four or five stalks had to be tied together for the required length. The wives of the master of sacrifice fought for the remains of sacrificial food.

The fault of the times.

Not of karma.

The sustaining strength of the Gayatri Mantra. The weapon was indeed grand but the wielder did not know how to use it.

Sacred verses reduced to mere words. Sounds dancing on the tips of tongues, faltering and whirling helplessly with displaced words, never reaching the temple of the heart.

The physical body, fused from the five elements, shamelessly sought worldly pleasures and grew in strength. Woman power,

---

[37] A king who became a sage through untiring penance.
[38] A piece of wood used to light the sacrificial fire.
[39] Sacred grass used in sacrifices and other rituals.

pushed aside carelessly with the back of the hand, was helpless. It withdrew into the loneliness of the four walls of the women's quarters and then deeper into the prayer rooms and the emptiness of the northern rooms—their walls blackened by the fumes of sacrificial fires praying to the sun. The very foundations of the Namboodiri houses, soaked in the incessant tears of these women, began to crumble. The new generation, delivered onto the ground wet with tears, shut their eyes tight, fearing the light. They even forgot to cry.

The great Goddess of Illusion, Mahamaya,[40] slept, unconscious. The four functional castes turned into watertight hereditary rights. Even then the few utterances of the sacred verses echoed in the air. The eight guiding spirits[41] joined their forces and sent destructive shooting stars.

Brahminism coughed and spat.

'The beginning of Kali Yuga! No doubt at all!'

'The signs are becoming clearer.'

What could a lone Akkithar, scholar of scholars, do? When a thousand similar priests indulged in love-play? Can one committed performer bear the entire burden, when a thousand other performers made elaborate preparations for the amorous Festival of the Moon?[42]

Chematiri Otikkan stopped pacing; his feet pierced the earth. What now?

It was time to have a bath and prepare for the daily routine.

---

[40] The Mother Goddess in the form of illusion can cover or reveal the truth depending on the sincerity of the worship offered or the purity of life the person making the sacrifice leads.

[41] The reference is to the eight Namboodiri families which are considered to be the original ones that Parasurama brought from distant lands and installed in Kerala.

[42] A poem written approximately 400 years ago. The text describes a festival held in honour of the Moon God by courtesans to obtain the fulfilment of their sexual desires.

Pachu and Vasu, unable to understand the reason for their elder brother's wakefulness, muttered to each other and finally fell asleep when they should have been awake.

3

Two dining halls, one facing east, the other, west. Between them the kitchen. At mealtimes each dining hall could accommodate a hundred plantain leaves[43] laid out in a single stretch.

At noon and in the evening, the bell outside the dining hall was rung continuously—the tapping of an iron rod on a piece of rail. At the sound of this bell, the brood of young Namboodiris, who gossiped in private spaces and in common halls, felt the pangs of hunger and moved in a procession towards the bathing houses.[44] The hangers-on among these parasitical Namboodiris argued vehemently over trivia, such as the third Namboodiri's new bungalow, his private earnings or his secret affairs.

Both dining halls had to be cleaned twice or thrice every day after these communal meals.

These hangers-on, who also functioned as special courtiers, would then withdraw into their respective dens for an afternoon nap. They also discussed and decided what type of 'companions' they would require for their evening's relaxation.

The overall management of the household was personally handled by Achan Namboodiri[45] himself. He had total control. Each of his younger brothers had his own particular hobby. The second in line was crazy about Kathakali and was a famed teacher of the Vedas. The third and fourth were interested in elephants and

---

[43]Traditionally in Kerala, meals are served on green plantain leaves.
[44]It was customary among Namboodiris and the upper castes of Kerala to bathe before lunch and dinner to purify themselves.
[45]Achan Namboodiri literally means 'Father Namboodiri'.

in the supervision of small principalities. The fifth spent his life in the sixty-four squares of the chessboard. He also had a flair for brief affairs with women. The sixth specialized in card games. He was thorough with the various moves and steps of the game and played through the night.

The House of Thazhamangalam was wellknown throughout the state of Cochin. Every year, their rental from properties topped 200,000 measures of paddy and an equal quantity as monies from the temples they controlled. They also owned petty principalities all over the land, including forests which spread into the Tamil country. In effect, they were wealthier and more powerful than the King himself.

The day-to-day expenses of the inmates ran to about a hundred kilograms of rice. More than fifty Namboodiris were permanent residents—servers, attendants and relatives—besides an equal number of women. Then there were those who claimed blood relationships and arrived under the pretext of helping with the daily rituals and offerings of worship. Friends, parasites, assistants—all helping each Namboodiri in his brutal pursuits. A crowd of Namboodiris, Nairs and temple attendants.

Achan Namboodirippad married thrice and had children by all three wives. He managed his household with the same tradition and foresight as his father, who had prepared a hundred-year plan. His father had heard of the cloth mills established by foreigners in Coimbatore and Bombay and invested a year's profits from his income in shares. After all, the goddess of wealth is fickle! When rulership and authority peak, dharma will be forgotten. He knew that time would not wait for any man, and so, year after year, he invested a portion of the profits in company shares.

'He is demented!' Other Namboodiris made fun of him. 'Thazhamangalam is indeed weird. Company shares!'

He paid no attention to such mockery but taught his eldest

son the mantra for the Kali Yuga:

> Please the white men.
> If possible, become a partner in their trade.
> Learn the English language in secret,
> Oppose it publicly.
> And condemn it loudly as the language of barbarians.

'Can the tongue accustomed to chanting the Vedas utter that barbaric language?' thundered Achan Namboodirippad, who repeated the Gayatri Mantra a thousand times every day.

What does Mazhamangalam[46] say in this respect?

What was the accepted custom?

All this by men who had concubines all over the country and four or five legally wedded wives. By what law? That of Sankara? Or Manu?

∽

One day, a traveller from a village next to Kalpathi River[47] arrived at the Thazhamangalam House. He was wearing the traditional costume of Brahmins fashioned from a torn length of cloth. The melmundu around his waist was threadbare. He was so thin and emaciated that the weight of his sacred thread appeared to crush him. His long hair, drawn into a knot at the back of his head, was unkempt. Nobody noticed a traveller in soiled clothes who had not seen water for many lives. Why should they? How many such people arrived daily seeking food? And not just one meal! Even if he lingered for a year or claimed a monthly salary, nobody would know. No one knew except the overseer Kesavan.

---

[46] A Namboodiri who codified the rituals of purification.

[47] A river near Palghat, in northern Kerala. Palghat lies on the border of Kerala and Tamil Nadu and has a sizeable population of Tamil Brahmins known as pattars.

However, this traveller met Achan Namboodiri in an outhouse adjacent to the house, where he rested on a rosewood bed with two dependent Namboodiris flanking him—both badly dressed and with scanty hair tied up—images of servility.

'Where is Kesavan?' Achan Namboodiri moved, his massive body suddenly alert. 'Kesavan, how many elephants do we own now?'

'Only Kuttikrishnan and Padmanabhan.'[48]

'That is not possible, Kesavan. Undoubtedly—no.'

'Yes, Your Excellency.' Kesavan Nair, a landowner among the clan of assistants to landowners, bowed low in supplication. He covered his mouth in an attempt to hide the overflowing betel juice.

'Isn't there a clumsy one? That beast... What is its name—something unusual...'

'Yes. Akbar.'

'Ah! Where is it now? Wherever it is, tomorrow you will release him in our forest near Palghat.'[49]

'But, Your Excellency, that...er...'

'What? Haven't you understood what I said?'

'Not fully.'

'Oh Lord! Kesavan, I didn't think you were so dull.'

Once again, Kesavan agreed.

'Have you forgotten the dinner for the Viceroy, the day after tomorrow?'

'So...so...?'

'He is very fond of hunting. He has asked whether it will be possible to shoot an elephant. So when he arrives should he not see an elephant in our forest? Now do you understand? Untie the chains and let him loose.'

---

[48] Namboodiris were so rich that they could keep elephants as pets.
[49] A town in northern Kerala.

'Master, isn't it too much...'

'Come on, Kesavan, you think it is too much. Why can't you understand when I tell you something? I, too, am not very happy about this. But do as I tell you. Where is my brother Neelakandan? Find out if he is in his bungalow.'

Kesavan left, his paunch heaving.

'What am I to do with such brainless fools?'

His sycophants murmured in implicit agreement.

The traveller from Palghat who had waited till his turn came appeared in front of Achan Namboodiri. He prostrated before Achan, weeping, his palms pressed together in respectful greeting.

'Are you a Pattar? Where are you from?'

'From Palghat.'

'Well, have you been waiting for a long time? Have you eaten?'

'Yes.'

'Then?'

'I have studied the subject of land survey. Shastri[50] said that in your house...'

'Is that so? Our Venkichan (Venkatakrishna)? The reader of scriptures?'

'Yes.'

'Besides the science of land survey, have you learnt English also?'

'Yes.'

'Can you converse with the white men?'

'Yes.'

'Then stay here today. I am going to Palghat tomorrow. There is a dinner in honour of the Viceroy the day after. Let's go together. After that…'

Achan Namboodiri valued a person who knew English, whoever he might be. In this case, Brahmin. Good. So much the better.

---

[50]The title given to a Tamil Brahmin teacher; one who knows the Shastras.

'Go to the office room, meet the storekeeper and get whatever you need.'

The Iyer walked away, his eyes brimming. Achan Namboodiri continued to play with his silver betel leaf box. The overseer led his brother Neelakandan to him.

'Did you send for me?'

'I had asked Kesavan to inform you. Have you understood?'

'Not altogether.'

'That elephant which was caught from…?'

'You mean Akbar?'

'That clumsy creature. I have been advised that he is not a good elephant; he's physically inferior.'

'Is he that bad? I'm not so sure.'

'Anyway, day after tomorrow, I have decided to hold a dinner party for the Viceroy at Palghat.'

'I heard about it.'

'The Viceroy is a great huntsman and is keen to shoot an elephant.'

'Brother, if you have already decided… Even so, to allow Akbar to be shot…'

'Neelakandan, do you know that most of our forests are in the Malabar[51] area? We do not have the necessary title deeds and documents for them. Are you aware of that?'

'So I have heard.'

'Most of it was earned by our father. Malabar is under the direct control of the British.'

'I understand all that. But still, to kill our tame elephant for that…'

---

[51] While the native states of Cochin and Travancore were ruled by kings, Malabar, the northern portion of present-day Kerala, was part of the Madras Presidency during the British rule.

'Your loyalty is to the elephant, is it? Ha! Ha!' Achan roared with laughter. Neelakandan moved aside to avoid the spittle.

Neelakandan had heard people say that his eldest brother was the very image of their father. Now he couldn't help noticing how, like his father, his brother appeared to be a conservative, traditional Namboodiri, but on closer examination, one realized how very progressive he really was! Though Neelakandan was unhappy at the thought of sacrificing an elephant which was a dear friend to him, he was impressed by his elder brother's cunning. Other Brahmin households were busy selling land—their only means of livelihood—in order to indulge in temporary pleasures, hastening their downfall. Most such houses were steeped in debt. They had just enough to get by from one day to the next. That was all. Thazhamangalam owned six such poor houses and was steadily growing wealthier. Indeed, his brother's management was very efficient.

'You may go, Neelakandan. Forget about the elephant.' The protector of elephants escaped to his bungalow. There were more elephants to tend to, feed, discipline—so many things to look into.

For a long time he had dreamt of a she-elephant calving in Thazhamangalam House. They had bought Lakshmikutty at his insistence. Since only bull elephants were put to work, paying for a she-elephant, that too at Thazhamangalam? Sheer madness! The news bewildered everyone. However, one should never scrutinize the actions of the great and try to gauge their intentions. Instead, one should know the result beforehand and use it to justify the action.

Neelakandan had imagined that when Akbar was sexually aroused he could be left with Lakshmikutty. He had chosen a small field next to the bungalow for such a mating. A small lake for the water play of elephants. A grove full of special palms, plantains and dense wildwood. A sanctified bridal chamber for Lakshmikutty's nuptials.

He could watch from the bungalow.

An elephant should be born in his house.

Let Lakshmikutty and Akbar mate there.

The male elephant scratched his cheeks. His forehead was swollen rousing the she-elephant with his seductive scent. Penis swollen, he touched his mate with his trunk, scratched the earth with his feet, looked around for a lonely place and flapped his large ears. The she-elephant groaned in passion, helping her mate, lying between the two tree trunks where she was placed by him, shuffling, unable to bear his pressing weight, roaring in pain when he finally filled her. The wild scent of the elephants mating aroused the other elephants who pulled and strained at their chains. But Akbar would now be the Viceroy's prey. Then there was—

Gopalan.

Sankarankutty.

Sekharan. [52]

It shouldn't matter.

There were other bull elephants.

He could consult Ichatha, his younger brother, who was the only one who understood his craze for elephants.

The third Namboodiri felt a sudden tenderness for his brother. Ichatha liked not only elephants, but oxen, buffaloes, birds and dogs. Oxen and buffaloes! He, who couldn't tolerate any craze other than that for elephants, ridiculed his brother.

'He can't sleep without the odour of cowdung.'

Probably that was why he was so crazy about sweeper women.

ᔈ

'Kesavan, I was just thinking, even though it is not necessary, why not arrange a day's Kathakali performance along with the dinner

---

[52] Elephants are symbols of prosperity. In Kerala, elephants are used in temple festivals to carry idols in procession. As pets, they are named like the children in the family.

for the Viceroy? It will please my brother.'

The Kathakali crazy Namboodiri would be in seventh heaven if it could be arranged. A performance before the Viceroy of India! Achan Namboodiri was in truth indifferent to the art of Kathakali and often poked fun at its mute gestures and outlandish costumes. But in organizing this event he could fulfil two goals—an unforgettable experience for no less a personage than the Viceroy of the country and a pleasurable evening for his Kathakali loving brother.

'Master, your thoughts are in the right direction,' sang the assistant Kesavan ingratiatingly. The smiles of the dependant Namboodiris around expressed wondrous approval but did not mask their slavish sycophancy. Their facial movements were in perfect harmony with Achan Namboodiri's.

Brahminism tied its melmundu around the waist and bowed obsequiously. Vedas and Shastras prostrated respectfully before new money.

Time plays out its drama.

And then life is over. So what?

Is life so valuable?

'Are there any extra expenses today?'

The assistant shuffled. It was the usual question. But he wondered whether the Brahmin storekeeper had indulged in some petty theft. He might have given something extra to some willing sweeper woman.

'Only the usual expenses.'

'Make a special offering of rice payasam in ghee tomorrow. Let this journey be auspicious.'

'Yes, Master.'

'Well, Kesavan, I was told that there was some noise and yelling from Nambyattan's bungalow. What was that all about?'

Kesavan looked up at the sky, then down at the earth, and

finally in all four directions, everywhere but at Achan Namboodi's face.

'What? Some woman...something like that?' urged Achan.

'Their impertinence! Immoral people! You know that Raman; it was his niece,' Kesavan exploded.

'Our palanquin bearer Raman?'

'Yes, it was his niece who went to your brother's house.'

'Hmm...'

'How can I tell you, Your Highness. It would be best if you were to pretend that you hadn't heard anything because it was nothing unusual.'

'Why? Was Nambyattan upto some mischief?'

'Yes.'

'And then?'

'Master was playing chess when this useless woman appeared on the scene.'

'Hmm...'

'He asked her why she had come, when no woman ever came to the bungalow. Then he asked her to leave.'

'She didn't go?'

'Not immediately. She stood there muttering something and then it happened suddenly.'

'Any harm done?' asked Achan.

'Not much. But they had to carry her away.'

'Is she dead? What a nuisance!'

'She may not have died. I didn't check. It seems she was pregnant. Need I say what happens when the young master gets angry? Her arrogance!'

'Kesavan, call that Raman and give him whatever is needed. If she is dead, we will bear the funeral expenses. What else can we do if people are not careful... As for Nambyattan, he is headstrong. Did he kick her?'

'Yes.'

'Kesavan, please arrange for a substantial offering tomorrow at the temple, and Namboodiri, we need a remedial prayer also. Do it now, immediately. Isn't it the custom?' Achan enquired of his dependants.

'Yes, yes, killing a woman is a great sin. But if the remedial rites are performed, it will doubtless be atonement enough. After all, she was only a maidservant.'

4

At dusk, Mathukutty sat on a seat in the veranda of her ancestral house, her mouth glistening red from chewing betel leaves. The ornaments on her earlobes wove dreams on her soft cheeks.

'Oh! Brahmin priest, what makes you pant and run so fast?'

'A Namboodiri has arrived at the guest house. A huge man. An alarming presence!'

'Who? Why? Didn't you ask him?'

'No. He didn't give me a chance. He walked in and sat on the veranda seat and imperiously called out "Mani".[53] When I went up to him he was fanning himself with his melmundu.'

'And seeing that, you came here?'

'No. It was his order. "Hey, Mani, bring me betel leaves and nuts." After that, came the questions: "Who is the owner of this guest house? Are you the cook here?"'

'So that made you run here.'

'I gave him betel leaves and nuts which he finished in a single mouthful.'

'You didn't ask who he is?'

'No. Instead, I told him that the guest house and the house belong to you.'

'Then?'

'He growled like a lion in acknowledgement. That was all.'

Mathukutty trembled inwardly. Who could it be? Such

---

[53] A pet name for young temple priests who are slightly lower than Namboodiris in the caste hierarchy.

a powerful Namboodiri! Surely not anyone who lived in the neighbourhood, else they would have heard of Karott House.[54] And what about his arrogance! To occupy the seat in the veranda and issue orders! Must be an unusual man. She must take a look.

'You may go. I will come there; meanwhile give him what he asks for,' she said aloud.

She washed her face and feet, chewed betel leaves, lime and betel nuts, straightened her fine mundu[55] and held the melmundu in her hands. Properly attired, Mathukutty walked towards the guest house.

In the guest house, on the seat in the veranda, Thazhamangalath Nambyattan Namboodirippad was making elaborate preparations to chew betel nuts. Mathukutty looked at him. His body looked as if it had been carved from sandalwood and bathed in milk. His eyes glowed.

'Are you Mathukutty?' his strong voice pierced Mathukutty's ears. She was hardly conscious of it.

'Yes.'

'I have heard about you. The one and only Karott Itty's daughter, the Golden Mathu, am I right?'

If anyone else had said the same words, she would have spat on his face. Golden Mathu! An ill-omened, hidden insult. But… this man… Mathukutty felt a delicious languor invade her body. Her heart was filled with tenderness.

She had begun this practice[56] before she was fifteen. Her mother

---

[54] Under the matrilineal system of Kerala, the mother's family—which people used as their family name—has a distinct name.

[55] Costume commonly worn by men and women of Kerala. It is a piece of cloth worn around the waist.

[56] The reference is to prostitution practised as the family trade, handed down from mother to daughter.

had been her teacher in the art. She knew the mantra of seduction by heart.

'What are you thinking, Mathukutty?'

Again that authoritative voice. She found that she could only obey.

Although she was now thirty and had perfected the art, she felt shy in his presence. She could not raise her eyes to his. Oh, God!

'Mathukutty, as I was walking by, I saw a fairly decent guest house. I was feeling very tired. So I thought I would take a little rest.'

'My good fortune,' the prostitute felt redeemed.

'I've heard about you, but never had the opportunity to meet you. Please send a messenger to the temple to inform them that there will be one more person for dinner.'

'If you won't take it amiss, you could dine here. There is a Brahmin cook.'

'I think it may be a problem for you. I am a very self-willed and stubborn person.' Nambyattan Namboodirippad's deep voice thudded against Mathukutty's lower abdomen.

'You can order whatever you want through the Brahmin priest.'

'But I can't order you around, Mathukutty, is that what you mean?' Namboodirippad laughed aloud, appreciating the humour of the situation.

Oh, God! That magnetic laugh! She could only mumble, 'If you say such things…'

'All right, send for more betel leaves and nuts. And is there a Muslim boy around?'

'Why do you ask? There is a Muslim priest around.'

'Does he live nearby?'

'Yes.'

'Is there a Muslim boy who plays chess? I have heard about him.'

'I will find out.'

'All right. Ask him to come here.'

'Who should I say asked for him?'

'Me, oh, you don't recognize me...that useless Mani, didn't he tell you? Duffer! Have you heard of Thazhamangalam?'

Mathukutty's whole being trembled. The prince of Thazhamangalam in her humble abode! An overlord more powerful than the reigning King himself.

Oh Lord!

'I wonder what conveniences and comforts you are used to.'

'It doesn't matter, Mathukutty. Just send for that Muslim.'

'Can't you postpone the chess game to another day? Tonight, after dinner...'

'Yes, indeed. I was a little overwhelmed. I am very fond of the game of chess. Still, Mathukutty, I like this game too...'

The finger that he pointed at her breasts seemed to tickle her heart.

Her body was mesmerized by all of Nambyattan Namboodirippad's movements. She felt as if she was being blessed and stroked with a peacock feather.

She must tell the Brahmin priest to ensure that all his needs were met. He calls himself a self-willed man! An undefeated and fascinating magician who manipulates sixty-four types of horses on the sixty-four squares of the chessboard, the left-handed archer Arjuna, commander of the army of the chess game! Let there be new personifications in the art of armed warfare, let there be new formations; may Sri Krishna bestow courage through verse[57] to future Kurukshetra battles.[58] For here was Thazhamangalam Nambyattan

---

[57]The reference is to the Bhagavad Gita, a philosophical poem supposed to have been recited by Sri Krishna on the eve of the Mahabharata war, when Arjuna refused to fight his grand-uncle, cousins, teacher and other relatives. Krishna's words shook Arjuna out of his gloom and made him fight.

[58]The historic site where the eighteen-day battle described in the epic Mahabharata was fought between the Pandavas and the Kauravas.

Namboodirippad, the great teacher of teachers, Bhishma himself—not at rest on a bed of arrows,[59] but on the full creamy breasts of the likes of Mathukutty.

The soul of Karott Itty descended from the sky and blessed her daughter.

༄

The days were confined to their hourglass measures. The courtyard of the guest house was littered with discarded chess pawns, shaped from the stem of banana plants.

The player knew his moves.

Mathukutty knew her man.

She was certain that she would never be able to receive anyone else. Mathukutty concentrated wholly on Nambyattan. It became a kind of worship, an unshakeable faith.

> Whosoever worships whichever God
> With concentrated desire,
> I reward their unshakeable faith
> Giving them the god they desire.[60]

Spring blossomed. Days seemed to shrink to mere seconds. With a sense of fulfilment and reflection, thoughts of her earlier births came to Mathukutty's mind.

She may have sinned. Yet no one had told her that it was a sin. It was considered the family tradition: prostitution traditionally inherited and practised from youth. She never stopped to think of right or wrong. But...now.... Now she could not accept anyone

---

[59] This refers to the bed of arrows on which Bhisma, the grand-uncle of the Pandavas and Kauravas of the Mahabharata, lay after he fell in the war. He could choose his time of death.

[60] The Bhagavad Gita, Chapter VII, verse 22.

else. Only him.

'When will you come again?' Mathukutty asked as she wiped her overflowing eyes.

'I can't say. Even this was not planned. Anyway, Mathukutty, I will not forget the gold.'

That taunt ripped through her.

'You shouldn't say such things. Those days are over when I used to spread my bed only after receiving gold coins. Now even if the heavens are offered, I will not sleep with anyone else.'

'Siva! Siva! Have I made a mistake? Am I being trapped?'

'No, you will not be troubled on my account. I shall wait for you. Always. Whenever you come this way I'd be happy if you could step in.'

'I won't forget what you said. If you need anything send a message through Mani. Do not hesitate.'

'Oh Lord! My good fortune.' Mathukutty walked around[61] Nambyattan as he prepared to leave. Touching his feet, she placed his hand on her head.

Nambyattan, who had hurt many women and never given a thought about it, shuddered as though struck by a meteor. His mind swamped with memories—vague, unformed shapes. A mass of darkness fell upon him screaming. Akbar, the elephant shaking his limbs, roaring in pain, seeking the fragrance of the she-elephant Lakshmikutty, fattened on green palm fronds and ready for mating in the small forest prepared in the backyard of the Namboodiri homestead. Akbar's long trunk seeking the hole on his cheeks made by the bullet in vain, slipping and thrashing about. The four directions fell apart when he roared in pain. Akbar fixed his

---

[61] Circumambulation of temples is a part of regular worship. It is also customary to circumambulate elders or people respectfully, seeking their blessings before undertaking a journey.

Outcaste

unwavering gaze on the Viceroy's gun, which still smoked. But when he saw his own attendants, false protectors, running towards him he closed his eyes. Blows from the hands that had stroked him! Unable to bear such treachery, the animal fell dead.

Nambyattan Namboodirippad's breath came fast and shallow. His right eyebrow twitched. The two vital nerves in the spine, Ida and Pingala, opened. Sushumna,[62] the nerve which lies between the two, reared its head. The long nerve which lay coiled thrice around the spine awoke. The thousand-petalled lotus blossomed, open-eyed, creating the effulgence of a thousand blazing suns.

He had to travel about fifteen miles to reach home. He struggled to move away to escape from his thoughts. Time and place became mere illusions. Oh Mother! Annihilation personified!

That palanquin bearer Raman's daughter, who fell before him protecting her swollen stomach, as he kicked her!

Chakyar's wife!

How many had been forced to admit being checkmated by him? Riding on two elephants, enjoying all kinds of checkmating with either the elephant or the pawn—willing or forced.

'My little son, what is this that I hear?' His mother's voice tinged with tears echoed in his heart. His inner being shuddered. 'Don't inflict such pain on others. It is a sin.'

The game of chess all day. At night, the hunt for women. One midnight, he entered his servant Pakku's house.

'Hey, Pakku.'

At his voice, Pakku trembled. He had a beautiful wife.

'No, please don't insist.'

---

[62] According to the *Yogashastras*, the human body has three vital nerves—Sushumna, Ida and Pingala. The nerve which lies within the spinal cord is called Sushumna (the sleeping one). Ida and Pingala lie on either side of the spine. In the centre of the head is the confluence of all nerves, Sahasradalakamala, the thousand-petalled lotus, signifying enlightenment.

A good looking woman in tears was a beautiful sight.

'What a nuisance. Your tears are salty.'

Pakku had loved and married this girl who came from the south. The very next day a funeral pyre was lit at Pakku's house. A foolish girl lay dead. After that, no one ever saw Pakku again.

Mother! Goddess of Illusion!

On his way back, Nambyattan Namboodirippad turned away from his usual route. He did not go home immediately. He felt he had to go to the Otikkan's house. He had to see Akkithar first, who had trained him to recite the Vedas, the one man who had taught him without any expectations of reward. The one and only Akkithar! And what a grand reward he had given his revered teacher! For that, he, Nambyattan, should burn in a fire of corn husks.[63] There was no escape from a teacher's curse.

Yet, Akkithar had not cursed him, in spite of Nambyattan's impertinent confrontation. 'It would be better if you left on your own. Otherwise, I will throw you out,' he had said.

'Nambyattan!' cried Akkithar.

'Call me Namboodiri.'

Oh, God!

Sorrow scorched Nambyattan Namboodirippad's heart. How hurt Akkithar must have felt that day. Akkithar of the famed Otikkan House was spurned by a sixteen-year-old Namboodiri, a mere disciple, younger than his own son.

---

[63] The reference is to Prabhakara, who in a fit of revenge, wanted to kill his teacher by throwing a rock at his head. But he overhears a conversation between his teacher and his wife, during which the teacher regrets the severe punishment inflicted on Prabhakara when he failed to recite what had been taught. Repentant, Prabhakara pleads to be forgiven and asks his teacher to tell him the penance for attempting to kill one's teacher. Reluctantly, the teacher tells him that the only penance for such a sin was burning in a slow fire. Prabhakara prepares a fire of corn husks and burns himself.

'It is best that you leave.'

He had left that very day, never to return.

Thirty-two years had passed. In between, Nambyattan used to get news of Akkithar, the great sage, and his relentless penance, which evoked only contempt in him. Penance! A mere charade!

He must fall at those very feet and beg to be forgiven. All that Akkithar had done was to advise him against his undesirable activities. But he had resented it. A nondescript Otikkan advising Thazhamangalam Namboodirippad!

It was extremely fortunate for Nambyattan that Akkithar was still alive. He thought of the Brahmin cook Ambi's wife, a helpless woman. Akkithar had said, 'You shouldn't be doing such things, Nambyattan.'

'It is best that you leave.'

Nambyattan crossed the gate to the Otikkan's house and stood there for a while. His body was covered with the fine red dust of the road. He could see Chematiri Otikkan in the outhouse, teaching poetry. Pachu and Vasu were also there, surrounded by several disciples. The ambience of the ashram[64] of a great sage!

Nambyattan Namboodirippad was filled with a sense of peace.

Chematiri Otikkan welcomed him.

'I have been asked to tell you to go to the temple.'

So Akkithar knew. His teacher! The great Akkithar!

He could see the past, the present and the future in the palm of his hand.

Nambyattan Namboodirippad, who stood tall and straight, felt himself shrinking to the size of a finger. There was not a single cell in his huge body which did not contract. That body, cast in sandalwood and bathed in milk, was now covered in perspiration. He could feel the right side of his body twitching. The effulgence

---

[64]The thatched huts in which the sages lived, meditated and taught their pupils.

of the greatest Truth, so far covered by the veil of Illusion, entered his being and blazed. In that radiance, the principle of the whole Universe became clear.

> I am the intelligence of the intelligent[65]
> The glow of all shining spirits.

Please forgive me for all my sins. Nambyattan prayed aloud.

---

[65] The Bhagavad Gita, Chapter VII, verse 10.

5

'I would like this girl to learn some poetry,' Thazhath Namboodirippad said, leading his daughter Paptikutty to Chematiri Otikkan.

For Chematiri, the four horizons shrank to a small circle of light around Paptikutty at that moment.

It was customary for students to stay at the Otikkan's house while they studied. He never refused anyone who aspired to learn. Paptikutty, however, did not have to stay at the Otikkan's house as her own home was close by. Though there was no rule that forbade girls from learning Sanskrit, only a few actually did.

Paptikutty! Would she become another Gargi?[66]

How could he refuse to teach her?

Should he tell the Namboodiri that his was a gurukula,[67] where ordinary people paid for learning by serving the teachers? Among equals, it was knowledge for its own sake. Wealthy overlords paid for learning in a thousand pieces of gold or a thousand horses.

Even in ancient times knowledge was not imparted free of charge. One had to know the intention of the pupil. Otikkan thought of putting Paptikutty to the test, to find out whether she

---

[66] A woman who lived in Vedic times, Gargi was noted for her intellect and courage. She held lengthy arguments with her husband, the sage Yagnavalkya.

[67] In ancient India the system of education was termed gurukulavasa, meaning the student stayed with the teacher, helped in his household and was in turn taught various subjects such as Sanskrit, poetry, astrology, mathematics, philosophy etc.

really deserved the knowledge that was his to give. Like Ekalavya,[68] who was asked to offer his right thumb!

Paptikutty, do not ensnare me, he pleaded silently.

'Namboodiri, let's do it this way. Do not make any regular arrangements. Let her come whenever she is free.'

Thazhath Namboodiri was very happy.

She was his first born, so what if she was a girl? A little darling, as beautiful as a bunch of creamy coconut blossoms growing in abandon.

'Let her study a bit of *Shakuntalam*. Please teach her Vedanta also, if you can.'

This golden stalk! Oh, God! Was it possible?

The predictions of the Shastras never fail.

૭

'Paptikutty!' Chematiri called her one day. 'You have to make a payment to the teacher. Serve the teacher in some way or pay some money. And in return, knowledge will be given. These things are not possible in your case. So...'

Paptikutty, who was still very young, did not understand the real meaning of his words. But she gazed at her teacher's face and sensed that he was saying something which she ought to understand. All her other four senses stood ready to aid the sense of hearing.

---

[68]This refers to a story from the Mahabharata. Ekalavya, a hunter's son, wanted to learn the skill of archery from Dronacharya, the teacher of the Kauravas and Pandavas. Drona advises him to practise archery before a statue of himself. Ekalavya's single-minded determination and perfection astounds Drona, who did not want any other archer to surpass his favourite student, Arjuna. So, as the traditional offering from student to teacher (gurudakshina), he demands Ekalavya's right thumb. Ekalavya gave it to him unhesitatingly, even though he knew that he would never again be able to wield a bow and arrow.

When Chematiri finally spoke, all the five senses together grasped and retained what he had uttered.

'For you, there is only one way to fulfil your duty to your teacher. Do what you can when you can.' These words were wrenched from Chematiri Otikkan's throat. The same illustrious person, who had time and again declared at the sacred bell[69] that his Vedic recital would never falter, discovered that he was choking.

What could he advise her, a ten-year-old, her earlobes still unpierced, still too young to wear the traditional costume of Namboodiri women?[70] It seemed to him that there were no adequate words in Sanskrit or in any other language.

Could he say 'Never be a mother'?

How could he? No, it was not possible.

Then what?

'Come with me,' Otikkan walked slowly to the bathing house near the pond. Uncomprehending, Paptikutty followed, walking respectfully behind her teacher, careful not to step on his shadow.

Vararuchi[71] had tried to kill the Paraya woman. But had he been

---

[69]The practice of taking an oath is preceded by the ringing of a temple bell in the presence of the deity, probably to rouse the deity and make him/her witness the promise.

[70]Young girls of upper-class Hindu families began wearing an undercloth tied in a specific way by the age of ten, even before puberty, after which they were not allowed to move freely with boys.

[71]A Brahmin, Vararuchi, when he realized that he was destined to marry a low caste girl, steals the child at birth, inflicts a wound on her head and throws her into a river. However, she was rescued by a childless Brahmin couple and Vararuchi eventually fell in love with that very girl. Later, on seeing the scar on her head, he realizes that she is the same low-born girl he had tried to kill. He and his wife never stayed in the same place for long. All their children were born during their wanderings. Vararuchi would ask, 'Does the child have eyes, nose and mouth?' and when his wife replied in the affirmative, he would ask her to leave the child behind. Thus the children abandoned at birth were brought up by people belonging to

able to prevent the destiny shaped by time? Had not Vararuchi's seed grown twelve times in the Paraya woman's womb? And those sons later grown to establish the twelve castes that dominated the world?

'Paptikutty, now with water, make your payment to me as your teacher.'[72] Chematiri Otikkan's face shrivelled. His eyes reddened. His heart thudded like a huge war drum. The saintly qualities acquired over the years shivered seeing the emergence of the killer instinct. A strange numbness seized him.

'Look, child, step into the water, face southwards and close your eyes.'

What did the Otikkan want? wondered Papti.

'Now, when I say so you may immerse yourself. But do not do it before I tell you to.'

Once you dip underwater, I shall not allow you to emerge, he resolved. Chematiri Otikkan rubbed his hands together to warm them. There was a wild churning in his stomach.

Oh, God!

'Now, you may dip yourself.'

Paptikutty stood in knee-deep water and dipped her head in the pond. Her small back was like a floating banana stem above the water.

Otikkan prayed to the presiding deities of the four horizons, spread his palms and sprang forward with all his strength. At that very moment Paptikutty rose from the water and stood erect. She saw Chematiri Otikkan flailing his limbs in the water.

A rush of power coursed through the veins of her young body, barely ten years old. She was energized. She grasped her teacher's

---

different castes. As adults, they met once a year to mark their parents' annual death ceremony. This is a story told in Kerala to exalt the unity and tolerance among the various castes.

[72] The custom of making offerings with water signifies purification from all sins and impurities.

legs as he bobbed up and down, thrashing about in the water, and with all her strength, pulled him back to the steps of the bathing house. Then she stood watching the Otikkan, who lay on the steps, his eyes closed.

As the blood which had rushed into his brain cooled, Otikkan opened his eyes. At his feet stood his pupil, water dripping from her body, holding her small chin in her entwined hands. Drops of water rolled down slowly on her soft, innocent body.

A young girl as pure as the icon of Siva. His beloved disciple!
He was no teacher.
A murderer.
Not a doer, but a killer.
Oh, God!

'Paptikutty, dry your hair. Else you will catch a cold. After that, you may go. Let us not have any more lessons today.'

Paptikutty's lips moved. The words crept out from the depths of her heart: 'Payment for teaching.'

The teacher, who was in the act of raising himself by placing both hands on the ground, slipped and fell face down. Wet as he was, he perspired. His throat ached.

'You have given it to me. I am happy. Come here.' The numb hands of the teacher were placed in blessing on the wet head of the disciple.

∽

The disciples who lived and studied in the Otikkan's guest house assembled. In the gatehouse Chami sat alone. Chami was an Ezhava,[73] an untouchable. He could not sit along with the others. If he so much as approached the other students, they had to bathe

---

[73] One of the lower castes in Kerala, their ancestors are supposed to have migrated from Sri Lanka. Their main occupation was toddy tapping.

to purify themselves. Every day, as the Otikkan began to teach, Chami would stand up in the gatehouse and listen carefully to what he said.

'Have you understood what I taught? Do you have any doubts? If I have not explained clearly, please let me know. Do not hesitate,' so the teacher called out to Chami every now and then. Whenever it was time for the Otikkan to bathe he went over to the gatehouse to be near his low-caste disciple. In the presence of his illustrious teacher, the disciple's dark, sunburnt face took on a faint reddish hue. At such times, his pure devotion rose and foamed like the waves of the sea. He felt as though he was in the presence of God.

Otikkan had pondered for a long time before he took on Chami as his pupil. The *Dharmashastra* was not against it. As a teacher, he could not reject a person yearning for knowledge. He had tested Chami.

'What do you wish to learn?'

'Astrology.'

'Do you really want to? Or are you prompted by the thought of the money you will earn? How much have you learnt already and from whom?'

'I've studied a bit at home. My old patriarch taught me.'

'Asan Chami, I suppose? What more do you wish to learn?'

'Please decide and advise me, Master.'

'Then we will begin at the very beginning. Do you agree? Do you understand the meaning of verses?'

'Yes, Master, to some extent.'

'First of all, you must learn Sanskrit thoroughly. Master that language like a scholar.'

'Is there anything that I have to do?' Chami's father enquired.

'Nothing at present. I shall ask Chami himself at the appropriate time. Let him be in a position to pay.'

Teaching an Ezhava boy Sanskrit! And that too, the teacher

was Chematiri Otikkan of the Otikkan House!

Just imagine. What impertinence!

But the great Akkithar told Chematiri Otikkan: 'It is not enough if you teach him grammar and astrological calculations. Mere scholarship won't help him. You must also teach him to earn his livelihood. Only then will this education mean something to him.'

Chematiri hadn't consulted Akkithar before he began to teach Chami. Even so, he listened to his father.

Chematiri Otikkan sat on the elevated platform and continued his teaching.

'There is not much difference between this tree, the earth and ourselves. That is what the Shastras say. Everything is made of the same matter. It is like the experience of seeing the pot as the clay. Different in form, that's all...

> The fire dwelling within various shapes of matter takes on
> the shape of the outer covering—
> The same inner soul which resides
> in differently shaped bodies seems different
> though it remains constant,
> unchanged and beyond the outward shape.[74]'

The teacher repeated the verse several times with full conviction.

'That boy Chami there, I here, the tree in the field—theoretically we are all one, but very different materially.'

Otikkan's gaze went beyond the architectural barrier of the building and visualized something profound. He sat near his disciples on a cloth spread on a slightly elevated seat in the veranda. The thoughts that filled his mind took the shape of words and overflowed. The teacher took a closer look at the truth visible only

---

[74] *Kathopanishad*, Section V, Verse 9.

to him and then continued.

The Mother representing the inner truth of human beings quivered and took many incarnations. The four yugas of creation blossomed and withered many times. In their bushes of dried leaves, many years were consecrated. Purusha[75] did penance on the snowy peaks, with the fire of annihilation burning in his third eye.[76] The Mother slept on his head and lap, waiting for Creation.[77] In the Milky Ocean,[78] Mahavishnu slept—the divine sleep—on the cold coiled snake, Anantha, without realizing the passage of yugas. On the lotus, which sprang from Vishnu's navel, the four-faced Brahma remained as pollen dust, creating newer and newer forms. The new forms crawled out, from the caves of the Earth, as Chami, Chematiri and Paptikutty, wandering out on their separate paths. Chematiri felt that every human being's story had a very long and complicated origin.

'Then why are we asked to have a bath when we go near Chami?'

The teacher's eyes sought out the person who had uttered these words. Paptikutty shrank, shocked at her own indiscretion.

'You may ask so. It is a valid doubt. A good question, Paptikutty! I am happy that you had the courage to ask it. Even though there is no difference in all our inner beings, there are many differences in our outward appearances and lives. We are forced to accept those outward manifestations, as dictated by our karma. The karma of a spiritualist is different from the karma of a worldly person. Also,

---

[75]Male energy.

[76]Lord Siva's penance on the Himalayas after his first wife, Sati, immolated herself. Kama (Cupid) was sent to disturb Siva's penance. However, Siva opened his third eye and burnt him to ashes.

[77]The reference is to the two wives of Siva—Ganga, who resided within his matted locks, and Parvathi, the daughter of the Himalayas who was placed on his lap.

[78]According to Hindu mythology, Vishnu, the preserver, rests on a coiled serpent, Anantha, who floats in a sea of milk.

there is the custom...'

Chami, seated in the gatehouse, also heard Paptikutty's question. A Brahmin girl, of the highest caste, to ask such a question! 'Then why are we asked to have a bath when we go near Chami?'

That seemingly insignificant question, which sprang from a precocious young girl, echoed in the outhouse and the women's quarters of the Otikkan House. Afterwards, it crossed the gatehouse and leapt into the world outside. A magical arrow—the impact of which changed the times and fashioned the concentrated salty tears of women into a sword.

One arrow it was when she picked it up, ten when she aimed it, a thousand when it hit its object.

The Mother of Creation felt suffocated. She, the true representative of Power who bore the cornucopia of nectar which surrounded the foetus of all living souls that sought birth, had to submit to the brutalities of the performers of sacrifices, trapped within the four walls of the women's quarters.

She was at the end of her patience. With her tear-stained face bowed low in the depths of dark storehouses, she prayed soundlessly for the sun's compassion. Aruna,[79] the charioteer of the Sun god, lashed the white horses drawing the Chariot of Day. Time prepared the altar for a new incarnation.

---

[79] In the Hindu pantheon of Gods, Aruna is described as the charioteer of the Sun god. The word 'Aruna' in Sanskrit means 'red' and refers to the red hue surrounding the sun when it rises and sets.

6

In the prayer rooms of the King's palace, those Namboodiris known as 'resident husbands'[80] to the palace women sat in the veranda, dressed in freshly washed white clothes, chewing betel leaves. Kingly meals, undisturbed rest, a game of chess or cards—that was their daily routine. These 'resident husbands', dreaming of the princesses who went to sleep in their royal bedchambers after supper, tried to contain their frustrations by lying face down. On rare nights, when fortune favoured some of them and attendants appeared with flickering lamps to beckon them, they left their friends and entered the bedrooms of royal beauties. These men even managed to make a show of kindness and consideration to their spouses; on rare occasions they pretended to take pride in their fatherhood. Later they had the misfortune to wait on their own Kshatriya offspring, ready to obey their commands.

Chinnammu Thampuran's companion Namboodiri went in search of Ittiri, the priest in charge of performing rituals in the palace.

In the bungalow, Chinnammu Thampuran waited for him.

---

[80] During the later half of the nineteenth century and the first half of the twentieth, when feudalism and joint family systems were in vogue in Kerala, upper-class women from Kshatriya and Nair families were allowed to have more than one husband. These women were never formally married. They never lived in their husbands' houses, but instead continued to stay in their own homes. Men who were chosen as their partners visited them there at night. Usually these 'husbands', known as 'resident husbands', were from the Namboodiri caste. This system of marriage was known as sambandham (relationship).

In the royal families, women did not have any gender specific titles, so the same masculine title of 'thampuran' (royal lord) was used for females also. True to their titles, the likes of Chinnammu Thampuran, Gayathri Thampuran and Aminikutty Thampuran were as autocratic and domineering as men. They discussed and decided the salaries for their resident husbands.

Stud bulls!

'Namboodiri, you may have to run to Kottayam[81] and pay a visit to the spiritual guardians of the clan,' said the companion Namboodiri.

'Is it to perform a purification ceremony?' asked Ittiri.

'No, it is a sacrifice with sesame oil,' said the resident Namboodiri. 'Please come over. The mother Thampuran has arrived.'

Keezhembram Ittiri stopped midway in his ritual recitation of the Vedas and rose.

'What is it, Your Excellency?'

'Namboodiri, did the resident hint at anything?' Chinnammu asked.

'No, he did not. It is not in his nature to do such things either.'

Chinnammu Thampuran sat on the low swing cot suspended from the roof of the veranda, her corpulent body spilling out of it. Prosperity in the form of excess flesh hung from every part of her.

'I was telling him that he should see you, Keezhembram. You may sit.'

The swing cot sobbed, chandeliers winked and ear ornaments shone, flashing a smile. Brahminism sat obediently, its top knot bobbing in acquiescence before this personification of darker and baser instincts masked by an aura of prosperity.

'Did you check whether there are enough betel nuts and leaves

---

[81] A town in central Kerala.

for a good chew?' That was a hint for the resident Namboodiri to withdraw inside with ease, his white, freshly ironed clothes uncreased.

'Look Keezhembram, my uncle, the King, does not take any interest in such things.'

Keezhembram Ittiri did not understand what she was referring to. Still, he nodded in assent. For him, whatever she said was the King's decree. Ittiri, accustomed to swinging to and fro in response to the minutest change in the inflection of the royal voice, now bowed nodding vigorously, right, left, right, left…

'Of course, the King doesn't have the time for such things,' Chinnammu continued.

'No, of course not. His Excellency has so much work. God above! Mortals like us can't even imagine how much,' the priest continued his accompanying music.

'As you know, Keezhembram, my Namboodiri is not so smart.'

The resident Namboodiri, who had gone inside to collect the betel leaves and nuts, heard what she said and shuddered. What was she referring to? His physical disabilities? Would she get rid of him? If his monthly salary ceased, the three children at home, by his wedded wife, would suffer.

'Listen,' her voice droned, 'we are not talking of one or two. There are three grown girls in this very house. Something has to be done immediately. I can trust you, Keezhembram, so I am confessing this to you. My sister has more daughters than sons. They have all come of age. We are prepared to give some amount by way of dowry.'

'Don't worry, I understand. I will ask around. Two or three people have already approached me.'

A white lie by Keezhembram! Still, the false but sweet comfort that it offered brought a rare light to Chinnammu Thampuran's slit-like eyes.

'Is that so? Then there is no point in delaying things. I hope these Namboodiris are not some riff-raff, untrained in the recital of the Vedas.'

'How can you say such things? Will I ever think of harming you? Siva! Siva! Is it possible? Won't it amount to treason?'

'Well, I have no doubts about your sincerity. But still...' Chinnammu retorted.

'Let's not delay. Have you had enough betel nuts and leaves?'

'There is no hurry,' the ritualist murmured while he plucked the veins of the betel leaves, his eyes roving over Chinnammu Thampuran's glistening, coppery hairy ankles.

'If it can somehow be fixed in this month itself, it will be good. We don't mind giving some money. Keezhembram, your efforts also will not go unrewarded.'

'Siva! Siva! I am not saying that I don't need the money. But with you, will I behave as though I am only eager to earn the silver? Isn't it my duty...'

'See me before you go.' Saying this, Chinnammu leaned on the folded mattress placed on the swing cot. She slowly raised her buttery legs which had been dangling above the floor. Keezhembram found the sight unbearable.

'Wouldn't it be better if I left for my house today itself?'

'Yes, do not delay. When you are ready, please come this way.'

The heavy breakfast that she had eaten was taking its toll on Chinnammu, whose eyelids began to close slowly. Keezhembram took one more look at her and went out. He made elaborate mental preparations to cast a net over poor Namboodiri families in his search for bridegrooms for the royal women. All of the land stank with the foul jokes cracked about these husband hunters for palace dwellers and aristocratic Nair houses.

Chinnammu, sleeping while the day was still young, was haunted by the vision of royal maidens, who peeped through the curtains of her consciousness. The Namboodiris who usually came to participate in the temple festivals pretended to be acquaintances of resident husbands, cracking jokes and finding reasons to prolong their stay at the palace, exchanging pleasantries with the palace women who had not yet acquired husbands. Chinnammu, who had borne four or five children, knew that the gold bordered sari and melmundu would not remain tightly tucked when such delectable temptations came their way.

'Keezhembram is not all that bad. He is very greedy. That's all.'

Chinnammu was the niece of the ruling king. Her first 'husband' was Pangyat Kunhappan, the King's friend. After some time, for some reason or the other, he stopped visiting her. Then it was the turn of a Namboodiri from the North, trained in martial arts, to be her resident husband. This, too, lasted only for a while. After that came the present Namboodiri. Having studied some poetry, he had come to the palace with the intention of studying further. He belonged to a poor family. The taste of royal food, the respect shown to those who wore freshly laundered white clothes—he had grown to like both. At times, the hanging lamp beckoned: 'Your turn tonight.'

∽

Keezhembram presented himself before Chinnammu Thampuran when he was ready for his journey.

'Haven't you heard, Keezhembram, in olden days, by the time the girls of the palace were twelve or thirteen, they were blessed with resident Namboodiris.'

'Even today it's not so difficult.'

'Do you think so? Some of the hot-blooded young Namboodiris have begun to declare that the younger sons of Namboodiri houses should have legal marriages,' insinuated Chinnammu.

'Siva, Siva! They must want to divide the traditional joint families and live separately... I don't want to hear of such impertinence.'

Keezhembram had also heard that in a Namboodiri house somewhere near the Vadakkunnathan Temple,[82] a young Namboodiri had presided over a meeting of like-minded youngsters and preached that all Namboodiris should learn English, stop the practice of more than one marriage for the eldest son, introduce legal marriages within the caste for younger Namboodiris, stop illicit relationships with members of the lower castes and other such ridiculous ideas. But he pretended that he had not heard of such talk.

Learn the barbaric language!

Legally wedded wives for the younger Namboodiris!

Unfamiliar customs!

'Don't pay any attention to these rumours and worry unnecessarily. Let me now go home. I shall bring three bridegrooms.'

'Please keep this money for your travel expenses.'

All the seven nerves in Keezhembram's body awoke. He decided to repeat the prayer for good fortune without fail. The silver coins jingled in his palms, as though quarrelling amongst themselves.

Within ten days, three good looking Namboodiris were brought before a dreamy Chinnammu Thampuran. Keezhembram paraded them like a mahout. In order to prove the worth of the human commodities that he had brought, he persuaded them to exhibit their teeth, tongue and feet, quoted the desirable traits that they possessed and negotiated the amount to be paid.

'Let us have all the three initiated as husbands simultaneously,' Chinnammu said gleefully, her joy mounting.

'Yes, yes,' Keezhembram also chattered in agreement.

Kunhaniyan, one of the young Namboodiris, whose voice had not roughened into that of an adult, said, 'I have to go home today itself.'

Chinnammu Thampuran asked hesitantly, 'Why? Haven't you

---

[82] A famous temple dedicated to Siva situated in Thrissur, central Kerala.

informed your people? How can you go off today itself? Tonight, you have to be here to participate in the function. Return tomorrow.'

The third daughter, Ramanikutty, was barely fifteen and Kunhaniyan, sixteen.

They would make a good couple.

After twilight, the three young Namboodiris bathed and prayed. Keezhembram literally led them by the ears to the bungalow. The resident Namboodiri put on a show of hospitality and smiled warmly. He welcomed them with gifts of clothes.

In the hall, the wedding ceremony, which consisted of the presentation of a ceremonial cloth to the bride by the bridegroom, was arranged. Three wedding saris. Three brass lamps with five lit wicks. Three oval-shaped wooden seats for the bridegrooms. Chinnammu presided over the function, Keezhembram acted as the priest. The resident Namboodiri turned into a silent, watching Brahma.

Each of the three young women had already gone through one customary wedding ceremony when some unknown man had tied mock-wedding talis[83] around their necks. Now, they were thrilled at the prospect of having three new toys to play with.

'Keezhembram never told me that it would involve all this,' Kunhaniyan, ensconced in Ramanikutty Thampuran's bridal chamber, mused morosely.

To be a resident husband at such a young age! He had lost his father rather early. The affairs of the household were run by his elder brother. He had two unmarried sisters. Even if they were to be married to men who had more than one wife, there was the problem of their

---

[83]In Kerala, till the 1950s, a girl had to undergo three wedding ceremonies—the first tirandukalyanam, when they attained puberty; the second, kettukalyanam, when a tali (a chain with a leaf-shaped pendant, symbolic of wedded status) was tied around her neck by some distant relative or a caste Brahmin. These were mere rituals in anticipation of the real wedding, the putamurikalyanam.

dowries. When he was harassed by all these problems, Keezhembram had said, 'Come on, Kunhaniyan, there is a way.'

Kunhaniyan was under the impression that Keezhembram was talking of the usual ritual of kettukalyanam. He would get about a hundred rupees for taking part in such a function. Sometimes, apart from rightful candidates from the same royal clan, Namboodiris were also allowed to participate in this function. Though the ceremony of tying talis around the necks of twenty young princesses at the same time was celebrated like a festival, it was considered undignified for a Namboodiri to participate in such a tali-tying ceremony or to act as the resident husband of a princess. Such Namboodiris were not allowed to participate in religious rituals. Of course, they received money as compensation.

How many times had he, along with other unmarried young Namboodiris, ridiculed these customs!

One man to fasten the tali, another to assume the functions of a husband, yet another to fulfil sexual urges. It sounded like the words from a poem of the Vyasa of Kerala,[84] Kunhukuttan Thampuran.

And now?

Tears sprang unbidden to Kunhaniyan's eyes.

Oh, God! Even he had been reduced to the status of a resident husband. The indignity of having to wait for the hanging lamp which would be brought down to lead him to the bedchamber! Kunhaniyan's mouth went dry. The ornamental cot moved to and fro as in a dance. Ramanikutty, with the curiosity of a child with a new toy, came up to him.

As was customary, the three Namboodiris were presented to the eldest Thampuran, the ruler of the country. Chinnammu

---

[84] A poet named Kunhukuttan Thampuran translated the epic, Mahabharata, into Malayalam and was given the title of Kerala Vyasa, equating him with the author of the Mahabharata.

Thampuran walked with them, giving instructions regarding the customs of the palace. She presented them with new clothes and instructed the accountant to include their names in the account book, with the salaries and payments due to them. Thus, their monthly salaries and daily expenses were recorded. All the details were worked out. An auspicious beginning.

The eldest Thampuran talked to all of them graciously. But with Kunhaniyan, he showed a special interest. He called him aside eagerly and asked, 'What is your family name?'

'Amalakkad.'[85]

'Haven't you informed your people at home about this new development? Your father...?'

'I don't have a father. I have informed my elder brother.'

'Do you have any younger brothers?'

'No, only an older brother.'

'How old is he?'

'Eighteen.'

'Only eighteen?' After a moment, the Thampuran asked his niece, 'Chinnammu, for which daughter have you chosen Amalakkad as the bridegroom? You told me, but I have forgotten.'

'For Ramanikutty,' the niece answered, feigning humility.

'Please send all three of them here. Let me have a look at them.' The older Thampuran showed affection towards his nieces, as was expected of him in his capacity as the King. He presented each of them with a brocade mundu and a gold ring.

'Chinnammu, ask Amalakkad's betrothed to stay back. All the rest may go. You may go as well.'

---

[85] In Kerala, when the joint family system was in vogue, a person traced his/her identity to the joint family they belonged to. Each family had a name such as 'Thazhamangalam', 'Karott', 'Pangyat', 'Keezhembram' and this name was a prefix to the individual's name.

'What prompted such a request from the eldest uncle? What is he thinking?' Chinnammu wondered. One had to think of him not only as the most senior uncle, but as the ruling King, too.

The King, who was lying on a sandalwood bed, asked Kunhaniyan to approach him.

'Look, Ramanikutty, my child, you may come forward as well. Let me see the two of you. You may stand there.'

Ramanikutty Thampuran stood two feet away from the king.

Gazing at them, the King smiled charmingly. He looked towards the inner apartments and called out.

'Ikkavu, are you there?'

The queen appeared dutifully behind the door.

'Come here. Take these children in and give them whatever they need.'

The childless King grew compassionate for a moment.

'Amalakkad, how old are you?'

'Sixteen.'

'It augurs well. Ramanikutty, come closer. Come and stand next to your Namboodiri. Together. Let me see.'

Embarrassed by the King's orders and yet unable to disobey them, Ramanikutty moved hesitantly till she stood by the King, almost touching Kunhaniyan.

'I am very happy. You should always stay like this. Till death. Maybe even after that. I should not hear anything to the contrary. Ikkavu, please take them inside.'

The King, who knew his nieces only too well, took a deep breath. His unusual eagerness transformed Ramanikutty for a minute into Kunhaniyan's real married partner.

'Do your dharma together.'

Kunhaniyan walked away.

'Let it be so.'

Ramanikutty followed him, her eyes on his feet.

7

The unseen ghosts that dwelled in the dark closets of Namboodiri houses, where sunlight never entered, frightened the young girls. The unmarried girls grew old waiting in the presence of bare bodied, lecherous Brahminism, contemptuous of femininity. Afraid of losing their virginity to the mere caress of the sun's rays, even when they stepped into the courtyards of their own houses, these young women, who were always accompanied by maidservants, covered themselves with shawls and carried umbrellas to hide their faces. Even before they could distinguish night from day, their ears were filled with love stories recited by their maidservants, who were free to indulge in such amorous games. These Namboodiri girls pretended to be shy and covered their ears, while in private they grieved over their fate.

'I think I am in trouble,' Thazhamangalath Achan Namboodirippad muttered, pacing the outer veranda of his thirty-two-room house, which stood in a spacious compound. His minions craned their necks to peep through the three majestic doors opening to the veranda, built in the style of temple gopurams. In this posture they remained, mere shadows of Achan Namboodirippad, invisible, merging with his presence.

Only his faithful attendant, Mangazhi Vasu Namboodiri, was filled with an unbidden anxiety.

'Now what? Anyone there? Ask that Kesavan to come to my room,' Achan Namboodirippad ordered.

Kesavan, the overseer, arrived and waited in his landlord's room, touching the pretty factory-made tiles and feeling their smoothness.

Every now and then, he looked out through the trellis work into the veranda. Achan's face reminded him of a cloudy sky which had cleared to some extent. He wondered what would happen and why he had been called.

After a long time, Achan Namboodirippad appeared with Vasu Namboodiri, who took great pains to be a short, faithful shadow to Achan, following closely behind.

'Kesavan—anyone there? Ask everyone to leave my room and stay out.' The order skittered around the whole house, thrusting all living beings away from his presence.

'I think I am in trouble. Ask those Muslims to come over tonight.'

'As you wish, Your Excellency.'

'Let it be done discreetly. You must be with them. Wait there, near the northern exit to the pond, next to the doorway. At midnight. Do you understand, eh? After that, everything should be done with great speed. Explain everything to them—that Hameed and Mammunni. Tell them that I asked them to do it.'

'Your Excellency, what should I say to the Muslims? At midnight? What is to be done near the pond?'

'A bit of trouble. It concerns that Namboodiri woman, Unikkali, who is staying here to help my mother. A useless woman! We have to eliminate her. Explain everything to the Muslims. It should all be over before dawn.'

'Oh, that girl! Amme!'[86] Mangazhi Vasu Namboodiri staggered at the thought. His parched lips fell open. His tongue caved in.

'Water,' he tried to call out, but no words emerged.

---

[86] This is a commonly used form of address to call out to the Mother or Mother Goddess in times of crisis. This importance given to the Mother and dependence on Her may be symbolic of the respect given to the institution of motherhood throughout Kerala—there are 108 temples in Kerala consecrated to the Mother Goddess.

'What, what is it, Kesavan, what's happened?' Achan Namboodirippad was thunderstruck. His own faithful follower fainting?

The woman Achan mentioned was Mangazhi's nephew's widow, who was staying at Mangazhi's home in dire poverty. Achan's mother had mentioned to Mangazhi that she needed a woman to help her with the preparations for worship, so Vasu Namboodiri had brought her here. But now, before the sun rose the next day, some Muslims would snuff the life out of her. By Achan Namboodirippad's orders.

Blood rushed, boiling, to Mangazhi Namboodiri's head; his vision blurred. Unable to raise his head, he rolled on the ground.

Oh, God! Her fate!

She was barely twenty years old. His nephew—her husband—had died of cholera soon after their wedding.

He wanted to plead with Achan Namboodiri to not do it. What had she done? Whose fault was it?

'Vasu, aren't you feeling well?'

Vasu Namboodiri could not recognize Achan's voice. His eyes filmed over; Achan's face turned hazy. Achan's appearance seemed to change. A head with horns. Eyes flashing fire. A rope in one hand and a pestle in the other. A huge buffalo next to him. Achan Namboodirippad was transformed into the God of Death, Yama himself. 'Ayyoo!' Vasu Namboodiri tried to sob out loud, but his voice was stuck in his throat.

Slowly, very slowly, Vasu Namboodiri sank into a horrendous dream. When he woke up, Kesavan was standing by him. He was lying in another room.

He wanted to call out, 'Kesava!' But his tongue had turned heavy and lifeless. It slithered like a snake which had gobbled its prey. His throat was blocked with thick phlegm. His eyes filled and his eyelashes were frozen and spiky.

Oh, God! What had transpired, what was to happen? The

Muslims would suffocate and kill her. His elder brother's widowed daughter-in-law! She, who had come here at *his* request!

A helper for the mistress of Thazhamangalam House. The work itself was not too tiring. She had to help the mother prepare for the daily ritual worship, collect karuka[87] and other flowers and make cotton wicks for the brass lamps. It was easy and did not matter much. But Mangazhi had overlooked what really mattered. She was below twenty and in the full bloom of youth. Nor was Achan Namboodirippad too old. To even think of Achan in that way was a sin, he admonished himself. Achan was a Brahmin who regularly recited the Gayatri Mantra a thousand times!

'No, Namboodiri, don't do it,' Vasu Namboodiri tried to roar. But his voice was dead. His tired body forgot how to move. His open mouth remained twisted to one side. 'I shall take her back to my house.' Vasu Namboodiri rolled fretfully on his bed.

'Kesava, please go and fetch that Nambi or Moose.[88] I think Vasu has had a stroke.'

So, after all, it was not an accident, but a deliberate act.

The child-widow Unikkali lay rubbing her bare neck[89] in a dark corner of a room in the northern quarters, like a speck of an atom which had accidentally slipped and fallen from its regular structure, an unspeakable sorrow burning her vitals. Before she could realize what was happening or guard herself, a large muscular hand grabbed her unadorned wrist and crushed it into submission.

Later, she didn't utter a word about the incident. Even if she had raised her voice in protest, would anyone have listened to her?

---

[87] A kind of green herbal grass with needle-like pointed leaves grown all over Kerala, worn by Namboodiri women in their hair as a sacred leaf; also used to prepare medicinal oils.

[88] The terms used here denote an Ayurvedic physician.

[89] The reference is to the shedding of the tali after the husband's death; widows do not wear any ornaments, and hence their necks are bare.

Days later, the mother of Thazhamangalath Achan Namboodirippad told him. 'Kuttan, please make arrangements to send her back to her house. Otherwise, we will be subjected to all kinds of gossip.'

Achan Namboodirippad's paunch had shuddered.

Towards the end of the night, behind the door from the northern section leading to the bathing pond, Yama's messengers stood in the form of men. The power of Achan Namboodirippad's command led the wronged Unikkali into the hands of these messengers.

∽

The next day, before noon, Kesavan Nair saw a bluish corpse floating in an unused well covered by bushes, in the compound of the Namboodiri house.

'She must have been bitten by a snake. How many times can one warn a person not to go near the well at night?' Achan Namboodirippad was heard accusing no one in particular, loudly and aggressively.

'Narayana, Narayana,' uttered his mother, entering the prayer room.

In the veranda, Vasu Namboodiri, his head smeared with ayurvedic oil and medicines, waiting to be cured of his paralytic attack, stared mutely. His tongue was tired and lifeless. One more half-grown mango tree was burnt to ashes,[90] motherhood, breast milk and tenderness destroyed. The two young beings—a woman and her unborn child, the sweetness of motherhood dawning on them—crossed the boundaries of the yugas by burning into ashes

---

[90] In Kerala, when a person dies and is cremated, the funeral pyre is usually made of mango wood. There is a custom of each person growing a mango tree so that it can be used to make the funeral pyre when he/she dies.

in the compound of the Thazhamangalam House.

Achan Namboodirippad consoled the grieving relatives who came from Mangazhi's house by saying, 'When something leaves one's hand one has to make it disappear from one's eyes also. That is the right thing to do. After all, she was here for a few days. So her death rites and the feast following the rituals should be performed in a befitting manner. I shall take care of everything.'

The people who came from Mangazhi's house heaved a sigh of relief and thought, 'Oh, God! Look at his generosity!'

'As for Vasu, are you insistent that you should take him home? For the time being, let him be here. It would be convenient for his treatment.'

'As you wish, Your Excellency.'

'All right, I shall do the needful.'

At dusk, Achan Namboodiri's first wife, on her way to light a wick and pray before the jasmine bush in the gardens of the central courtyard, swooned and fell. After a while, she opened her eyes and gazed about her vacantly.

'Unikkali! Unikkali!'

She thought she saw an apparition in the air and was seized with fear. She raised her hands as though to ward off an unseen spirit, then turned around and screamed in fear.

'Narayana, Narayana,' Achan Namboodirippad's mother continued to chant in the prayer room. This old lady, bypassed by death, sat on an oval wooden seat left behind by time, and trembled. She invoked her special deity, Siva, and prayed. 'Oh Lord! Please redeem her soul.'

8

With a single cloth around her waist, Ittingayya rushed from the inner quarters and dashed out of the house. Achan, reclining in the veranda and absorbed in matters of the household, sat upright.

'What can we do if she behaves like this? We may have to chain her.'

'I have been thinking the same thing,' droned Kesavan, pulling up his mundu which had slipped below the waist.

The mute Vasu Namboodiri, eyes afire, pointed at the gatehouse and stared round-eyed. His twisted mouth contorted even more.

'If she runs around half-naked like this, it is going to be a problem,' Kesavan Nair commented and looked towards the gatehouse. The eldest wife of Achan Namboodiri stood in the doorway and began to gesticulate in the air, as if her way was blocked.

Her young sons tried to pull her indoors.

'No, I won't come in. Unikkali is there.'

The sons did not know what to do.

Vasu Namboodiri was staring aimlessly, his wrinkled face like a pickled mango. He slithered inside, climbed on the cot and lay there staring at the ceiling, hands folded on his chest prayerfully. A deep sigh escaped his lips.

Nambyattan, the chess player, stood respectfully in front of his eldest brother. His huge body glistened. His face, outlined by a thick beard, gave off an inner glow.

'Yes?'

'I wish to visit Gokarnam[91] and Mookambi'[92]

'When are you going? Please take whatever you need for your expenses.'

'I don't need anything. I must set off today, no later.'

'What?'

'I plan to undertake this pilgrimage on foot. I just wanted to inform you before leaving.'

'So…'

'Permit me to go,' Nambyattan prostrated before his eldest brother.

'What, what are you doing?'

Was he in trouble?

Mangazhi Vasu paralysed.

His wife on the brink of madness.

And this chap?

Nambyattan rose, stood with folded hands and said, 'Elder brother, you are the one who did the Upanayanam[93] for me. Our father is dead. When one goes on such journeys, it is customary to seek the advice of teachers and the blessings of elders. The teacher's advice was sought and given. As for blessings—grant me blessings.'

'What are you saying? I don't understand anything.'

'Hereafter, I wish to lead the life of a wandering mendicant.'

'Go then and return safely. Will you be away for a long time?'

'No.'

Achan Namboodirippad watched his younger brother

---

[91]A place of pilgrimage in Karnataka.

[92]A place of pilgrimage in Kerala.

[93]Brahmins are supposed to have two lives—the first of which begins with birth and ends with the close of childhood. To mark the occasion when he is initiated into true Brahminhood, the Upanayanam ceremony is conducted, when the boy wears the sacred thread, which is symbolic of Brahminhood binding the wearer to truth and proper conduct.

descending the stairs and sat still for a long time. Not only had he carried Nambyattan in his arms when Nambyattan was a baby, he had also initiated him into the recital of the Vedas. What had happened to him? For some days, Achan had watched a change in his brother. No shouting, no yelling, no chess playing. He no longer encouraged people to visit him at his bungalow. The chessboard had been relegated to the attic. What was the matter with him? Why was he making his pilgrimage on foot? He would probably be eating stale food served in charity houses. Perhaps his time for lavish meals was over. Now, by his stars, perhaps it was time to eat a single scanty meal a day in various parts of the country. After that…after that who knows what was in store for him? When and where was he destined to fall and die? Achan Namboodirippad put an end to his stream of thoughts and resumed chewing betel.

'Kesavan, is that Tamil Brahmin surveyor around? Send for him.'

The Brahmin from Palghat arrived.

'Swamy,[94] didn't you say you are familiar with the English language?'

'Yes.'

'In that case, please teach English to the young Namboodiris of this house. They will need it in the coming days. You may start tomorrow itself. For the time being, you can hold the classes in Nambyattan's bungalow, which is vacant.'

∽

The younger brothers of Namboodiri families and their relatives continued to stay at Thazhamangalam House, indulging in feasts, illicit affairs, chess or card play and tending to elephants,

---

[94] The literal meaning of 'Swamy' is 'lord'. It is a term used to address the Tamil Brahmins of Kerala.

unmindful of even the change from day to night. When they met, the important topics of discussion centred on the length and width of their undergarments and similar subjects. During the feast after the ceremonial recital of the Vedas, they boasted about their lordliness and felt thrilled.

In the outhouse, Mangazhi Vasu Namboodiri stayed alone, on medication and a special diet. Gradually his skin began to shrivel. After midday meals, he peeled the dead skin from his own body, taking pleasure in that exercise. Every now and then, he stared at Achan Namboodirippad. Unable to face that unblinking gaze, Achan Namboodirippad opened his silver betel leaf box and continued to chew diligently.

His second and third wives stayed in the house. They would easily serve his need for women. The thought of his crazed first wife gradually grew intolerable. He did not know of any antharjanam who stepped out of her house without a shawl, an umbrella and a serving woman. 'She is of course very ill, still...' Normally an antharjanam who entered the inner quarters of her husband's house on the day of her wedding crossed the outer veranda again only as a corpse, borne on a pyre of bamboo, after sacred verses were whispered into its ears.

Achan's mother, who sat on the wooden seat in the prayer room reciting her prayers, became restless and anxious.

Should she call Kuttan?

She thought of her son's first wife. The pomp and splendour of that wedding! She was such a modest girl that one did not feel like looking away from her. So attractive and dignified! Despite the trials she had endured, her face had retained its serene beauty. Though she had conceived four or five times, she was still in good shape. Oh Lord! May she be blessed with sense and recover from her present illness. Please make her well.

'Ittingayya, if you continue to behave like this, it will be a problem for all of us. Is it possible to keep an eye on you all the time?'

The matriarch walked slowly to the northern side. 'Children, please ask your father to come here.'

'Grandmother is calling you, Father.'

'Kuttan, you have to do something about Ittingayya.'

'Yes, I shall. I, too, have been thinking about it.'

'Please ask Chematiri to come. Let him make an astrological calculation. After that, we can think of taking remedial measures through people like Kaattumadam or Kallur.'[95]

'Will Otikkan come after Nambyattan was so rude to his father? Anyway, I shall send word.'

'He won't refuse. One hears so much about his kindness of heart and good deeds. Kuttan, send word for him immediately.'

Achan Namboodirippad, who returned to the outhouse, was very upset. What should he do? He could not disobey his mother. But how could he request Chematiri to come? What a shame it would be if he did not turn up! Someone spurning Thazhamangalath Achan Namboodirippad's request to visit his house! He must specifically mention that the request was his mother's. That would have a better effect. Chematiri Otikkan had lived in this house when he was young and Achan's mother had known him from that time.

Thirty-two years ago, Akkithar of Otikkan House had walked out of the gates of Thazhamangalam, hurt and shamed by the insulting words hurled at him by his dear disciple. Now, at noon, two days after his mother's request to Achan Namboodiri, Akkithar's son Chematiri entered through the same gates, accompanied by the special messenger sent to bring him.

He had brought his Ezhava disciple, Chami, with him.

'You may stay here at the gateway.'

---

[95]Kaattumadam and Kallur were famous Namboodiris who practised exorcism.

Chami, who was thrilled at the prospect of spending a few hours in the company of his teacher, waited humbly, unaffected by the heat of the midday sun.

'Come in, come in, it's a long time since we saw you. How is the elder Otikkan?' said Achan.

'He is all right. He leads a strict and disciplined life.'

'Siva, Siva, I am anxious to see Akkithar himself, but even this is a happy occasion. After all, you came, Chematiri.'

'Did you think I would refuse to come if you sent word, Namboodiri?'

'I had my doubts. You father was very unhappy when he left this place.'

'But it was he who asked me to go without any delay.'

'Is that so?' Achan Namboodirippad gasped in surprise.

'I cannot stay for long. I am very busy. And I have brought a boy with me.'

'Then don't delay. Have a bath. Who did you say has come with you?'

'An Ezhava boy. Please give him something to eat. He is my disciple.'

'Yes, yes, I will make all the arrangements.'

After his bath, Otikkan went indoors. The mother waited for him there. When he saw Achan Namboodirippad's mother, who had not stepped beyond the precincts of the house for more than fifty years, Chematiri Otikkan became a young boy again. He had stayed with his father in this house for a long time. At that time, the present Achan Namboodiri's father had been alive. His first two sons had passed away. After that, this Achan Namboodiri was born. Otikkan and he were of the same age and they had begun their training in the recital of the Vedas together.

Otikkan woke from his reverie when the mother said, 'I just wanted to see you.' He recalled the many times he had eaten the food she served. He was a mere child then and used to sleep inside. She was the one who used to oil his hair, matted from a year-long penance, combing it into shape. How many years had passed since then!

Everything had changed one day, when his father called him after lunch, interrupting his playtime. He had not finished his training in the Vedas, but his father had decided: 'Unni, we are going home. Take leave of mother and come away with me.' Thirty-two years had passed since that day.

'I haven't seen you for a long time, Unni. I do not know whether it is correct for me to call you Unni now. I heard that you have completed the Yaga.'[96]

'You must call me Unni. In fact, you shouldn't address me in any other way.' Chematiri Otikkan's eyes filled with tears.

'Come closer, let me look at you. I can't see too well now.'

The mother looked him over carefully and burst into uncontrollable sobs. It had been thirty-two years since she last saw him. Otikkan also couldn't suppress his tears.

'Unni, you have grown so old. Your hair has turned grey. Oh my God! You look exactly like your father.' In a trice, the gap of thirty-two years was covered. Chematiri was once again the young Namboodiri boy from Otikkan House.

'Please have your meal.'

Chematiri Otikkan sat in the kitchen of Thazhamangalam House, which to him had become a hazy memory over the years, a spark of remembrance from a previous birth. As always, the mother of Thazhamangalam served him.

'I have some salted mango for you, Unni. You always insisted

---

[96]The literal meaning of 'Yaga' is 'sacrifice'. After the performance of a sacrifice, a Namboodiri is considered to be an expert in all aspects of the Vedas—the recital as well as the ritual.

on pickled mango, no matter what other delicacies were served.'

Chematiri tasted the salted mango with the tears on his cheeks; the mother had not forgotten anything. Through the keyhole in his mind's closed door, Chematiri's memories rushed out.

'Your father...?'

'He is all right. He keeps to a very strict routine.'

'Does he observe the fast every fifteenth day, even now?'

'Yes.'

'Oh, God! Otikkan is a truly holy man.' For a moment she shut her eyes and continued, 'He and my children's father were of the same age. They were great friends.' The mother's face glowed compassionately with the pride that comes from lineage. Something greater than pathos flitted across her face.

'I cannot delay any further. Mother, please sit on that wooden seat. I wish to circumambulate you and prostrate before you.'

'No, that is not necessary, Unni. I am happy, you have my blessings. Your life will be fulfilled.'

'Even so, please sit down. The moment I reach my house, my father will ask me whether I circumambulated and prostrated before you when I met you.'

'Dear God! Your thoughts are always so pure.'

Weeping, the mother of Thazhamangalam House pressed her hands in blessing on Chematiri's greying hair as he lay prostrate before her. To Chematiri, those tears seemed like a shower of nectar. His head felt cool in that outpouring of love.

'Kuttan must have told you about the affairs of this house.'

'He did. I shall consult my father and then give whatever advice I can.'

'Good. That's what we need. The older Otikkan's predictions never fail.'

Even as Chematiri sat in the outhouse and discussed the effects of bad times with Achan Namboodiri, his mind was filled with memories of the mother, the great mother of Thazhamangalam House!

Chami stood at the gate and surveyed the mid-noon sky. At night, he had often stood gazing at the sky, having acquired a fairly good knowledge of the stars. It was only now that Chami realized how noble and exalted the clarity of daytime was, especially the spotless mid-noon sky. It was as clear and luminous as the written word. He could perceive all his lordly teacher's instructions in the clear, dazzling firmament. In the clarity of nothingness, the sky seemed to be a case of glass, the depth of which could not be plumbed by mere sight. The truth that lies beyond sight and form! The insight which evolves and goes beyond one's physical vision. The clarity of matter without letters. The sun's rays spread in all directions. The immersion of the sun in the greatness of the universe, gazing at which, the self ceased to exist. His master had explained that the person who looks must have an inner vision. There are signs everywhere. One has to train oneself to understand their language.

'Have you eaten anything?' Chematiri Otikkan's voice brought Chami down to earth.

'Yes.'

'Let's go.'

Along the way, the teacher explained and interpreted the commentaries on the sacred verses, written in the form of chants, and the disciple assimilated them wholeheartedly.

He was born an Ezhava. Traditionally, they practised astrology of sorts. He had ancestors who had learnt to recite Sanskrit verses without mastering the proper pronunciation. But that was all. Somehow he had had the luck to be the disciple of a great Brahmin like Chematiri Otikkan. Under his guidance, he had learnt the application of mathematics to astrological calculations.

'It is not enough to learn. You must meditate. Mere knowledge of the Shastras is not enough. Do you understand?'

'Yes.'

'You must meditate on your favourite deity. Hold the image of that figure firmly in your mind. You must have self-discipline. Choose an auspicious day, think of your ancestors and teachers and begin to meditate. In the beginning, it is very difficult to concentrate on the figure of the deity. Later it will get easier.'

'Yes, Your Excellency but…'

'What? Speak up! Do not hesitate.'

'I have not gone through the usual formalities. I have not made my dakshina to you.'

'Are you in such a hurry to make that payment? Didn't I tell you that I will ask for it when the time is ripe, when you have progressed with your learning? Only then will you understand its significance.'

In that burning heat, Chami walked behind the Otikkan, watching Otikkan's shadow, the one who was the incarnation of Varahamihira in the Kali Yuga. The texture of knowledge that filled the mind of the disciple almost transformed his body and set it aglow. The teacher was thrilled.

9

After the festival at the temple of Karanthitta, all the young Namboodiris had assembled in a room at the entrance to the temple. A young Namboodiri spoke in a high-pitched and emotionally charged voice, a voice that made even the enshrined Siva deity tremble!

'How long can we live like this? Behold! Over our heads, time is sprinting. We, who go through life eating at feasts and glibly chanting the sacred verses, have forgotten our sisters born of the same womb. Think of the increasing number of child widows! Before girls are ten or twelve, they are married off to elderly men who are already married. With marriage comes a burst of rivalry and competition among co-wives, and perhaps the delivery of a child in the midst of all this turmoil. But before long, they are widowed. As for the younger Namboodiris, the aphans who are not allowed to marry into their own caste, they go around having illicit affairs.'

The older ones among them went in search of a place to sleep. The other young Namboodiris, belching after their sumptuous meal, felt uneasy.

'Why are you all silent?' he continued. 'Shouldn't things be more humane in our own houses? Are you all aware of what is happening within the four walls of the women's quarters? Do you know of inmates who wear wet clothes continuously for want of a change? Not out of poverty, but to suit the arrogance of their menfolk! Their insensitive brutality! Haven't you heard of the Namboodiri who tore his wife's earlobes because she was a little late for his puja? Another great man, in his anger, tied all his wives together.

In another house, a young girl had her head smashed in with a coconut for the sin of talking to a half-caste relative. Siva! Siva! Must I go on?'

Most of the assembled Namboodiris had already heard many such stories. But they feigned ignorance and stared at each other.

'But what can we do?' lamented a young Namboodiri while he stretched out on an elevated seat in the room, mindful of his overfull, and therefore unyielding, stomach.

'That is what we have to consider seriously.'

'I will tell you. First, all of us must learn English.'

It was Chematiri Otikkan's son, Ichatha, who came up with that suggestion. For quite a while that young Namboodiri, already proficient in Sanskrit, had wanted to learn English.

'And will that do? I think not. There are a few more tasks to be achieved. Quite a few. We should all unite and ban this practice of illicit relationships with women from other castes, this "sambandham". That is the next thing to be done. Then—'

'What! What will happen to all the women of the King's household?' wondered a man who seemed to have taken an oath to maintain the continuity of progeny in all the palaces.

'I don't know,' replied Ichatha. 'Let them find a solution to their problem. Let them marry into their own caste.'

A cold silence, similar to the one which follows a heinous murder, spread around the temple premises. Marriages within the caste in palaces! The days of wearing freshly washed clothes presented by the palaces would end! The news would then spread to aristocratic Nair families. They would also be content with marriages within their own caste. And then?

'Then there are other issues to be considered. May I start with a question. Do you have any idea as to who rules us now?'

'The King of Cochin, of course.' None of them wanted to waste an opportunity to prove their intelligence and knowledge.

'That is not what I had in mind, not the fortunes of this small region, an area that can be contained within the letter "O"; I mean this country, India, the land known as Bharata. Who is ruling it?'

'The white man.'

'Very soon they will go... It may happen sooner than you think.'

'Nonsense, I think the young Namboodiri is touched in the head.' The white man going away? Sheer folly and madness!

'They are the chosen divine beings of Kali Yuga. Sri Rama had blessed their ancestors, those monkeys who helped him build the bridge over the sea, long ago.'[97]

'So, do they have tails?'

'Don't they? Of course they do. You can be sure of that.' The white man departing, it seems!

'I am going to sleep. I don't want to listen to this kind of nonsense,' a Namboodiri said and stood up.

'At the moment, you won't understand what I am saying. A time will come when you will be forced to understand. By then, you won't be in a position to do anything.'

Yawning, they rose and went away, one by one. Ichatha of Otikkan House alone stayed with the slim, dark and young Namboodiri.

'Aren't you going to lie down, young Otikkan?'

'I was thinking about what you said, Namboodiri.'

The young Namboodiri looked at him carefully, fascinated by the source of that sweet voice. The youngest son of Chematiri Otikkan! A young priest in the making, not yet sixteen.

'If you are not in a hurry to sleep, come with me. We will take a walk.'

∽

---

[97]In the Ramayana, it was an army of monkeys who helped Lord Rama to reach Lanka, where he killed the demon Ravana.

The young Namboodiri began, 'Young Otikkan, haven't you heard about Servants of India Society? Gokhale, a man from a poor background, who gave up his respected job at Fergusson College? And Mohandas Gandhi, who took pride in being known as the political disciple of Gokhale? That great man who befriended the labourers of South Africa who had been reduced to slavery, and who conducted experiments by inflicting pain on himself? And on the other side of the spectrum, revolutionaries such as Rama Prasad, who robbed villages to form an armed battalion to wage war on the foreigners to conquer them?'

Through the wide path adjacent to the bathing house in the pond, the young Otikkan walked with Unni Namboodiri, who was advocating the mantra of freedom.

The faint starlight threw a veil on the village.

'Young Otikkan, do you know English?'

'My uncle has promised to teach me.'

'Who? Pachu Otikkan? He knows English? Whom did he learn it from?'

'I don't know for certain. In the marketplace, there is a Christian priest who wants to learn Sanskrit. So he has become friendly with uncle. He comes to our house every now and then. Sometimes, uncle goes to the marketplace too.'

'So, his teacher is a foreigner.'

ಬ

That night the young Otikkan and the dark, skinny Namboodiri undertook a minor world tour.

The Namboodiris spent their days feasting to assuage their hunger and spent the nights at the houses of prostitutes, slaking the fires of their lust, whiling away time as the night turned to dawn. At dawn, they revived their appetites once again for another day's boring routine of eating and sleeping. As long as this routine was maintained, they pretended that they had achieved the ideals of human life.

Often, in order to get their daughters married, old Namboodiris married yet again, collecting more dowry on each occasion. But more wives meant more children. Quarrels among the many wives of one man had become common in Namboodiri houses. The older Namboodiris, fearing these noisy brawls, sought the company and the houses of lower caste women, where they slept undisturbed.

The two young Namboodiris studied the dark stains on the walls of Namboodiri houses, whitewashed with a veneer of Brahminism. They sensed the strength of centuries reflected in the old, ugly performers of Vedic rites and shuddered. They sighed, staring at their own fists, which were not strong enough to be raised in revolt.

On that day, unknown to anyone else in the village temple, after the festival feast, a spark of fire emerged when the two young Namboodiris' spirits rubbed against each other. Much later, that spark struck at the very heart of Brahminism. The sacred thread, which had become a burden, and the untended top knot—a wild growth—caught fire from that flame.

∽

Thazhath Paptikutty had come of age. In a dark room specially decorated with rice-flour paste, she sat for three days, beautified, bejewelled, in penance—as though she was getting ready to change the shape of the times that lay ahead. Paptikutty's large and shapely eyes were limpid, filled with the liquid of love. As her eyelashes brushed against her eyelids, the very foundations of the Namboodiri houses felt the tremor of that movement. Time wrought changes in her limbs, seemingly in preparation for a change in the texture of future events.

One day Thazhath Namboodiri visited the Otikkan's house.

'Otikkan, my daughter wants to continue her studies for a

while longer. Is there any way?'

There was no way. For a Namboodiri girl who had come of age, there was no way of continuing her studies.

'There is no need for that. What she has studied is enough.'

'But she is insistent. I am at a loss.'

'Is that so, Namboodiri? Then, we are only seeing the beginning of her stubborn insistence.'

'What are you saying, Chematiri?'

'I...I...said...' Chematiri stuttered. What could he say to this man, who was Paptikutty's father?

'Namboodiri, I can suggest a way out,' Otikkan began. Before he could go any further, his son Ichatha approached him. 'What do you want?'

'May I go with uncle to the marketplace?'

'What did Pachu say?'

'Uncle said he will take me.'

'Then you may go. Aren't you going to see that foreign priest who is learning Sanskrit?'

'Yes.'

'See Namboodiri, Pachu is learning English from a foreign priest. The foreigner wants to learn Sanskrit in exchange. This boy, Ichatha, is also fascinated with the idea of learning English.'

'What is the use of learning English?' Thazhath Namboodiri asked.

'He wishes to go to Madras and write the public exams, if it is possible. I do not think it would be possible.'

'Siva, Siva, Otikkan, you have always been fond of some new idea or the other!'

Thazhath Namboodiri had to find a solution for his daughter's insistence to continue her studies. Namboodiri girls who had attained maturity were not supposed to step out of their houses, much less continue their studies. They were not allowed to see men—not even their teachers. Even the kind of education that she had already received was far too much. A sufficient grip of the Malayalam alphabet, some arithmetic and a great deal of Sanskrit—a Namboodiri woman should not even dream of acquiring knowledge beyond that. Even so, Thazhath Namboodiri's daughter wanted to study more. Obstinacy! What else could it be described as!

'Namboodiri, you could do it this way. There are many texts kept in this house. If she is so insistent, let her take them home. After she reads them, return them to me. She must be very careful. If she has any doubts, I will write out the answers on a palm leaf. The process is very difficult. But if anyone, even a low-caste person, comes seeking knowledge, we should not turn them away. There is no greater sin than rejecting such a seeker. Thazhath Namboodiri, do you know that we perform the funeral rites of those who have initiated us to recite the Vedas? Why? The belief is that he is like a father to us. In the order of priority, first comes the father who has given us a physical body. The second is the teacher, who gives us spiritual knowledge. Therefore, the teacher automatically becomes your spiritual father. Are you aware of this? So the intention of teaching is to show the way to the final release. Is there any karma which is greater than training a person to be worthy of that knowledge?'

Thazhath Namboodiri, who had mastered only the daily rituals, was perplexed. What did Chematiri mean? Whatever he meant, it was clear that he was fond of Paptikutty.

'So, Namboodiri, you may go now.'

Chematiri Otikkan's eyes watered. A clear vision of the days to come filled his mind's eye and his round face, suffused with many emotions, swelled and ebbed.

Thazhath Namboodiri wasn't done. He wanted to consult the Otikkan about his daughter's future. 'I wanted to tell you something else as well. The horoscope from Cheriyedath House matches that of Paptikutty's. The dowry requested is also suitable. I want to give my consent. But the hitch is that the elder brother is unmarried.'

There were only two men in the prospective bridegroom's house. The bridegroom was a highly scholarly Namboodiri trained in Vedic recital. He had enough to live on. But he was the younger brother in a family with an unmarried elder brother. What was the way out?

'Chematiri, both the elder Namboodiri of Cheriyedath House and I want this wedding to happen. Please find a solution.'

'I have heard that there is no remedy in such a case. However, if the elder brother has some kind of ailment, the next in line may marry to keep the line alive. That is customary. Anyway, why not decide after consulting an expert in the Vedic rites?'

When Thazhath Namboodiri left, Chematiri Otikkan's mind was in turmoil. The time was at hand.

Now what? The very foundations of Brahminism would be destroyed.

'I wanted to see you, elder brother,' said Pachu Otikkan, who had been standing by him for some time.

'Yes?'

'That foreign priest wishes to hear the Vedic recital. He knows the sound and method of chanting. He has already read a book on this subject written by another foreigner.'

'So what do you want me to do? Do I have to teach Vedic recital to that barbarian?' snapped Chematiri.

Pachu Otikkan was dumbfounded. He had never heard his elder brother speak in such a fashion. Why was he so angry? He had had no hesitation in accepting a low caste Ezhava boy as his disciple. He had allowed his own son to learn English. Maybe a non-Brahmin should not be allowed to hear the sacred verse. Still, this unreasonable anger! Pachu was about to leave the place. Brahmins will be born in countries across seas. Foreigners will be born in their land. Their father has said so himself, and so did the sacred books. Family attachments would grow through the wife. Reverence for forefathers would dwindle. Ancestral land would be sold. Climate change was at hand. Rainfall would be scanty. Comets and whirlwinds and sudden fires would become common. Oh God, there were terrible times ahead! But fearing destruction, should we start killing now? Pachu wondered. Something had happened to upset elder brother, what could it be?

'Pachu, I'm sorry. I lost control... Should I be the one who teaches the Vedas to…' Chematiri Otikkan fumbled. 'Tell your foreigner friend it isn't yet time for him to hear Vedic recitals. Tell him that if he stays on for a while longer, he will get a chance to do so and receive Vedic tuition without any difficulty.'

Oh! Pachu Otikkan was relieved. He could now escape from the presence of his elder brother. He was filled with an inexplicable fear and was afraid to clear his doubts. When his brother was around, he found it difficult even to teach the younger Namboodiris.

༄

Cheriyedath Thuppan, known as Tundan, came to the Otikkan's house when Chematiri Otikkan was sitting upstairs, deep in thought. With stunted limbs, he resembled a dwarf oarsman. The name 'Tundan' seemed apt, meaning 'a piece of a man'. Without a doubt, he who had bestowed such a title was a poet.

'I have been wanting to see you for a long time, Otikkan.'

'Anything special?'

'Nothing much. The subject of a marriage. The horoscope of the Thazhath girl agrees well with that of my younger brother. I, too, like the match. But there remains this question of the younger brother marrying when the elder brother remains unmarried. If my brother has to wait till I marry, then his wedding will never take place. Is there a way out?'

'That is a subject for the Vedic experts to decide. What right do I have to give advice?'

'Still, your opinion...'

'No, that is not required. If you want this marriage to take place, please go and see a Vedic expert. Whatever remedial rite is prescribed, perform it. That is the correct way.'

'If that is so, I shall go right away. How is Akkithar?'

'He is all right. So you have decided to see the Vedic expert, haven't you?'

'Isn't that better?'

'There is no doubt.'

Chematiri Otikkan's eyes followed Cheriyedath Tundan, who walked away with a rolling gait. On waking up this morning, whom had he first seen?[98] Thazhath Namboodiri wanted a solution for his daughter's obstinacy to study further. Then came the topic of her marriage. Paptikutty, the daughter of Thazhath Namboodiri—his dear disciple!

'Pachu, who is there?' he called out.

On hearing his elder brother's voice, Pachu spat out the betel nuts he had been chewing and came up to him. 'Vasudevan.'

'I will come as well. Call the younger boys also. I would like us all to recite the sacred verses for some time.'

Disciples and poetry. These would help one to obliterate all bad thoughts. Otikkan felt better.

'Let that Chami also come and join us. Let him sit aside in the courtyard. Vasudevan, you will all bathe afterwards, won't you?'

These regular meetings strengthened the ties between the teacher and the disciples. Unconsciously, they merged in spirit—the wedded and the unwedded, the disciples, the high and low castes, sons and fathers—all of them were transformed into a group appreciating

---

[98]In Kerala, there is a superstition that the day's events would go well or not depending on the first person one sees upon waking.

the world of poetry. An inseparable and lasting relationship, greater than blood ties, brought them together.

'Can't you hear properly? Listen carefully and understand how it is recited. When you recite a poem, others should automatically understand the meaning of the verses.'

Chami sat at the distance prescribed for untouchables and listened. The hour-glass filled and emptied several times. Saraswati, the goddess of speech and words, seemed to have taken her seat in the upper storey of the house of the Otikkans. A unique Brahminic aura, cleansed by traditions practised during several births, pervaded Chematiri Otikkan and lent the atmosphere a fiery glow of purification. The recitation, both alphabetical and chronological, ended. Then Chematiri Otikkan began to recite alone without pause. With his thick hair tied into a side knot, his large red-tipped eyes half-closed and his voice filled with the emotion suited to the meaning of the verses recited, his whole demeanour reminded one of Sri Sankara and Melpathur.[99] Watching their elder brother's face, his brothers couldn't sit still. They rose and stood near him.

For a long time, there was no recital of verses, only silence. Chematiri Otikkan sat with his eyes closed, impervious to all who surrounded him. In his mind, he was with his father, who sat in meditation in the temple. His father, whose incessant penance continued for more than thirty years, a relentless penance which included the fifteenth-day fast, meditation, chanting and prayers for more than three quarters of the day. Day by day, his father increased the ascetic quality of his penance. Oh, God! Why, perhaps by some chance... One could not say anything. In his father's case, all calculations went awry. Even death was waiting to take his orders.

---

[99]The reference is to Melpathur Bhattathiri, who wrote *Narayaneeyam*, a book of verses on the life of Lord Narayana (Vishnu).

'Oh, God! Save us!' Hearing Chematiri Otikkan's words, those who stood near him started. How long had it been? No one knew. At one moment they were all reciting verses, according to age and discipline. After that, only Chematiri continued to recite. Then even that had stopped. The glow on Chematiri Otikkan's face stupefied those who were around him. Wiping their eyes, one by one they rose and stood next to him. Chami, who saw this wonderful sight, brought his palms together and looked at his teacher's face.

'Why did you all stop reciting? I was in a trance. Now...we will continue tomorrow. That is best,' said Chematiri. Gazing fondly at the satellites who surrounded him, with eyes that saw beyond the present, Chematiri Otikkan also stood up.

The disciples' minds were filled with an unusual sense of peace created by the experience of the past few hours. No one was anxious to break the silence. The low-caste Ezhava, Chami, the spiritual Otikkan, the young Namboodiri who did not know the letters of the language, the grammarian who knew the customs of the country, all of them saw their spirits in each other. After a few minutes, they resumed their own thoughts and routine activities.

Chami felt that his life's mission had been fulfilled. He felt as though he had accomplished the impossible task of crossing, on all fours, the low-roofed cave of Punarjani.[100]

Transformed into a twice-born Brahmin, he walked down the path among the rice fields.

---

[100] A mythical cave through which all sinless people are able to cross on all fours.

10

A sturdy banyan tree lowered a hundred roots to reach the earth. Only one special root grew upwards, connecting the upper and lower sources. That cardinal root split asunder the walls of the human head, reaching out to the sun and carving the only path to the divine source of the devas[101] and the sages.

Three-hundred-and-thirty million gods. A distinct god for each of the three-hundred-and-thirty million living beings. A god for every man. The nectar-like inner vision of seeing oneself as one's true god. Salvation of self through dependence on self. The symbols may vary; forms are not reality—they are immaterial.

All the hundred nerves of Thazhamangalath Nambyattan Namboodirippad awoke, filled with a virile awareness. He could feel the powerful flow of the force of ascension, the strength of a fall.

Suddenly, he felt the soft touch of Golden Mathu. The lower tip of the hundred-and-first nerve twitched. Suddenly the doors, hitherto closed, opened. And in the force of the tempest unleashed, the sound of Om[102] struck against the original source. The spirit

---

[101]In Hindu mythology, human beings are divided into three categories—devas, manushyas and asuras. Devas are human beings who, through their pure thoughts and actions, have attained some degree of divinity and have been elevated as semi-divine beings. Manushyas are human beings and asuras are demons. This division is perhaps according to the gunas (qualities) they possess—devas representing the sattwaguna (pure), manushyas the rajasaguna (prone to activity and not so pure) and the asuras the tamasguna (dark and evil). It can also be interpreted as manushyas attaining a certain kind of purity and becoming devas or indulging in evil and becoming asuras.

[102]Om is the primal sound, a combination of three vowels—Aa, Uu and Am.

ruling his heart opened his eyes.

The figure of Akkithar filled the mind of the wandering Nambyattan and showed him the path. He, whose beard had grown and entwined itself with his hair, walked on. Exhausted, he arrived at the house of the Karott family. Time stood still and waited after making the appropriate offerings for this auspicious moment. Gazing at his own feet, he called, 'Mathukutty!'

His voice had softened. Yet, there was the strength of an order beneath the layers of that gentle voice.

'Oh, God!'

Like an echo to that call, Mathukutty arrived at the gate and stood in front of Nambyattan, who was covered by the dust of his travels.

'Mathukutty!'

'You.' Words gave way and she withdrew. She wondered what had happened to the sandalwood sheen of his body and the devil-may-care tone of his voice.

This wandering mendicant looked nothing like her Nambyattan.

Nambyattan noticed Mathukutty's pale face and her swollen belly bearing creation's vessel of nectar, and realization dawned. Maybe it was...then...

'Mathukutty, this...this...'

'After you blessed me with your visit—'

'Oh, God! That too!'

Suddenly, in his mind's eye he saw another pregnant woman, who had come to his bungalow one mid-afternoon. The niece of the palanquin bearer, Raman. He had risen from his place by the chessboard. After the act, he had calmly brushed the dust off his feet and resumed his play. They had had to lift her from where she lay and carry her out.

The pilgrim's eyes filled with tears, seeing which Mathukutty sobbed aloud, 'I won't in any way be a burden to you. There will be no scandal.'

'Siva, Siva! That's nothing, Mathukutty. For me, those days are over, the times when a good name, the slurs on it and so on were important. Come here, Mathukutty, take this temple offering. Hold out your hands.'

He opened a small bundle covered with a banana leaf, took a portion of the offering—the size of a gooseberry—and prayed before placing it reverentially in Mathukutty's cupped palms.

'Early in the morning, after your bath, before you eat anything, have a little of that offering. He will be a brilliant child. Have no doubts.'

'Aren't you going to stay for some time?'

'No, I must reach my house today. We shall meet again, if destiny permits. Please come here. Oh, God! May you have a happy life!'

He placed his strong hands on Mathukutty's head. His eyes overflowed. The tears fell on Mathukutty's head and formed a pool. Then, it flowed on to her cheeks, merging with her own tears of love and forming a bigger flow before it finally fell at her feet. At that moment, the entire universe took shelter in these two beings.

ꕤ

Thazhamangalath Achan Namboodirippad sat in his room in the upper storey of his house and watched Nambyattan approach through the gateway. Vasu Namboodiri, who stood next to him, rolled his bloodshot eyes and pointed his fingers to the gate, uttering some gibberish.

'Oh, Nambyattan, is it really you? I am glad that you have come. I was somewhat worried.'

'I wasn't able to achieve what I wanted to. Instead, I wandered here and there.'

'We will talk about all that later. Have a bath, meet Mother and then come back to me.'

Nambyattan Namboodirippad stepped into his bungalow, which seemed empty and lustreless without the people who usually frequented it. The young Namboodiris, learning English from the Tamil Brahmin, rose hastily to their feet. The teacher looked embarrassed.

'Good, Swamy, let the children learn some English. You may sit and teach them. Let me bathe and change.'

He heard the sound of someone clearing his throat and turned. It was the palanquin bearer, Raman, who was bowing low, his melmundu tied to his waist, hands over his mouth, the very personification of utter servility. Nambyattan Namboodirippad felt weak.

'How is everything?'

'Your Excellency, she died.'

Nambyattan sat down, completely shattered.

'Oh, God!'

The murder of a woman!

Oh, great Mother! Please punish me. I am the greatest of sinners. Punish me with a special hell.

He wept.

The change in the young master frightened the palanquin bearer. He had never seen the young Namboodiri so distraught. This overlord, who feared no one, reduced to this? Now what?

'Raman, from now on you need not come to work here.'

These words made Raman desperate. Was his means of livelihood to be terminated? There were ten or twelve souls at home waiting to be fed. He had hoped that the overlord would help him financially. Had he been foolish to approach the Namboodiri? The palanquin bearer's knees shook.

'Your Excellency, I...'

'I have thought everything through, you may go. Don't come here again. That land near the river, known as Kaithamuri—those four to five acres are yours and the income from that land will keep you from starving. Go and inform the office that you will cease to work here. You may go.'

Raman had not expected that much; he had only hoped to get some money. The forms of the other girls in his house began to appear in front of the greedy palanquin bearer's eyes. He imagined all of them pregnant with swollen stomachs. They would all then breathe their last, kicked by the overlords, and one after another, he would get more land and houses. He sat inside his palanquin and grunted in satisfaction.

'Yes, why are you waiting? You may go.'

Nambyattan felt that his private mountain of sins was so huge that no gesture or generous offerings of land or other material and spiritual gifts could demolish it. A long, tragic procession of his sins came into his view. It occurred to him that while his soul burned in the heat of the sorrowful sighs which emanated from those innumerable hurt beings, the blessings of those who accepted his generosity might redeem and console him to some extent. He could not fathom the depths of the brutality in which he had revelled for nearly thirty-two years, from the days of early manhood.

The very first act of insult was directed towards his own teacher.

A teacher—the equal of father and God!

A veritable sage!

After that, it had been a perpetual game of hiding behind the power and protection offered by his famous family.

In truth, he had not slept well for days. The moment his eyelids closed, he could only see the ghostly dance of orphaned souls, specks of light which shone from the burial ground of wounded spirits.

No, Mother, I cannot bear the thought of rebirth. Let it all end in this one. Combine all punishments in a single stroke. I have the strength to bear that burden on my shoulders.

He should burn in a slow fire for cursing his teacher.

Maybe this was the truth, the suffering had already begun.

Not for thirty seconds did he enjoy a sense of peace. Even momentary peace had become a mere memory. Blood trickled from the pores beneath his hair.

Mother, I await with outstretched hands. Give me whatever you think I deserve. The sins committed for aeons by generations of Thazhamangalam men—Mother, here I stand, your son, Nambyattan.

Nambyattan sat on the steps of the bathing house for a long time, unaware of the passage of time. He fell into a rare and content trance as he watched his face reflected in the water. The reflection seemed to contain the ten incarnations of Lord Vishnu.[103] The different stages in his long and purposeless journey were clearly revealed to him. He watched the magnificent sight of all the fourteen worlds[104] shrink and fill his cupped hands. In that moment, he was transformed into a stationary point in the eternal movement of time.

---

[103] According to Hindu philosophy, when evil forces threaten to rule the world, the Divine will take a form (human or animal) and vanquish it. Thus, Lord Vishnu is supposed to have taken ten incarnations—those of a fish, tortoise, wild boar, man-lion, dwarf, Parasurama, Sri Rama, Sri Krishna, Buddha and Kalki. Nine incarnations are believed to be over and the tenth is expected, heralding the total annihilation of the universe.

[104] The universe is divided into fourteen worlds, some of the more well known worlds being Brahmaloka, Satyaloka, Devaloka, Bhuloka and Nagaloka. The first three represent different layers of heaven, the fourth the earth and the fifth the netherworld.

11

The feast following the recital of the Vedas was an occasion for competition. Both teams tried to outdo the other. It was not enough if one team's arrangements for the feast excelled the other's. The other team's efforts had to be sabotaged, if possible.

Lack of attention could lead to disaster. The participants had no compunction when it came to spoiling the other team's plans. For example, lizards fashioned from salty dough were deliberately thrown in the rice and milk pudding to spoil its taste. An insect in the milk pudding! A bunch of human hair in the rice! Nothing to do but discard it all—such were the tricks used.

Both teams had senior and seasoned Vedic chanters. Still, as the chanting commenced, members of the opposing team tried to make the other falter. One slip and they had to live in ignominy, at least till the next Vedic recital.

After the Vedic recital and the feast the famous Pooram festival began.[105] It was probably the most celebrated festival in the region, with more than a hundred gods taken out in procession amidst the rhythmic drumming of the Panchari.

The leader of the Southern team was Thazhamangalam, backed by both power and prestige. The Northern team was led by the House of the Otikkans.

'Kesavan, remember, the opposite team consists of Chematiri and his people. You have to work hard during the Pooram festival.

---

[105]Pooram is a grand temple festival, with caparisoned elephants and an orchestra of drums and fireworks.

If your attention strays...' Thazhamangalam warned. That would be the end. Smoke would rise from the lamp of the Southern team, the elephant would run amok. The entire Pooram would be spoiled. It had happened before.

'Upturned, it can be used for the feast after the Vedic recital, turned upside down, it will be handy for the Pooram festival.' These famous words of advice from Chematiri while his team prepared for the festival had reached Thazhamangalath Achan Namboodirippad's ears and he repeated them like a sacred chant. Each time he uttered those words he shuddered and felt diminished in some way.

For Thazhamangalam's feast, dishes and delicacies, from salt to payasam, were served in silver vessels. A gold vessel with a spout was used for the water ritual.[106]

'Oh! Ho! What an obvious show of wealth and pomp by Thazhamangalam! Can the Northern team beat them? Let's see,' boasted the Southern team.

And they did.

From salt to sweet curries, the Northern team served the delicacies in golden bowls. Not one or two, but four bowls for each delicacy. For the final water ritual, water was poured from a silver vessel with a spout.

Was Chematiri a magician?

---

[106]The water ritual is performed before every meal in a Namboodiri house. The plantain leaf placed before the seated Namboodiri is washed with water after which ghee, rice, ginger and jaggery are served. Water is poured into his hand and taken around the leaf while reciting the Gayatri Mantra and the water is drunk chanting the Amrithamasi ('This is nectar'). Once again he takes water and a rice ball and consumes them chanting the Amrithopastharanamasi ('I am drinking the nectar'). At the end of the meal, he washes his hands and drinks the same water chanting the Amrithabhidannamasi ('I am washing the food down with nectar'). The significance is that the food a Namboodiri eats is converted into nectar through the offering made to God.

The magic lay in his words, 'Upturned you can use it for the feast after the Vedic recital; placed upside down, you can use it for the Pooram festival.' How was it done? From the headgear worn by caparisoned festival elephants, convex bowl-shaped decorations dipped in gold were taken out and polished to be used for the next year's festival. 'Bowls' of different sizes. Salt, pickle, desserts such as rice pudding and jaggery pudding—all were served in different sized, shapely bowls.

What an ingenious idea!

Upturned they became small bowls. Placed face down, they turned into the blobs in the headgear of the caparisoned festival elephants.

'Kesavan, be careful. That Chematiri is not an ordinary person. He has eyes everywhere. Please inform all our people. This year's Pooram...'

Thazhamangalam had more money. Even so, the best drummers joined the other side. If they were with the Southern team one year, they went over to the Northern team the next year. Chematiri's team knew the trick to achieve this. 'File one or two cases against them in court,' Achan ordered. Failure seemed imminent on all fronts for Thazhamangalam, the first family of Cochin.

The King would be present to watch the Pooram festival. Achan Namboodirippad was disheartened. Nambyattan used to be of great help. He would be there, in person, from start to finish. It was an occasion for him to settle scores with many people. But now, he was so utterly changed. The other brothers did not take an active interest in the whole affair. The only capable one now lacked the will. His elephant-crazy brother alone would stand by him. Even that, only because of his interest in elephants.

Nambyattan had not been averse to sparking a few physical assaults either. Once the Vedic recitals commenced, he would be on the spot until it was over. The horoscope for the Pooram festival was cast there.

'Kesavan, have you made all the preparations for the festival of Vedic recital?' asked Achan. 'Let there not be any competition.'

'Yes, Your Excellency. There is no need for a competition. Why create unnecessary quarrels? I feel that there is no need for that,' Kesavan simpered.

Mangazhi Vasu twisted his already contorted mouth and laughed, his red eyes going round and round. Achan Namboodiri was afraid to look Vasu in the face.

Mangazhi Vasudevan, who had been his shadow from time immemorial! Had Vasu been with him to help during these festivals, he would not have had any problems. He could even reach out and catch the moon. That shadow had turned into a macabre form, following him around, frightening him. He was unable to free himself from its terrifying presence. He closed his eyes and did not look back.

As for his household, there too...

Screaming.

Beating of the chest.

A voice without a body.

And the moment he stepped out—

A twisted face with an ugly, twisted laugh.

Frightful glances from rolling eyes.

His younger brothers did not even know how the affairs of their house were managed. They were interested in their own bungalows, hobbies, games and tawdry activities. That was it. They were willing to obey their elder brother's commands but were indifferent to everything else. Nambyattan was the only one who had stood by him, even though at times he had acted somewhat hastily. His had been a fearless nature. Now, he too had become deranged. Meditation and prayer was all he thought of.

'Kesavan, shall I call my brothers and consult them?'

'That would be a good idea.'

The thought of his brothers gave a fillip to Achan Namboodiri. They could be effective in their own way, if they wanted to be, in a variety of activities from the recital of Vedic verses to employing underhand methods, if the need arose. They were experts in the game of cards as well as in the management of household affairs.

His father had advised him: 'Kuttan, do not antagonize your brothers. Most of the Namboodiri houses follow the practice of pushing out the younger brothers or forcing them to leave of their own accord. Once such a practice sets in, before you know it, the house and the family will perish.'

That would not happen at Thazhamangalam. Each of the brothers had his own house, lands, attendants, every comfort and signs of power that they wished for. His great-grandfather was the person who had begun to multiply their wealth. Even before that, they had had enough to live on. Wealth consolidated and managed efficiently over two or three generations had caused the family fortunes to grow considerably. Thoughts of his grandfather and father caused a surge of blood in Achan Namboodiri's veins.

∽

Nambyattan Namboodirippad stood inside the house, in front of the door that led to the prayer room. Inside, the mother of Thazhamangalam sat in worship on the wooden seat reserved for the wife of the head of the family. Reverently, she accepted the temple offerings from her son and applied the sandalwood paste on her wrinkled forehead and body.

'I did not know what to do. That's why I sent for Chematiri Otikkan. He is blessed with a unique strength of character and good behaviour,' she explained to him.

'Only on my return home did I realize that Ettan's[107] wife has been unwell.'

'It all began with the death of Unikkali. Oh Siva! Don't make me suffer any more.'

When had he last talked so freely with his mother? Very long ago, and even then, rarely after the sacred-thread ceremony. If she wanted something, she would mention it, but the request was normally directed to his elder brother. Her needs were few. What did she need? Everything was provided according to custom. Till they grew up, it had been her responsibility to look after the children. After that, her sphere of activity had been restricted to worship and the overall supervision usually assigned to the head of the household. She did not have to step inside the kitchen, the family being wealthy enough to hire servants. Nor did she have to make preparations for worship. There were people assigned to do those jobs. Whenever there was a ritual or a ceremony, his elder brother consulted Mother, and she explained the existing customs. Her husband was dead. Her children had grown up and they in turn had had children. She spent her time praying, playing with her grandchildren and reading the *Bhagavatham*[108] and *Kilipattu*.[109] That was the range of her activities. In less wealthy families, the women had to assist in the kitchen. Usually there were four to five wives in the household. Each one was allotted some work. One was to sweep the kitchen, another to sieve the rice, the third to

---

[107] A term used for elder brother.

[108] An epic relating the story of Lord Krishna.

[109] The literal meaning of *Kilipattu* is 'Song of the Parrot'. This is a specific reference to the poems written by Tunchat Ezhuthachan who wrote the *Adhyatma Ramayanam*. Here, the reference is to his poem *Bhagavatham Kilipattu*. He relates the story as though it is sung by a parrot. As he belonged to a lower caste and couldn't recite sacred verses, he resorted to this technique of using the parrot's voice to recite the verses he wrote to make it acceptable to his high-caste readers.

collect and arrange flowers for worship and so on. As soon as these women entered the household, the mother of the house advised them on their duties and customary practices. They went about their duties with no further thought. It was those who bore children who worried: food was always scarce. But what about those who were childless? The young widows? Oh, God!

'I hope you are not going on one of your journeys immediately.'

'I've not decided,' said Nambyattan. 'For my part, I want to undertake such journeys frequently. The rest is in the hands of destiny.'

Was it Nambyattan, her own son, who uttered those words? The mother gazed at her son, unable to believe her eyes. What had happened to him?

'I was planning to go to the house of the Otikkans tomorrow.'

'That's good,' said Mother. 'I had thought of asking you to do just that. If it is possible and convenient, please try and meet Akkithar.'

'I am going there for that very purpose.'

'Oh, Siva! Save me.' All of a sudden, the mother turned away from her son and looked at the idols of the gods placed on the three-legged stool. Perum Trikkovilappan,[110] Bhagavathi,[111] Vettekkaran[112]—all of them were there. The mother felt that their faces bore a closed expression conveying discontent and displeasure. Would those faces never clear again in response to her daily worship and offerings of flowers? Unconsciously, the figure of Unikkali,

---

[110] Siva, who is the family deity of specific Namboodiri families and is the presiding deity of the temple at Talipparambu in North Kerala.

[111] The mother goddess. According to the Dravidian pantheon of gods, there are three gods—Ayyan (the god who rules the forests), Amman (the goddess who rules the land) and Andavan (the god who rules over the mountains). The Aryanized version of these deities are Ayyappa, Bhagavathi and Subramanya respectively.

[112] A local version of the hunter god Ayyan.

who used to assist her in her worship came to her mind. The face of Bhagavathi seemed to resemble Unikkali's. The mother blinked once or twice. Then she looked at her son. The son also turned his gaze to each of the gods placed on the stool and then at his mother, who sat on the wooden plank. He felt that his mother had turned into a stone like the idols of her gods after a life of suffering and perseverance. The mendicant son's heart filled with compassion. A sorrowful expression flitted across his otherwise strong and masculine face. The mother and son continued to gaze at each other for a long time. The blessing which emanated from the heart of the mother, purified through sacrifices, added a new glow to the son's maturity. At that moment, he became a devotee who had a vision of the Supreme Being and who exulted in the unity of his self with that Being. In that bliss, he felt himself dissolving into a sublime nothingness.

12

In the palace, the prayer hall was filled with the golden glow from a wooden lamp called the matampi. In that smokeless radiance sat Young Otikkan, Ichatha, not knowing what to do. Scratching his matted hair, the young Unni Namboodiri sat by him.

Embarrassed, Amalakkad Kunhaniyan tried to make light of the status accorded to him, marked by his freshly washed clothes that were obviously received from the palace. Two or three young men, aspirants to 'resident husbandships', sauntered in after their supper. All of them waited for the arrival of the hanging lamp heralding their visit to the bedchambers.

The Young Otikkan's face blazed with fury. In the luminous light of the wooden lamp, his attractive face flushed excitedly while the young Unni Namboodiri's face reflected an air of stillness.

On Ramanikutty's orders, the attendant arrived with the customary hanging lamp. Kunhaniyan, probably the youngest among them, was allowed to meet his wife every day. As a rule the 'resident husbands' waiting to be called to the bedroom assembled after supper at the bathing house or the prayer hall to play chess or cards. Kunhaniyan was never seen in those places whenever the Young Otikkan had arrived in search of him.

'Don't you ever give yourself some rest?'

The other residents also raised their voices in derision.

'Go to your own house once in a while or you won't live very long.'

What sort of madness was his! What excess, what folly!

Kunhaniyan also felt slightly peeved, even though he had

actually began enjoying Ramanikutty Thampuran's company.

'Go and inform her that he is not coming today,' Young Otikkan exploded with rage. 'Hey you, go away and tell the lady or the assistant, or whoever it is, that Kunhaniyan is not free today.'

The holder of the lamp was thus shooed away by the Young Otikkan. 'Are these young Namboodiris out of their senses?' he wondered.

'Hey, you, I told you that you should be off,' Young Otikkan bellowed.

The naturally timid assistant, alarmed at the harsh tone, fled indoors.

'Hey, Ichatha, let Kunhaniyan go. Why do you trouble him so?' a young Namboodiri intervened.

'It is not a problem for me. But Thampuran...' Kunhaniyan interjected feebly.

'Thampuran! She is your wife and still you call her Thampuran! Of course, when you accept a salary, you have to work for it. You may go.' The Young Otikkan's offensive words flayed Kunhaniyan, shaming him.

'Shame on you, Ichatha, such emotional fervour is uncalled for. Shouldn't you think of *his* situation?'

The Young Otikkan also felt that he had said too much too hastily. He had not intended to sound so harsh. The criticism that lay uppermost in his mind rushed out when an occasion presented itself. Not being very mature, he had been unable to soften or temper his words.

'I am not going. Not just today, but never,' said Kunhaniyan, stung.

'Hey!'

The flame of the wooden lamp flickered back and forth. The palace, swathed in the silence of that cold night, shook and trembled. There was an electrifying change even on Unni Namboodiri's normally calm face. The Young Otikkan stared at Kunhaniyan, who looked crazed. He looked as if he had witnessed a strange phenomenon. In the prayer hall, the stillness grew alarmingly.

There had been occasions when 'resident husbands' were discarded by their wives. There were also instances of these unlucky men freeing themselves when fed up with the despicable deeds of their wives.

But...

Kunhaniyan fell into a stupor in the wake of his own powerful words. The next day, an hour after sunrise, Kunhaniyan went to Chinnammu's bungalow. As usual, the young Brahmin cook had prepared his breakfast. Kunhaniyan sat staring listlessly at the boiled bananas served on a plantain leaf.

'I will serve him. You may go.'

Hearing Ramanikutty's voice, Kunhaniyan's head sank lower. He knew that if he looked her in the face just once, he would change the decision he'd arrived at after a sleepless night. Ramanikutty, who personified the purity of the idol of Siva used in daily worship, had the power by her sheer proximity to force him to give up his decision. All his resolutions would falter when faced with her innocence.

'Aren't you going to drink your coffee?'

Kunhaniyan did not see the coffee growing cold and a thin film of cream that had formed on top. His fingers began to tap a rhythm on the leaf before him.

'Yesterday,' began Ramanikutty.

What could he say? That henceforth he was going to his own house. That...

'I heard everything,' said Ramanikutty. 'Who were the others in the prayer hall? Some people were making fun of you, isn't it? Let me ask you something: What wrong have I done?'

She knew everything. In any case, it was not a secret. There had been other Namboodiris in the prayer hall. Before dawn, they would have faithfully relayed the news to the high command, hoping to gain some favour. In their anxiety to stay in favour, they would not have paused to think of the larger consequences.

'How have I erred?' she persisted.

Kunhaniyan concentrated on the boiled bananas, peeling their veins off carefully, one after the other, placing them together and apparently admiring their appearance.

Whose fault was it?

'Is it my fault that I was born in a palace?'

Oh! Gods who protect humans! He thought.

'Why are you silent?'

'I do not know what to say. I thought of returning home today.'

Even though she had heard the news from other sources, the confirmation of the same from her 'husband' shocked Ramanikutty. Nonplussed and exhausted, she leaned against the wall for support.

Chinnammu, who had eavesdropped on her daughter's conversation, came into the dining room.

'Won't you come back after two days? Has anything happened at home?'

A query from the King's own niece!

It sounded like a royal command.

What could he say?

The previous night he had taken an oath on his dead father that he would not be a paid husband any more; so there was no question of continuing as a resident husband in the palace.

He had bragged to Unni Namboodiri and the Young Otikkan, who had left before dawn. 'I am going today. That is the truth. After that, if Ramanikutty needs me, she must come to my house.'

But that was not the custom. It would never happen.

Then what? Then, let her not come at all.

'What is the occasion?' Chinnammu demanded an answer.

Kunhaniyan was moved by a rare courage.

'I will tell you. I am going back to my house. I do not think I will come back here. If Ramanikutty so wishes, she can come and stay in my house. It may not be easy for her.'

Kunhaniyan drank the coffee that had gone cold in a single gulp and stood up. In the heat of that outburst, he had addressed Ramanikutty by name. She was thrilled. For the first time, he had not referred to her as Thampuran. That, and the bold words he used, were new to her. No woman in the palace had been addressed by name by their Namboodiri husband.

Chinnammu's obese body shook with anger. Such arrogance! Did he know whom he was playing with? Did he realize what he was demanding? Ramanikutty to stay in *his* house!

The women from the palace never stepped into the courtyard unless accompanied by armed attendants. They slept in their own homes. They were members of the family of the ruling king. Yet a nameless fellow, a virtual beggar, dared to suggest that his royal wife should go and stay in his house.

The man's impertinence!

'I am not angry with anyone. But in truth, I feel very uncomfortable. I shall not remarry. But...but, I cannot stay here. Ramanikutty, come here. Let me tell you something.'

Again, he had called her Ramanikutty. He was actually calling her by her name! The pure quality of that voice aroused Ramanikutty. The young niece of the ruling king lifted her eyes slowly and looked at her husband's flushed face, a face she had seen only a few times.

'Come, let me tell you something.'

What was he going to say? He had mentioned that he was not angry with her and that was enough for her.

Ramanikutty's feelings for her husband were different from what she had felt for him until then. The veil which covered her, birth after birth, dropped away and she saw the many wonders which were revealed to Lord Krishna's[113] mother when he had opened his rosy lips at her request. She visualized a distant birth in which she went around the sacred fire; the white puffed rice shedding from the palms of her hands into the sacrificial fire;[114] the fire god appearing as a physical presence blessing her.

'I love you. When all the present restrictions are removed, you can come to my house. I do not want to hurt anyone. But the tears of too many young girls have seeped into the walls of our houses. I realize how true Young Otikkan's words are. That is our sacrificial ground. The pillar for conducting the sacrifice has been raised. The sacrificial fire is burning, unblemished. Now, let me go.'

Slowly he wiped his flushed face, making it even redder, and walked out of the dining room. Without looking back, he went to the prayer hall. He took off the freshly washed clothes he was wearing. Then, he picked up the cloth he had worn when he had arrived at the palace. It was soiled, but he didn't mind. He walked out, his head held high.

Ramanikutty did not know how long she stood in the dining room, leaning against the wall. Was she thinking of anything? If she was, her face revealed nothing. She did not weep. Her heart was too empty for even that.

When Chinnammu saw her daughter having her lunch and going about her routine as usual, she was relieved. She felt that there was no reason to worry. The impertinence of that young Namboodiri! The instigation, of course, came from the two young

---

[113] This is a reference to the story of Krishna rebuked by his mother for eating mud. In her anger, she asked him to open his mouth. When Krishna obliged, his mother saw a stupendous sight of all the worlds of the universe with all its living beings. Recovering from a faint, she realized that this was no mortal child, but an incarnation of the Divine.

[114] This is a ritual performed during the marriage ceremony of Namboodiris.

Namboodiris from the North. She gnashed her teeth in frustration.

Young Otikkan and the emaciated Unni Namboodiri continued their 'pilgrimage', spreading their message. Compassion, which had fled from the Namboodiri houses, afraid of the wild bushes and forests that grew in the compounds, now turned and looked back. The Namboodiri women, prohibited from seeing the sun's rays, ran and hid themselves when a few rays of the sun stealthily crept through the cracks in the doors and entered their inner quarters. The Namboodiri men, who had shredded the apparel of Vedic qualities into pieces and worn them proudly around their bodies, jumped up hastily, trying to cover the cracks through which the light filtered.

They blamed each other; they tried to contain the sparks of fire emanating from their own flesh and blood with the palmyra fan.

And yet, the sun rose, once again.

13

The Chakyar[115] employed all his humour and inventiveness to present to a discerning audience the story of Ittitathri, a young woman who on the evening of her husband, Indinyayakkappan's annual death ceremony transformed herself into a man by fixing a lotus stem in her vagina, thus developing a penis and taking on the name Ittitathran. The audience laughed and enjoyed the innuendos in the recital of the story. They dwelled on the nuances of the story of the transformation of Ittitathri's sexual organ, and honoured the Chakyar's theatrical skills with a gold chain, usually awarded only to the bravest in the land.

In the Koothambalam[116] adorned by a hundred pillars, the young Namboodiris and the adolescent girls who had not yet had their ears pierced or begun wearing their traditional costumes were tickled by an unexpected yearning as they sat gazing at the Chakyar's accompanying drum. The young Namboodiris just initiated into the chanting of the sacred verses twisted their sacred threads and played with the deerskin they wore. They retied their waist strings made of sacred grass and fervently prayed for opportunities to form

---

[115]A caste below the Brahmins (Namboodiris) and above the Nairs in the caste hierarchy of Kerala. The Chakyars are temple dancers who perform the dance dramas of Kudiyattam, Chakyar Kuttu, etc. The Chakyar Kuttu is a one-man show, a satirical commentary on society through the narration of an epic story, performed on temple premises. It is believed that Chakyars are children born to Namboodiri women whose husbands were declared outcastes.

[116]The hall adjacent to temples, where performances such as Kudiyattam, Krishnattam and Kathakali are held during temple festivals. These halls are noted for their architectural grandeur.

secret liaisons even before their formal initiation into Brahminhood.

There was a section of women who grew up revelling in the plentiful throwaways from the temple premises and the opportunities to form illicit relationships due to the shortage of men in their own castes—causing prolonged warfare. They got food without any exertion, the privilege of pleasing the Brahmin caste, pure physical pleasure. All they did after they came of age was to welcome the Namboodiris who came visiting at festival and feast time, indulge in vulgar exploits, gossip and procreate; thus increasing their numbers. This routine was easy and pleasurable. The justification was that the fulfilment of the first three virtues—dharma, artha (money) and kama (lust)—of the fourfold desirable human goals would automatically lead them to the fulfilment of the fourth virtue, moksha (liberation). Dharma and artha could be earned by serving the Brahmins. Kama was indeed a hereditary birthright and the very pulse of life itself. As for the young Namboodiris, they went around grunting like stud bulls with no other thought or aim in life. The powerful words uttered by Young Otikkan and his mentor, the slim, dark, young Namboodiri, made them aware of their own moral laxity. So they avoided the two of them and went about their activities secretly.

∽

An enraged Chinnammu sat in her bungalow and glowered. How dare that young man despise his relationship with the ruling king's niece! Requesting her to come and stay at his house if she so desired, a house which was as poor as that of the proverbial Kuchela.[117]

---

[117] This refers to the story of a poor Brahmin, Kuchela, Sri Krishna's friend. Persuaded by his wife he reluctantly visits his friend Krishna with a request to alleviate his poverty. Krishna gives him a warm reception and eats with relish the pounded rice prepared by Kuchela's wife. Kuchela never made his request to Krishna. But by the time he returned home he was blessed with a house, wealth and other comforts by Krishna.

When the ritualist Keezhembram came to her, Chinnammu's turbulent mood softened.

'Is there a way out of this tricky situation? Ramanikutty is so restless.'

'Oh, Oh! I didn't realize that he would be so petty. What can I say except that it is a kind of foolhardiness. I feel ashamed for having brought that worthless lout here.'

The seven vital veins in Keezhembram's body had gone numb with the cold food he was accustomed to for days together. His chilled hands were always happy to hold the ceremonial fan[118] in support of the despicable activities of the Thampurans.

'I don't think he will come back. He went off in a stubborn fit.'

'Let *me* try. I will go and find out.'

Even though Keezhembram was an employee of the palace, Chinnammu Thampuran knew that the incentive of additional money alone would move him to action. She went inside to fetch an initial payment of ten silver coins. 'Keezhembram, even if he is unwilling to return, you should not come back empty-handed. Please bring another Namboodiri.'

'Don't I know what to do? Do you think it will be so difficult to get a Namboodiri for your family? Siva! Siva! Remember, she is the great King's own niece.'

'Shouldn't we ask Ramanikutty's opinion?' asked Chinnammu's resident husband, who had hidden himself in the room, with great hesitation.

'Yes, yes, raising such useless questions. You don't help, but are always there to create problems. It is becoming very difficult, Keezhembram.'

Without waiting for her to complete her tirade, her husband

---

[118] Ornamental fan made of peacock feathers were used to fan the king and the temple deities on ceremonial occasions.

slunk back into his hole in his freshly washed clothes.

'So please, go your way,' she looked at the shining figure of King George the Fifth embossed on the coins placed next to her and continued. 'Please keep this for your travel expenses.'

'May God protect us.' The ritualist ran his eye over Chinnammu's plump body and uttered his blessing with closed eyes.

∽

Before long, Keezhembram jingled enough silver coins to bring to Chinnammu's bungalow a young Namboodiri who had spent most of his time attending feasts and visiting prostitutes.

'Is he trained to chant the Vedas?'

'He is from an aristocratic family, well placed in the hierarchy of the original eight houses of Namboodiris. They have fallen on bad times and are not so prosperous any more.'

'That will do. So let us have the ceremony this very day. After that, we shall arrange a small feast too. What do you say?'

The Namboodiri, who had come with the high hopes of becoming a resident husband, daydreamed of the night to come and salivated.

'Mother, please come here,' Ramanikutty poked her head through the door to the veranda. 'Let me make it very clear to you. I do not want any other Namboodiri. There is no point in scolding me later. I am making my stand clear right now.'

Those words, spoken with a quiet firmness, wounded Chinnammu's bloated frame.

'You run along. These things will be decided by us.'

'Yes, yes,' the ritualist nodded.

'Namboodiri, all you want is money, isn't that so? I will give you enough. Go away. Do not trouble yourself on my behalf.' Ramanikutty withdrew without waiting to hear any further talk.

Keezhembram was in a fix. The Namboodiri who came

Outcaste

dreaming of a new liaison peeped inside and sighed. 'So, in the end, isn't it going to work out? Were you making a fool of me, Keezhembram?' he asked.

'No, Namboodiri, don't worry. Stay here for two days. Everything will be all right.' Keezhembram consoled the poor fool.

'Yes, yes, Namboodiri, you may go to the prayer hall. Go back only after two days. I will tell Keezhembram,' added Chinnammu. 'Let me try to persuade her, Keezhembram. She is very stubborn,' she finished.

The ritualist got up, thinking that his efforts had been wasted. He had dreamt of receiving more money for his work. He had eight sisters at home. Three of them were married. Had it not been for his personal problems, he would not have deigned to do this kind of slavish work. He had not been trained to do any job other than performing pujas at temples and rituals at rich households.

Keezhembram moved towards the prayer hall. His ninth sibling was a boy, an only brother who was blind, but very clever. He was the one who managed the household affairs. Keezhembram sent all his beggarly earnings to his brother who had used it carefully to conduct three weddings. One more wedding was almost fixed.

Oh goddess! Please give me a long life. My son is not yet four years old. His brother had said, 'We must arrange for Unni to learn English. He will then protect and maintain this house. Otikkan had remarked that his horoscope was good.'

Keezhembram sat in the prayer hall, worrying about his own problems. With a heavy heart, he recited the verse for ushering in good fortune.

5

On moonlit nights during the Tiruvathira[119] season, when the soft breeze wafted in after caressing the golden dome of the Sri Krishna temple at Trippunithara,[120] Chinnammu felt anxious. During the night of the Tiruvathira, when she sang the Mangalathira[121] and danced in the moonlit courtyard of the palace, her lips red from chewing a hundred betel leaves, her hair adorned with ten varieties of flowers and leaves, she thought of her daughter. What had happened to her? Months had gone by after Kunhaniyan had gone away. Another Namboodiri couldn't be arranged for her; she wouldn't permit it.

Absolute folly!

Kshatriya women were different from Namboodiri women. What had happened to her?

Chinnammu's step faltered as she was dancing to the tune of the Mangalathira. She was worried about her daughter. Through the open window, Ramanikutty's long and shapely eyes gazed at the outside world. In the distance, on the flagpole of Lord Vishnu's temple, was affixed a flying vehicle, the Lord's vehicle silently calling out to people to give up all worldly bonds and rise into the skies. Some unknown good fortune, the result of the good deeds of ancestors, had held her hands and led her to a good partner. By the time she had overcome her initial shyness and had begun to know him intimately, she had had to give him up. This poor woman, born ahead of her times, thought of her fate and let out a sigh painful sigh.

---

[119] A festival celebrated by women of Kerala in honour of Kama, the god of love, who was burnt down by Siva's wrath. It falls in the month of December, when the women in the house assembled in the inner courtyard to sing and dance.

[120] A town in mid-Kerala, near Cochin, the abode of the kings of Cochin and famous for the temple of Krishna.

[121] A song sung by Namboodiri women on the occasion of Tiruvathira, the festival of Kama.

From the courtyard downstairs came the arousing strains of a song of yearning. Ramanikutty felt the searing pain of separation. In that molten heat of suffering, the plethora of sins nurtured by the authority and wealth of the kingly palace melted and disintegrated.

14

'Wait. Don't step in yet.'

As Neelan's bridal party began the ritual of his bride's entry into her husband's house,[122] the elder Namboodiri, Cheriyedath Tundan, cried out this order, hearing which the bride, Paptikutty, and her party waited at the gate of Cheriyedath House. Neelan, the groom, who stood behind them in his new clothes carrying the pot which held the sacred fire, scratched the ground with his feet. Behind them came the Namboodiri women, who held their umbrellas and talked to each other, unaware of what was going on. One by one, the men tried to find out what was happening. They watched Tundan, who sat calmly in the front room skinning areca nut kernels.[123]

'Lack of common sense. What else can one say?'

'Some kind of obstinacy!'

'There are ways to tackle such a sticky situation.'

'Then why did he take the trouble to get his younger brother married?'

In the front yard of Cheriyedath House, the Namboodiris who

---

[122] In Namboodiri weddings, after the ritual of tying the tali, the bride is taken to her husband's house and ceremoniously installed as his wife and a member of his family. There are many rituals with regard to this function.

[123] Paan chewing is a part of the food habits of India. The main ingredients in making a paan are betel leaves, lime, betel nuts and, in some cases, tobacco. Some believe this is a digestive after a meal. But there are others who are addicted to it. It is a substitute for smoking, especially amongst women. Women chew for decorative purposes also, the juice reddening their lips.

had come to participate in the installation ceremony of the bride raised their voices.

'It is not possible to instal the bride,' Cheriyedath Tundan announced emphatically.

Why?

What was the reason?

State it.

'No, my brother knows the conditions. I have informed him. If those conditions can be met, we can proceed with the installation ceremony. Otherwise, we cannot.'

'Let us call him.'

Thazhath Namboodiri, who watched his first daughter's bridal ceremony interrupted, sat at the gate heavy-hearted. Granted, it was a case of the younger brother marrying while the elder remained unmarried. Still, the elder brother had conducted the wedding. Cheriyedath Tundan himself had taken the initiative to arrange the marriage. For the continuation of progeny; to ensure the family line continued.

The elder Namboodiri was not physically fit, so he had allowed the younger brother to marry.

The sin of such a marriage being conducted was ignored.

Shouldn't there be a son to show the gateway to the next world? A person to give the sacred water when he breathed his last? A rightful heir to perform the propitiation ritual for his ancestors? The Vedic priest had referred to the sacred scriptures.

In times of danger...

After going through all that, now...

'He readily agreed to the wedding. In fact he wanted the bride to be from Thazhath House.'

Thazhath Namboodiri sat cross-legged on the dusty ground.

Those who waited to sound the ceremonial ululation yawned. People who came to receive the bridal party holding the eight auspicious objects[124] were tired of standing and waiting. Their hands ached.

Paptikutty stood perspiring, holding the handle of her umbrella close to her thudding heart. Those who stood around sighed, seeing her decorated feet. What was the matter?

Who could they ask?

The bridegroom took off the green karuka garland, shook it and threw it away. He stepped into the front room and, reluctant to look at his elder brother's disgruntled face, switched his gaze to the roof.

'What is the matter? Whatever it is, agree with him.'

'Agree? Do you know what you are talking about?'

'Where is Chematiri Otikkan? Let's call him.'

'I was told that he will come only in the afternoon.'

'Who else is there?'

'Tundan will not listen to anyone.'

'Why is everyone so worried? We can't have the installation of the bride here. That's all. You can hold it somewhere else.' Tundan declared.

'Please give your permission. We can hold it anywhere you want.'

'What is the matter? Tell us.'

'My brother knows it.'

'Let's hear it too.'

'No.'

'They *must* hear. You *must* say it, brother. Let them also hear it,' Neelan exploded.

The elder brother frightened him into silence with a mere stare.

---

[124]Gold, a length of brocade cloth, unhusked grain, raw rice, a ceremonial lamp a polished brass mirror, sindoor powder and kajal were symbols of a woman's married state.

'Please go inside, Cheriyedam.'

Someone found a way out. Indoors was his aunt whose words of advice he might listen to. After the death of the mistress of Cheriyedath House, it was this aunt who had stayed on and helped run the household.

'If his aunt talks to him he might listen to her.'

Tundan was very fond of this aunt.

Someone sighed hopefully, seeing that Cheriyedath Namboodiri had slithered inside.

The bridegroom escaped from the uproar of the front room to come out and stand by his father-in-law near the gate.

'What is it all about? Please explain,' Thazhath Namboodiri pleaded with his son-in-law.

'I should not have married.'

Those soft but firm words boomed in Paptikutty's ears.

Paptikutty, who had been considered a lucky girl.

The bridegroom was a young man and this was his first marriage. The family led a comfortable life. There was no one else to share their wealth. She was indeed very lucky.

'I should not have married.' Those words uttered by her wedded husband tore at her heart.

The nuptials were not yet over. She had not even looked at her husband to her heart's content. Paptikutty felt the earth beneath her feet giving way.

'I should not have agreed to this marriage.'

'Why?'

'Why is your brother objecting now? Was it not performed according to his wishes? Is he not satisfied with the arrangements?' Thazhath Namboodiri looked at his son-in-law's expressionless face and lowered his head in disgust. The rising desperation within him found a voice which whispered: 'Agree to whatever he says. Isn't he your elder brother? He was keener on this marriage happening than anyone else. And now?'

'That is the root cause of all this confusion.'

He had married at his elder brother's insistence. Tundan had gone to great lengths to ensure that the remedial measures for the sin of the younger brother marrying when his elder brother was unmarried were completed. He had made the preparations for the installation of the bride. On the fourth day after the wedding at the bridegroom's house, he had said, 'That is best. The ceremony after the wedding should be held in the bridegroom's house.'

He was happy.

And now?

'Do not ask about it. It is better that you do not know about it,' Neelan somehow managed to stutter.

'Whatever it is, settle it between yourselves. How long can the bridal party be kept at the gate?'

'Let it be done.'

'Let the installation be performed in the central courtyard.'

And after that?

After all, they were brothers.

'Neelan, agree to whatever your brother wants.'

No, Neelan felt he couldn't. If he agreed... No, he couldn't face the consequences. It was better to drown himself.

How could he face Paptikutty? On the other hand, if he went against his brother's words...

No, he didn't have the courage to do that. He couldn't even dream of it. Disobey his elder brother... That would be like disrespecting one's own teacher.

And then?

Oh, God! Help me.

Cheriyedath Neelan looked sharply at his wife's face. Through the veil, he saw her eyes brimming with tears.

Oh, God!

He pressed his hands on the ground and leaned backwards.

'Begin, Neelan, let's not delay any more. Shouldn't we complete the next ritual also?'

Paptikutty stretched her tired legs and moved forward. Placing her right foot first, she entered the inner precincts of Cheriyedath House. Her firm footsteps caused a tremor around the inner courtyard of that four-sided structure. The festive sounds boomed and resounded like Death's sibilant whispers. The married Namboodiri women raised their voices and talked incessantly in an attempt to feign an enthusiasm that had lost its earlier vigour. In the place of the head of the family, the aunt made the offerings. Paptikutty sat on a decorated wooden seat placed in the central courtyard holding her tali, the symbol of the sanctity of marriage, and prayed. Surrounded by bits of unni appam, a delicacy made of jaggery and rice powder, strewn here and there by the young Namboodiris in their scramble to catch them, she picked up the polished brass mirror placed among the eight auspicious objects and examined her face. She decorated her forehead with the caste mark and wore in her hair a garland made of karuka leaves. On her henna-red finger, a silver ring twinkled. The entrancing beauty of those fingers sent shivers down the spines of the spectators assembled in the upper veranda. They were caught in a peculiar dilemma: unable to take their eyes off such beauty and yet afraid to continue gazing at its blazing quality, they stared through half-shut eyes.

In the northern quarters, preparations were made to observe rituals celebrating celibacy.

The hour stood ready for the post-wedding rituals. The western quarter of Cheriyedath House wore an air of spiritual fulfilment after breathing in the fragrance of incense from the sacrificial pit in the northern quarters.

The ceremony of the purification of the bride—according to Vedic rites—to become fit to bear a child, began. The fire fed specially with boiled buttermilk flared. Chanting, 'Oh Fire, purify me to bear the child of my husband,' Paptikutty mentally sacrificed herself to the purity of her purpose. She sat on the ox skin and performed the celibacy ritual for four days with four separate ghee offerings to the fire. After that, she was declared pure enough to bear children.

∽

In the western bridal chamber, Paptikutty waited for her first union with her husband. The eight auspicious objects and a burning lamp lent an air of purity to the sacred moment. Generations of pure tradition lit Paptikutty's face with a new glow of desire. The very thought of the ritual of bathing sent a thrill through her limbs.

In the soft, diffused light, the door to the bridal chamber opened noiselessly. Paptikutty, seated on the edge of the decorative cot of polished rosewood, stood up. She covered her bare breasts with her intertwined hands and gazed at the floor, seeing a reflection of all her previous births in her toenails.

'Look at me.'

What?

That voice!

It was different from the one she had heard from the man sitting in front of the fire during the wedding ceremony. Whose could it be? Slowly she raised her heavy eyelids.

'Oh, Amme!'

Her voice strangled in her throat, circling, refusing to emerge.

This was not her husband, but his elder brother.

Tundan!

Paptikutty stood in front of this stunted gnome. He smiled, no, showed his teeth and grinned like a devil. She began to perspire profusely.

'Look at me, I...'

The sacred verse beginning with the words 'Yours on...?'[125] rang in her ears.

Where was that Namboodiri who had sat by her and recited the mantra to open her vagina?

This man?

Paptikutty's vision blurred.

Again, she recalled words from the sacred verse:

I shall not give you cause to weep.

Where were the hands that had promised to wipe her tears?

Her husband's brother who was to be like a second father!

Father!

God!

In Paptikutty's heart, where the God of Death was howling, something else quivered and woke up.

No, no, it was not possible.

Struggling to save herself, she crawled towards the door.

Tundan sat on the cot swinging his stunted legs, enjoying himself.

'Don't be afraid. I have told him everything.'

So...

That was why...

The younger brother to wed.

The elder brother for post-nuptials.

That was why he had hastened the installation of the bride in his house. If it was held in her house, this would not have been possible.

'Don't be anxious. I wanted this very badly.'

---

[125] One of the verses recited during the wedding ceremony. It has romantic connotations.

Panchali![126]

Not five husbands, but only two!

Tundan and Neelan.

'Paptikutty!' cried Tundan.

He should be slapped soundly. Calling her by her name!

Husband's brother! She should not even see him. For a Namboodiri woman who was forbidden to even see the sun's rays, looking at any man other than her husband was equal to adultery.

And in this house?

Paptikutty leaned against the door. Water, water, she longed for some water. Her tongue refused to move.

Paptikutty, who had waited anxiously for her nuptials, cursing the length of each second, too shy to look at her own heaving breasts, now writhed, unable to get out of her bridal chamber.

The door was bolted from the outside—a precaution taken by the younger brother on behalf of the elder brother. Gatekeeper! God of Death!

'I shall go off after some time.'

His head should roll on the floor! Oh, for a kitchen knife! The detachment with which he said it! Like the polite words of a traveller who had stepped into a house for shelter on a rainy day.

The knowledge of the Vedas which had raised Brahminism to heaven had now entrapped one's own brother's wife to satiate a man's lust!

The Devas of the Earth!

Is there a God?

Then...

Goddess! Amme! Save me!

---

[126] Draupadi was the wife of all five Pandava brothers in the Mahabharata. This was not out of choice, but the result of a peculiar turn of events based on the words of the Pandavas's mother, Kunti.

For the first time in her life, Paptikutty understood the emptiness of those words.

He had the audacity to tell her that he had already informed his brother. That tongue which uttered such words should be plucked out and sacrificed!

Tundan, who had been shaking his stunted legs in enjoyment, got up. His grin seemed more like a grimace to her. He grabbed Paptikutty's wrists with their jingling brass bangles and pulled her towards him. Paptikutty, leaning on the door and panting helplessly, realized that he had the strength of a wild animal.

'Please sit here,' saying this the stunted animal caressed her youthful beauty, thrilled at the experience.

She remembered another sacred verse again:

I imagine your vagina as Godhead.

Only once had her wedded husband touched her, and that too as a part of the ritual, accompanied by sacred verses to purify her body, to sanctify her to bear his children. Just once. Another sacred verse rose in her mind:

I, Lord of Oceans, grant you the privilege of creation.

'We shall see each other at night,' her husband had said. She did see now—and what a sight it proved to be!

Has any human being suffered the twisted fate of seeing more? Her husband's face!

That very night, he too would come.

He was probably waiting his turn outside the door. A true worshipper of elders! Let his elder brother finish. A slavish dog waiting to lick the leftovers.

Cheriyedath Tundan moved closer to Paptikutty. He gripped the edge of her clothes.

Paptikutty's inner eye opened. The purpose of her birth was

revealed to her in that moment. Her weariness and inertia vanished. The concept of Illusion reared its head. The primal figure of the Mother Goddess[127] in a graveyard, wearing a garland of skulls, gleefully sucking the blood trickling from the decapitated demon's head, appeared in her mind's eye.

In that instant, the bridal chamber was transformed into a chamber of birth.

This was her second birth, the true fulfilment of the title 'twice-born'[128] given to her clan.

Paptikutty! The Goddess of Revenge!

The personification of power, an incarnation born on hearing the clarion call of Time itself to punish the evil-minded.

In Paptikutty's eyes, Tundan, who sat next to her, grew smaller and smaller until he was reduced to the insignificance of a mustard seed. Her parched and blistered lips grew moist with compassion. A smile, to seduce the whole universe, adorned her lips.

'Oh, God! That is enough for me. I am happy,' Tundan uttered, pleased with the change in her.

But the very next minute he hung his head, unable to face Paptikutty's scorching gaze.

To Paptikutty, he seemed to have turned into one of the Goddess's minions.

A mere slave at her feet!

'Shall I turn off the lamp?'

'No,' commanded Paptikutty's tongue, which had gained a new lease of life.

From now on, she would issue the commands... The male

---

[127] The image of Kali, the Mother Goddess, who after killing the demon Darika, drank his blood. Kali is supposed to be the goddess of Night, residing in burial grounds.

[128] Brahmins have a second birth when they are initiated to the study of the Shastras and bound by Truth to the sacred.

breed would have to obey her dictates.

Enough of obedience!

Oh Paptikutty, Mother of the Universe!

To Paptikutty, who now understood the secret behind her incarnation, the entire plan of action, from birth to her death and union with the ultimate, became clear. Her eyes shone with a sense of contentment.

'I...I.... Let me go.' Tundan stood before her, obedient, impotent, having surrendered all his powers to this Goddess. As for Paptikutty, she lay on the wide bed, covered with white sheets, the very personification of desire. She detained Tundan, who stood wagging his tail, awaiting her orders.

'Stop,' he begged. 'My younger brother is waiting.'

He did not have the courage to spend the entire night with this luminous flame of power.

A shining beauty, a seductive figure!

The expression on her face! Siva, Siva!

He could do nothing but obey her.

'Let me...my younger brother wouldn't have slept yet.'

Splendid! The hour was auspicious, excellent.

Two men to share her bridal night!

'All right,' Paptikutty assented.

Paptikutty, who now knew the secret of her birth, stretched out on the bed. She laughed, satisfied at the thought of those beings who would fall at her feet and surrender completely, mere beggars whose begging bowls would remain empty. This pleasure dimmed momentarily at the thought of her husband's helplessness. Her eyes moistened. She closed her eyes for a moment and prayed to the powerful Mother Goddess. Gradually, she mustered her former willpower and once again transformed into the Goddess of Revenge.

15

It was customary for all the temple trustees to meet and celebrate the eighth-day feast in the month of Karkitakam.[129] As the men of Cheriyedath House were also temple trustees, their responsibilities on the occasion were great. The Namboodiris who were participating came from distant places and included in their numbers Vedic scholars, humourous poets and various other types of scholars. The feast that was offered to them presented a veritable sample of the finest Malayali cuisine.

Cheriyedam Tundan was ready to go to the temple before noon. Neelan had left in the morning.

'Aunt, you are here, aren't you? I am going to the temple for a short while.' He said, looking towards the inner quarters.

Someone must have heard him; Paptikutty would be there. He never looked her in the face.

He should not.

Custom dictated that he should not see his brother's wife.

He never even talked directly to her.

At night…that was different.

On hearing his voice, Paptikutty came to the outer veranda.

'Chematiri Otikkan will be coming, won't he?'

'He usually does.'

'It would be nice if you could invite him over.'

Paptikutty had to be obeyed.

If only she could see her teacher, at least once. Paptikutty's

---

[129] According to the Malayalam calendar, Karkitakam is the last month in the year.

thoughts wandered wildly...

But it was a great sin!

And anyway impossible.

But still...

How long was it since she had seen her guru?

From the Otikkan House, the father would come, along with the younger Namboodiris.

She had to see them. Should she send her servant to invite them?

Paptikutty trembled in a fit of revenge.

She must seduce all Namboodiris, nay, all men.

Sita hesitated. Mother Earth opened up and saved her. Only Amba[130] had fulfilled her revenge. She was reborn as the eunuch Shikandi to kill Bhishma. Paptikutty was ready to reincarnate as many times as was necessary to extinguish the race of men.

Tundan mused, 'Will Otikkan come? I don't know. Anyway, I shall try.'

They would all come—Pachu Otikkan and Vasu Otikkan—to see their former disciple. All of them must come. Even the great king, the ruler of the country. She would attract all of them and bring them to her. Let this special penance take its own course; at the end of it, all the great houses would be destroyed. Oh you protector deities of renowned families! Where were you now?

The act had to begin with her husband's Namboodiri house itself. In the very presence of her husband and his brother, she would take all the Namboodiris who came to the feast to bed. One

---

[130] Amba is the eldest of the three princesses, Amba, Ambika and Ambalika, whom Bhishma abducts as brides for his brothers, Chitrangada and Vichitraveerya. On finding out that Amba was in love with another prince, Salwa, Bhishma releases her and allows her to go back to him. But Salwa refuses to accept her because she had been abducted by Bhishma. Amba promises to take revenge on Bhishma in her next birth. She immolates herself and is reborn as a eunuch, Shikandi, who is used by Arjuna to vanquish Bhishma.

by one, each one would take his turn.

Tundan and Neelan would serve as guards at the door.
Behind the closed door, there would be the Mother.
Personification of Power!
Cheriyedath Paptikutty!

She sent for the servant, in whose open palms she placed two silver rupee coins. The impoverished servant was thrilled when her hands made contact with the figure of the sovereign who ruled an empire over which, it was claimed, the sun never set.

'If you see the younger Namboodiris of the Otikkan House, please ask them to come. Tell them that I have requested it. Do it discreetly.'

At the time of her installation as a bride, the elder brother had stood in the way.

Why? The reason was known to the younger brother.

Obey the elder brother and do what he wants.

He obeyed.

Did anyone think about the woman from the inner quarters? The first night, when all the pores in her body had opened up with desire, the younger brother held the lamp and led the elder brother in. He had even stood guard at the door. When his turn came, he too went in.

It was so long since she had slept well! The endless procession of sleepless nights. The searing pain she endured each night. If only she could sleep. Paptikutty took a bath and was ready. She wore freshly washed clothes and made her red lips redder by chewing betel leaves.

She was sure that someone from the Otikkan House would come.

If they did…
Somehow…

It could be either Pachu Otikkan or Vasu Otikkan. Whoever

it was, she knew them well. Both had been, in name, her teachers. Hearing a sound from the outer veranda, Paptikutty looked up.

It was Pachu Namboodiri from the Otikkan House. A scholar. A middle-aged man who had learned the meaning of goodwill and compassion through the literary works he had mastered.

The presence of the old aunt in the house...she would be suspicious. But it did not really matter.

Let her also enter the witness box when the time came.

'Tell him he can sit in the outer veranda,' she ordered her servant.

Pachu Otikkan came in and seated himself.

'I haven't had any news about all of you for a long time. So I sent word hoping to see you for a short while,' Paptikutty greeted him.

'I am happy that you thought so, child. You were part of my household for some time. I couldn't visit you earlier because of other urgent preoccupations.'

'All is well with Akkithar?'

'Nothing is new. When you reach that stage in life, what special news can there be?'

'I want to see Chematiri Otikkan, but I do not seem to be able to do all that I want to do.'

'Even my elder brother thinks a great deal of you. You are... I do not know how to say it. Whenever we talk of you, he looks worried. I really do not know why he feels that way. We have to console ourselves by believing that it is all predestined. What else can we do?'

She had the feeling that she was temporarily losing everything she had learnt recently and reverting to the innocent, gullible girl that she had once been. No, she could not let it happen, she had to gather strength.

Paptikutty opened the door of the inner quarters and entered the outer veranda.

She posed, raising one leg and pressing her foot on the door frame, making herself all the more visible to Pachu Otikkan.

'Young Otikkan and Chematiri's wife, are they all right?'

'Yes, nothing to worry. You know that Chami, elder brother's low-caste disciple? One hears that he is not badly off. It seems that he has started to earn quite a living.'

'That is good. With the blessing of Chematiri Otikkan, everything is possible.'

'Cheriyedath Namboodiri has gone out, hasn't he?'

'Both of them have gone out. They will be back only after the ceremonial feast.'

'Then I too shall take leave and go to the temple, where I have some urgent business.'

'Can't you go later? That will give me some more time to talk to you.'

'Siva, Siva, little one, we have never thought of you as an outsider. You are my elder brother's special favourite. He has taught several young boys, but never a girl, only you. I do not know the reason. But I know that he has a special love for you.'

Oh, God!

If she were to dwell on her past, she would lose all her courage. She would falter at the very first step that she took and would ultimately have to face the punishment of being an outcaste without having achieved anything. Otikkan would report her to all the important dignitaries of the region. Rumours, counter-rumours and accusations would follow. There would be a trial. An outcaste—that was unthinkable. If he was trapped, he would not talk. Any talk would result in him becoming an outcaste and the last rites being performed while he was still alive. Never again would he be allowed to participate in a ritual or sacred rite. Afterwards, he would have to wander and beg for a livelihood. That too, in an alien place, not in the place of one's birth.

'There are some betel leaves and nuts in the room upstairs. Please accept it.'

'Don't inconvenience yourself.'

'It is no inconvenience. Later, I would feel unhappy if I hadn't offered you at least some betel leaves and nuts to chew when you visited me. Remember the number of times I have eaten the food served at the Otikkan's house.'

'Oh, child, I am so happy.'

'If you go up the staircase, you will find the betel box kept on the bed.'

Pachu Otikkan crossed the outer veranda and climbed up to the western portion of the first floor. As he stood, hesitant, he saw the betel box placed on a bed. The bed must be Tundan's; he always pretended to be sickly. That was probably why the bed was not folded, Pachu thought. As he had planned to bathe after he left, he decided to sit on the bed.

Paptikutty, too, went upstairs using the staircase in the inner quarters. She reached the western section and waited, hidden and silent. Pachu Otikkan, who opened the betel box and began the preparations to chew, was put off when he realized that there were no betel leaves.

'Here, I have the betel leaves.'

'What? You? Here? Child, what is the meaning of all this?'

What was she up to? Taking such liberties with him even though she had stayed at his house. He had seen her, but still... If anyone saw them now... Oh, no! He wished he hadn't come up.

Paptikutty approached the perplexed Otikkan and placed the betel leaves inside the box. Deliberately, she rubbed her pointed breasts against his shoulders. To Otikkan, who by then had lost control, she seemed to have changed into the goddess of love performing the feminine dance of spring. The sight of her body aroused all his nerves. Suppressed desires crashed in, wave upon wave. The hands which had hitherto fumbled with the betel box unconsciously touched Paptikutty. The touching of limbs sparked off a fire. In the ensuing heat, Otikkan lost his senses completely.

∽

Afterwards, Pachu Otikkan crossed the gate of Cheriyedath House, bowed by guilt, unable to endure the weight of sin conjured by his actions. Cheriyedath Paptikutty laughed contentedly as she watched his retreating figure, his hair left loose, his steps floundering.

She was determined to enlist all the Namboodiris of the land in the rituals of this new Mahamakam[131] battle. Remembering Paptikutty, all the Namboodiri houses should shudder and cry out in fear till the end of time.

That great priestess of the tantric order[132] undertook the penance of Kali, the destroyer, to change the presiding deity, and in the process rebuild Kerala, the temple of Parasurama. She gathered strength to dislodge the very roots of customs which were as ancient as the four Yugas. She had broken the first coconut[133] on the head of Brahminism and offered it to Ganapathy, the God of auspicious beginnings.

The figure of King George the Fifth, embossed on the silver rupee coin, smiled once again as it lay on the palm of the servant woman.

---

[131] A festival of martial arts conducted at Tirunavaya, near Thrissur, once in twelve years by the zamorin, the ruler of Calicut.

[132] Tantra is a section of Indian philosophy based on rituals such as animal sacrifice and explaining matter and mind in terms of sex and the energies of the body.

[133] Ironic reference to the custom of breaking a coconut at Ganapathy's shrine at the start of a venture. This is done to invoke the blessings of the god who is known as the Remover of Obstacles. The symbolic coconut Paptikutty smashes is on the head of the Namboodiri community.

Using a blunt pencil, Paptikutty wrote on a scrap of old paper the epitaph for all Malayali Brahmins.

One: Pachu Otikkan from the Otikkan House.

Two...

16

The inner courtyards recited the tales of centuries of suffering. The inmates—hapless Namboodiri women—inhaled the suffocating air of their dark rooms and continued their routine duties without the slightest deviation. While they slept, they screamed in fright at nightmares of jackals howling from the bushes in their compounds. Some inner conviction pushed them ahead, banishing thoughts of suicide from their minds and forcing them to sit in their prayer rooms and make offerings, facing northwards.

To blot out the decadent odour of the experience of sharing one husband among many wives, they recited their prayers louder than ever. When it dawned on them that the husband–wife relationship existed only when they were united by the sacred darbha grass as they sat in front of the sacrificial fire, they wept inwardly. In order to atone for the sin of an occasional unconscious mental berating of their menfolk, they celebrated their husband's birthdays wearing freshly laundered clothes and eating leftovers from their husband's meals.[134] The mothers of girls born into Namboodiri homes wept in distress, unable to strangle their baby girls at a tender age. They crept into their husband's rooms on the days when the current favourite absented herself during her monthly period, only to shudder later when the resultant pregnancy advanced. They circumambulated the temple till the eighth month of pregnancy, regularly performing the Tiruvonam puja,[135] praying for the birth of a son.

---

[134] Eating leftovers from the husband's meals was traditionally a way to show respect and submission.

[135] One of the rituals performed by pregnant women to bear a son, Tiruvonam

The Namboodiris, who had conveniently forgotten the plight of the inner quarters, pretended they did not see their own mothers starving, depressed and humiliated, with only a single cloth to protect themselves from rain and sun. Instead of being solicitous of their own wives' needs, they hastened to pay their dues for the nights spent with prostitutes.

While women of other castes were envious of the apparent happiness and prosperity of Namboodiri women who seemed to have enough to eat and clothe themselves, these women continued the routine of wearing wet clothes, fasting and reciting sacred verses to redress themselves of their sinful fate: being born female in an illam.[136]

'It is unfortunate. What can one do? There was no time even for the nuptials. It seems he died of cholera.'

The girl had been married off before she came of age. The wedding was celebrated with pomp and splendour. The bridegroom belonged to a superior Namboodiri family. He could recite the Vedas with a smattering of Sanskrit! Did it matter that he was old? All in all, it was a good proposal.

The mistress of Thazhamangalam House sat in her prayer room in meditation. She shed tears of compassion thinking of the premature widowhood foisted on her relative, Ittinechi's daughter.

'It's of no use... We have to console ourselves that it was fated to happen,' she consoled herself.

'Unikkali, why are you staring at me? I am afraid. What is the matter? Speak up,' Achan Namboodiri's first wife had run into the prayer room and began to mumble incoherently. But the words

---

puja involved feeding children and giving them gifts on the day of the stellar sign Tiruvonam every month.

[136] In orthodox Hindu families, just being born female was considered the result of the bad karma of past lives.

were alarming, forcibly removing the screen over those unforgettable events. Destroying her peace of mind, they seemed to perform a dance of skulls before the mother of Thazhamangalam.

'Oh, God! Please protect me. Go away and lie down for some time. You will feel better.' The hands which fumbled with the prayer beads began to shake uncontrollably.

'I don't want to stay here. If I stay here... Mother! I am going back to my house. I am taking my children with me,' Ittingayya declared.

If only one of the young Namboodiris would scold her and make her behave. But now could anyone scold her? She was deranged. Something had to be done. Maybe an oil ritual or something of that sort...

If only she could be shown to Akkithar...

Then everything may turn out all right.

But Akkithar never visited anyone. It was very difficult to even get a glimpse of him. It was great luck to see him at all; events would then take a better turn. That was the general belief.

He went to the temple very early every morning and returned home only after twilight. He went to bed early.

And in any case, can a Thazhamangalam wife wait and long to see anyone? That too, a man? Siva! Siva!

One of the eight outstanding physicians in the land had predicted that a complete cure was out of the question. His advice had been to do something to obtain the blessing of the Almighty. A cure through such a measure would bring happiness and she would at least be able to manage her own affairs. Until then, one had to be very careful.

It was not easy to persuade her to return from the bathing house once she entered it. She would linger there, seated on the steps. On further persuasion, she would take a dip and emerge without wiping herself.

'Oh, God, bless her with some good sense. The only consolation is that she doesn't harm anyone. No one at all.'

If by chance she saw Achan Namboodiri, Ittingayya would stare at him suspiciously for a minute or so. Afterwards, she would retreat into some corner and stretch out her arms, as though to ward off a fearsome sight that had suddenly appeared in the air. Days passed with no specific origin or purpose, existing only to provide endless nights and mornings for the House of Thazhamangalam.

In the front room, Mangazhi Vasu walked upto Achan Namboodiri who lay on a cot, calculating the accounts of this great Brahmin household. A smile poked its way on to Vasu's face, making it uglier than before. Achan Namboodiri was frightened when he saw this personification of unlucky events pursuing him relentlessly. The sight of this man brought back memories he wished to forget.

His brother Nambyattan stood by deferentially. His hair and beard had grown longer and formed matted locks.

'Haven't you heard? It is very unfortunate, the news of Ittinechi's daughter. Shall we ask her to come and spend ten days with us?' Achan Namboodiri asked him.

'I support whatever you decide to do. I've heard the news. We have to console ourselves thinking that it is the result of the actions of past lives.'

His brother Nambyattan, who once killed people with the ease with which he struck the pawns on the chessboard, now spoke of the fruit of the actions of previous lives! Everything about him had changed. Pilgrimage and meditation. What could one say?

'She is not even fourteen. Now what is to happen to her?'

'I, too, was thinking about that. Probably there is some truth in what that Young Otikkan and Unni Namboodiri are preaching,' said Nambyattan.

'What? What did I hear you say? From the very beginning, the people from Otikkan House have shown streaks of rebellion.

That Chematiri accepted a low-caste boy as his disciple, taking him around wherever he goes! His brother's friendship with that foreign priest! The son is supposed to be a reformed progressive! Revolutionary! Trying to put an end to younger Namboodiris marrying into other castes and having illicit affairs. Siva! Siva! All these activities...'

Nambyattan replied calmly, 'Carrying on these customs has spelt disaster for Namboodiri houses. There are pools of young widows' tears in all our houses. The sighs of ageing unmarried girls who have no hopes of getting married is overpowering. These are the reasons for our downfall. And added to all this, the relationships with prostitutes.'

'But that...' muttered Achan Namboodiri.

'Indeed, these customs have been prohibited by the rules of Sruti[137] as well as Smriti.[138] Be not in contact with either breath or flavour of low-caste women.[139] On seeing all this, our young Namboodiris are forced to protest.'

Was this his brother, the same person who used to hunt a different prostitute every night? This could only be termed as the result of karma!

'We can only think of these activities as a kind of impertinence and foolhardiness of those young Namboodiris. What are your plans, Nambyattan, are you in a hurry?'

'Not at all. I am at your disposal,' said Nambyattan.

'I want to see Akkithar. He is, after all, not the kind of person with whom all and sundry can seek audience,' said Achan.

'I want to see him as well. I shall be happy to meet him. I

---

[137] The part of the Vedas which describes the concepts of Vedic philosophy concerning the body, the world and the mind.
[138] The part of the Vedas which enunciates the canons of law.
[139] A verse from the *Manusmriti*.

have been thinking of it for a long time. I can go immediately.'

'So be it, get ready to go,' replied Achan.

Mangazhi Vasu Namboodiri, who stood next to Achan, prodded Nambyattan and drew attention to himself. He opened his round eyes wide. Tears began to roll down his lifeless cheeks. Thus he stood for a long time. Nambyattan, who sensed something, gazed at Mangazhi and the keen eyes of that renunciate filled. Achan, who was lying stretched on the cot, watched the two men looking at each other and weeping. At that moment, even he understood the language of the heart.

'Nambyattan, let Vasu also go with you. He too must want to see Akkithar.'

A glow of happiness spread on Vasu Namboodiri's lifeless, wrinkled face. Slowly, he followed the well-built Nambyattan Namboodiri out of the house.

17

As the afternoon turned into evening, Nambyattan Namboodiri of Thazhamangalam reached the temple of Siva near the Otikkan's house. Mangazhi Vasu Namboodiri followed, panting. Tired, they sat, resting for some time in the bathing house next to the pond. The thought that they had reached their goal refreshed them. Seeing the golden cornice over the sanctum sanctorum of the temple, Nambyattan joined his palms in worship.

'Let's bathe before going to the temple. Akkithar will be there. Both our inner and outer selves should be pure. Concentrate and pray hard.'

After their bath, dressed in wet clothes, Nambyattan and Vasu stepped into the temple. Softly, Nambyattan opened the door to the inner sanctum and touched the ground with his hands before placing them on his forehead.

'Touch the ground and place your hands on your forehead,' he told Vasu Namboodiri. They stepped into an unknown halo of light and waited deferentially. Afterwards, they went up to Akkithar, who was seated in lotus posture in the central stone structure which faced the sanctum sanctorum, and stood to his left, their heads bowed reverentially.

In the divine presence of those two godheads, one living and the other carved in stone facing each other, Nambyattan's mind dissolved and lost itself. Vasu looked at the firm, strong body of the eighty-year-old Akkithar and sighed.

'Now you may worship,' Nambyattan instructed with a gesture of his hands. 'Touch the bell softly. Do not disturb his meditation.'

Without realizing the passage of time, Nambyattan stood still in prayer in the granite-paved inner courtyard of the Siva temple. He had a sensation of weightlessness, as if he were floating effortlessly in the sky.

'Have you been around for a long time?' Akkithar stirred gradually from his meditation and turned his serene face to them, asking in tones used to chant verses. 'Let us go. It is time for me to leave. I hope you are not going back home immediately. Stay the night at my house.'

Holding a bamboo staff taller than himself in his left hand and a huge palm-frond umbrella that blocked out the sky in his right, Akkithar stepped into the path between the rice fields.

It seemed as though the five elements—sky, air, earth, sun and space—gave way to him respectfully. Mother Earth herself seemed to be moving with him, into the space left by his footsteps.

'Namboodiri,' he addressed Nambyattan, 'please tell your elder brother that there is nothing that I can do. It is all the result of your karma. There is nothing to do but bear it. Still, try and do some good deeds.'

What could Nambyattan tell Akkithar? A man of action and intense penance who had mastered the art of knowing everything before it happened.

'Think good thoughts. You may not always be able translate them into action. Even when we die, these thoughts live on. Haven't you understood that, Namboodiri?'

There was no need to explain anything to him. Why explain to a man who understood everything without anything being said? Words became meaningless, a mere draining of energy from the body.

'Namboodiri, you can clear whatever doubts you have. Do not hesitate. As you mature and develop a frame of mind to acquire knowledge, your guru will automatically come to you, the great Mother of the Universe herself. Therefore, try and acquire that frame of mind. That is all we need. For us, nothing else is possible.'

Those words first reached the ears, then entered the heart, and finally transformed themselves into a permanent experience. Not lifeless words, but words that personified the ultimate Truth.

Akkithar looked at Mangazhi and said, 'What can I say, Mangazhi? You will be all right by and by.'

Those words were enough to enliven Mangazhi, who had not lost his hearing.

Akkithar's predictions rang true. The results would follow hot upon the heels of his words. The words of such sages, who endeavour and succeed in attaining the ultimate truth through penance and strict routine, can create a whole world out of letters.

'Please forgive my foolhardiness. Oh, God! Only when you say that you have forgiven me will I have any peace of mind.' Forgetful of his surroundings, Nambyattan, who was generally known as the fifth overlord of the reputed Thazhamangalam House, prostrated on the bare ground before Akkithar. There he lay in worship. His limbs brushed against the rough stones strewn in the path; blood oozed. Akkithar, who normally walked rapidly, stood still. He turned slowly and looked at Nambyattan. He closed his eyes and remained so for a few moments.

'Nambyattan, get up. I have blessed you.'

After a gap of thirty-two years, Akkithar of the Otikkan House had addressed his former pupil by name.

'Call me Namboodiri.' Akkithar could still hear that impertinent voice filled with self-importance, nurtured by wealth and power.

'Nambyattan.'

How sweet was that voice to Nambyattan, who lay on the path paved with sand and hard stones! Akkithar did not call him 'Namboodiri', but 'Nambyattan', and that too, so fondly! 'Oh, God!

If only I could die at this moment,' Nambyattan wept, stricken to the soul.

'Aren't you satisfied, Nambyattan? Must you make me wait on this path much longer?'

Nambyattan had not thought of that.

'Here, hold this umbrella.' Akkithar handed over his hallowed umbrella to his disciple. Nambyattan held his trembling hands out like someone who was about to receive a rare and precious gift. He touched the umbrella thrice and placed his hands on his forehead.[140] Tears streamed down his cheeks. At that moment, their path in the fields seemed transformed into a heavenly way, sprinkled with holy water, a great path which spanned the distance between life and death.

Nambyattan crossed that path in a single step.

∽

Chematiri Otikkan stood at the gate, waiting anxiously for his father.

He spotted Akkithar coming along without his umbrella, pressing the long staff on the ground for support, and was thunderstruck. What had happened to that famous umbrella?

Like a shadow behind Akkithar, holding his umbrella, came Nambyattan. In that moment, Nambyattan looked so similar to his master that it seemed like Akkithar had transmigrated into another body. A follower of his father, next in line to him!

What could have happened?

'Am I very late? There was no need to come in search of me. It is not yet time for me to die. When it is, I shall tell you.' On

---

[140] The umbrella and the walking stick are two objects associated with sages and wandering mendicants. The handing over of the umbrella is symbolic. The person who receives the umbrella is the chosen spiritual successor.

hearing his father's sharp wit, the son moved aside.

'When you were late, I grew anxious,' said Chematiri.

'Nambyattan and Mangazhi have also come with me.'

Nambyattan? It had been a long time since he had referred to his disciple like that. What had happened to bring about this change? That umbrella in another person's hand, the silent Akkithar so loquacious—what was on his mind? One could never understand him fully. All studied calculations splintered where he was concerned.

'I will sleep soon after dinner, so if you need anything, ask my children. You can go back home tomorrow. What do you say?' Akkithar addressed Nambyattan.

'I am thinking of accompanying you to the temple,' said Nambyattan.

'Must you? Better not. I am not sure when I will be going.'

Nambyattan stepped into the front room along with Chematiri.

Vasu could not understand what was happening, but was filled with an unusual happiness. He looked up, twisting his distorted face and bringing his palms together in a gesture of obeisance.

The sound of students repeating lessons in English with the same studious determination with which they recited Vedic verses could be heard, rising and falling.

∽

Nambyattan walked, his heart overflowing with happiness. By noon he should reach home. In the heat of the mid-afternoon sun, this wandering mendicant perspired profusely.

Straining to keep up with him, like the unshakeable results of karma which cling to man, Vasu Namboodiri followed closely behind. Every now and then he would remind Nambyattan of his presence by poking him or by uttering incoherent words—eager and futile efforts to establish his physical presence.

Nambyattan's legs followed the urges of his heart and took him to Mathu's house, Golden Mathu.

'Mathukutty!'

Mathukutty, engrossed in watching her son play, heard that resounding call and rose. As if she had just taken a dip in holy waters, she felt purified. Holding the hand of her beloved son, she dashed to the gate.

Nambyattan was thrilled when he saw the young boy who clutched his mother's hands and jumped high, straining to balance on his heels in an attempt to appear taller.

'Won't you step in?'

'No, not now. I shall come some time later. This...boy...?'

Mathukutty, the famous courtesan, blushed and lowered her head bashfully. In the history of her clan, she could think of no precedent when anyone enquired about the fatherhood of children born to the likes of her. None of these women had even reverently welcomed their husbands home... As the husbands changed almost every day, who could the children call father? They had remained fallen women for generations. Prostitution was their family occupation, a clan which took pride in the lineage from the famous courtesan, Medini Vennilavu.[141] A house which had openly hoisted a flag to celebrate the Festival of Love. A tradition where Vatsyayana's *Kama Sutra* was memorized even before puberty. Grandmother, mother and a long hierarchy of women whose favourite chant was *Ambopadesam*.[142] Even though she had such a background, Mathukutty, in Nambyattan's presence, felt the power and sanctity of being faithful to one man. All the living cells in her body awoke and danced with happiness.

---

[141] A famous courtesan described in a book of poems, known as *Chandrotsavam*, written in the Middle Ages, describing the moon festival of love.

[142] A work on erotic love.

In the testing ground of Brahma, jeevas[143] somersaulted, spraying nectar.

'His name?'

'He has not yet been named. I thought it could wait till I met you and asked your opinion.'

'Good. Let him be called Sankaran. It is the name of my teacher, the great Akkithar, haven't you heard of him?'

'I have heard that he is one of the greatest of Namboodiris,' said Mathu.

'Siva, Siva, that is nothing. Who knows him fully? Sankaran, come here. Let me look at you.'

'For me, there cannot be a happier moment than this. You are the first person to call him by his name. Look, Unni, go over to him. Oh, Sankara!' Mathukutty choked, unable to say anything else. Vasu Namboodiri stared and made some incoherent sounds, shifting his gaze several times from Nambyattan to Mathukutty's son, who stood looking hesitantly at the stranger. A smile brightened his twisted face. He poked Nambyattan and mimed to indicate that the child would be a great man.

'Sankara, come here, take this offering from God.'

'Hold out both your hands and receive it.' Mathukutty made her son stretch out his small arms.

'This is the most blessed gift that I can give to you. It was given to me by Akkithar. Bathe Sankaran and apply it on him. Do not show any indifference. Remember the person who has given it. If you show indifference to Akkithar, even Lord Siva, who resides in the great Vadakkunnathan Temple won't forgive you. Please be careful.'

'I shall be, Your Excellency, I shall be very careful.'

'I have to leave now. You must take this boy to the Otikkan's

---

[143]The immanent divinity present in all of creation.

house, for the initiation ceremony of writing his letters.[144] After that I have told Chematiri to advise you on what to do. I have to go now, Mathukutty, but I will see you again.'

'Your Excellency, please stay for some time. Let my son prostrate before you to receive your blessings. He has never seen you before.'

Briefly, Nambyattan closed his large eyes, flickering with the tender shoot of an inner light. Time passed. He then looked at Mathukutty and his son, who lay prostrate before him after circumambulating him. Holding his son's hands, he raised him up and placed his palms on Mathukutty's head, blessing her. 'Get up. All will be well.' He turned and called Vasu Namboodiri, who had been standing staring at them, before he hurried away.

Mathukutty watched him—a hunter's body transformed into that of another Valmiki[145]—disappearing from her sight and wept bitterly. Seeing his mother sobbing wildly, not knowing why she was crying, the little boy joined her, tugging at her clothes and weeping. Holding her son to her breast, Mathukutty thrashed about on the ground like an epileptic. She picked up the sand from the ground where Nambyattan had stood and rubbed it on her head. As though in a dream, she entered her house, dragging her feet.

---

[144]A function at which very young children are initiated into the art of writing. They are made to write the first Malayalam alphabet 'Aa' on rice grain, spread on the floor after the puja to Saraswati, the goddess of the arts and learning.

[145]The first poet of ancient India, Valmiki wrote the Ramayana. He was a hunter by vocation before he abandoned everything to write the epic.

18

'Is it my fault that I was born a Namboodiri woman? Maybe I am wrong. I know that we are not supposed to see strange men or talk to them; it may even be a sin. Still, as a human being, would I not have certain desires? You men, who spend your lives moving from feast to feast and Vedic recitals, do you think about the desires of the young girls in Namboodiri houses? You think that cutting your hair and learning English are very progressive measures and you can thus achieve everything. And we should endure living death, isn't it?'

The slim, dark Namboodiri and Young Otikkan were seated in the outer veranda of Cheriyedath House, running their fingers through their matted hair, unable to look Paptikutty in the face. As she stood leaning on the doorframe of the inner veranda, trembling with rage, they sighed and looked down at their dirty toenails.

'If anyone gets to know that I talked to you people, there would be rumours and scandals. But I am not afraid. Do you think any other Namboodiri woman would be able to do what I am doing? If she is found talking to men, she would have to break the protective umbrella and leave her home.'

On one of their journeys, they had casually dropped by at Cheriyedath House to have a meal, to get news about the school friend of their youth and to discuss their progressive movement.

'Why are you quiet, Young Otikkan? At least I'm happy to see you. I do not know what fate has in store for me. Do not take to heart what I said. Think of it as the meaningless utterances of a helpless Namboodiri woman.'

Both the masters of Cheriyedath House were absent. So it was Paptikutty herself who had welcomed the waiting guests.

'No, no, we were the ones whose programmes didn't have a focus. Now I understand everything. Our path is very clear. Young Otikkan, have no doubt. Our inner courtyards are bursting for a change,' said Unni Namboodiri. 'Enough husk has been collected. A spark of fire is all that is required to ignite it. Let us go now. Bless us and send us on our way.'

Bless? A fallen woman like her? Paptikutty shrank in shame. 'I...I...'

'What he said is quite true. Paptikutty, you are our leader who can show us the way. The mother of Cheriyedath House,' said Young Otikkan.

She had gotten into the habit of calling Young Otikkan by his name during their student days. When she heard him address her as 'Paptikutty', the memories of those days of mischievous youth awoke in her and made her shudder. The unconscious usage of that term of address brought them closer to each other. A thousand mile chasm of unfamiliarity was bridged in seconds. Innumerable walls created by custom were broken. Time moved backwards. Once again, they turned into the school friends of bygone days.

As time prepares itself for a change, the purpose and motive that guide that objective unite. To be able to assist the phenomenon of incarnation, the world also changes its shape. As Vishnu transforms himself into Rama, Anantha, the serpent on whom he sleeps, turns into Lakshmana. A Balarama is born, to pave the way for Sri Krishna. Kamsa[146] too is born at that time, as a forerunner of Krishna.

---

[146]A cruel and despotic king and uncle to Sri Krishna. Krishna was born to kill Kamsa. Each incarnation of Vishnu was undertaken to extinguish a demon or an evil force. There has to be a reason justifying the incarnation. In that sense, Kamsa was the reason for the incarnation of Krishna.

How long could one stand and watch the downfall of the clans created by Aryans, the very sages who wrote the first of the Vedas, as generations of their own sons and grandsons drowned in their own carnal desires?

How did Paptikutty manage to say so much? She had not talked like that before. They did not know whether she had consciously intended to talk so. It was as though in a semi-conscious state of mind, she had been provoked by an inner command.

Young Otikkan had called her by name, Paptikutty, creating turbulence within her. 'Mother of Cheriyedath House'. He should not even think of her as Paptikutty, as a woman. That in itself would be reason to suspect her of adultery. The knots created by superior family traits, the insistence on the unadulterated purity of the clan—these unseen bonds did not allow people to even breathe freely.

'Let us leave.'

Young Otikkan and Unni Namboodiri got up with a sense of achievement. They wanted to talk at length with each other but were unable to do so. They regretted the fact that they had been so unmindful of the wails and sighs from the inner quarters of their own homes. A mental vision of their toiling mothers, wrists adorned with plain brass bangles, rose before them. Those hapless Namboodiri women, who moved slowly, dragging their feet within the northern and southern quarters of their houses, for seventy or eighty years! Those women who had given up their innermost desires to perform penance, to fast, to pray, in the hope of a better life in their next birth; to preserve their marriages; for the happiness of their children; for the happiness of the whole world. These antharjanams who fasted and prayed, sacrificing everything for the benefit of everyone else. Unmindful, the horse-hooves of time clattered above their heads and moved on.

Oh, God! Was there no solution for this plight? The inner

quarters lay closed, heavy with sorrow, which, over the years, seemed to have been transformed into pleasure, and became a familiar part of the psyche, like seasoned pain that gives a sense of inner joy and happiness.

Cheriyedath Paptikutty went into her bedroom and bolted the doors. She wept to her heart's content, lying on that bed kept perpetually ready for use. Her tears flowed, but she did not know why they surged from her.

How many names did she have on her list?

One—

Two—

Three—

She must look again at that old piece of paper. Although written with a blunt pencil point, the writing was clear. The names and detailed descriptions of bodies. She had also recorded the date and the hour of each union.

The horoscopes of those who were to be cursed.

She must have more names.

Not a single Namboodiri house should be left out. One person from each house, no more. She did not do this for physical pleasure, but to fulfil the purpose of the incarnation she had taken.

I who am surrounded by the Cosmic Illusion do not reveal myself to everyone.[147]

Slowly, Paptikutty began to understand the pain of penance.

The saintly Brahmins who were like her mentors.

Learned men, poets, those who recited the Vedas.

Their punishment for ignoring their true nature. The fatal attraction that arose from the illusion of mistaking the earth[148] for a

---

[147] Bhagavad Gita, Chapter VII, verse 25.

[148] A philosophical allusion to mistaking the universal for the specific. Another pair that is popularly alluded to is the rope and the snake, signifying the human

clay pot and desiring it. The punishment for such misguided desire.

Kali, the fierce Mother Goddess, born of Siva's own body. Kali's kicks could only be borne by Siva.

Henceforth, there was no time for sleep.

'Are you in there?'

It was her husband's voice.

Helpless and tired, Cheriyedath Neelan sat on the seat in the outer veranda. He raised his dust covered feet and placed them on the seat. 'The heat of this sun is unbearable. It seems to be an attempt to annihilate the whole world. Is there any buttermilk? Please bring me some.'

The stunted devil's younger brother, Neelan, said all this without looking his wife in the face. He did not have the courage to face that fiery beauty.

He drank the sour buttermilk noisily, cooling his parched throat.

'Oh! Oh! Hasn't my elder brother returned?'

'No. I haven't seen him. I was told that he will not be coming for lunch.'

'Is that so? Where has he gone?'

Neelan stopped talking as he did not know what else to say. He took a look at his dark body, wet with perspiration. Suddenly, he had a glimpse of the inordinately luminous beauty of the woman who stood by the door. Sheepishly, he sprang from his seat and went out into the courtyard.

He stared at the light which was still powerful even though the sun had begun to set. His eyes hurt, yet he continued to stare. Afterwards, he went back to the outer veranda. Oh, what a relief that he could not see a thing. He had a sensation of watching the dance of a thousand small suns. As it climaxed, the light stirred

---

problem of delusion born of ignorance.

the darkness and let it loose.

The night crashed in upon him.

Neelan went into his bedroom shivering. In the presence of his wife, he felt like a weak and ignoble eunuch entering the inner chamber of a pure woman. True, he had married her with fire as witness. But then? No. It was better not to remember all that had followed.

Without any visible change in her attitude, determined to wreak revenge for the false submissiveness she had to show during the daytime, Paptikutty stretched out on the bed, resting her head on her arms. She smiled contently, watching her husband waiting to obey her orders.

Neelan sat close to her on the cot. She was indeed his wife. But there were memories, now almost forgotten, which made him uneasy. They slept together, the whole night in the same bedroom. Not one night, but many nights. Many nights subject to only seasonal changes. Each morning he would wake, remember the lost hours and curse himself. He waited for the night but when it actually came, he trembled in fear and wished for morning. She would smile invitingly at him, a smile to seduce the whole world. But when he approached her, she subjected him to a chilling indifference, the push of an unseen foot.

The play of time! The loss of life![149]

Play with the fire that annihilates the whole world.

In that burning fire, everything burns to ashes.

'Look, what have I done to deserve this? Was it such an unpardonable mistake?'

'Oh nothing, nothing at all.'

Paptikutty looked at her husband and opened her long eyes wide, eyes that reflected the past, present and future. She thought:

---

[149] A verse from *Bhaja Govindam*, written by Sankaracharya.

indeed you have made no mistake. He had the gall to ask her what mistake he had made! From now on, she would not treat him as her husband.

'I had high hopes and great desires,' said Neelan.

She too had desired so much; seated within the women's quarters she had yearned, even though it had only been what a Namboodiri woman could legitimately yearn for.

'I am sleepy,' Paptikutty said indifferently.

Let her Namboodiri sleep. After that she could go downstairs. In the bathing house, the famed Kathakali artist was waiting for her.[150]

Renowned! A great name in the land! Wealthy!

Yet the country would learn to treat him like a diseased cur. He would have to go into exile. Never again would he enter a stage, a theatre.

This night.

A dark, ominous night.

Kali, Karali, the ominous night, the messenger of death.[151] Even the sage Kasyapa could do nothing. Let Siva of the blue throat arrive to swallow poison! She could wait.

Paptikutty's inner being boiled and foamed. She visualized in her mind's eye the earthquake of the days to come and was thrilled. Let it quake. She was waiting, ready.

Was her Namboodiri asleep?

Even if he was not, it did not matter. Let him know. Even if he knew, he would not be able to move his tongue in protest. He, who had sacrificed his wife to his brother, what could he say? Such a virtuous man who had lost his sense of discrimination.

---

[150] The reference is to Kavungal Sankara Panikkar, a famous Kathakali maestro, seduced and shamed by Kuriyedath Thatri, the protagonist of the actual events on which this story is based.

[151] Different forms of the Mother Goddess, the divine slayer.

Pooh!

Cheriyedath Neelan burned with passion and rolled in his bed, unable to control his arousal. Downstairs, the servant girl would be available. Two people may be able to sleep in the husking room.

Oh, God! What a fate.

Neelan fumbled and got up hastily. He hit the air with his fists.

Elder Brother! Elder Brother! He should wring the neck of that stunted animal and smother him. Watch him fall at his feet, writhing. Neelan roared with laughter as he visualized his elder brother writhing, the nerve below his earlobes broken.

He paced the bedroom with measured steps.

19

'For some time, we have been hearing scandalous rumours about the antharjanam of Cheriyedath House,' said Thazhamangalam Achan Namboodirippad, his voice lowered, as he sat in his front room chewing betel nuts. The wrinkles on the 'bad-karma' Mangazhi Vasu Namboodiri's distorted face tightened. His round, protruding eyes traced a continuous circular motion, unable to remain fixed on one point. A little to his front sat the ritualist, his legs crossed. The assistant, Kesavan, caressed his stomach, which had grown in size, a sign of prosperity. His expression changed from surprise to pain and alternated between the two according to the need of the hour.

'Kali Yuga! Kali Yuga! What else can one say? These good-for-nothing types who spoil the name of the clan,' the ritualist spluttered, bursting with rage.

'Trial of a fallen woman! We have to perform that too! It shouldn't look as though we omitted to do what we are supposed to do. After that, we can inform the King.'

'Yes. Without a doubt. The only way for us is to carry out this suggestion. We should clear all doubts and obtain irrevocable proof. Only then might the King intervene. Till then, it is the job of the ritualists.'

'I have requested Chematiri Otikkan also to join us here. We should take care of such things. No one should say later that we acted indiscreetly.'

'He will be here soon,' Kesavan babbled.

'Who and how many will be cited by her? What will happen?'

Achan was perturbed. He, who was used to secret liaisons whenever his three wives failed to satisfy him physically, grew anxious. Had he too unknowingly gone to that useless woman? 'One hears that she goes around in disguise.'

The ritualist pretended to be surprised.

Mangazhi Vasu sat on the floor by the cot. He looked towards the inner quarters, shut his eyes and made some incoherent noises.

'Thazhath Namboodiri will be very unhappy. But what can one do?'

Even if it was one's own daughter, if she was accused of prostitution, there was only one solution: to close the gates of the house on her and to perform the last rites for her, symbolizing her death as far as her House was concerned.

When Mangazhi Vasu saw Chematiri Otikkan crossing the gate and coming towards them, he made a subhuman sound that seemed to arise from the netherworld.

'Ah! Now everything will be all right,' said the ritualist, relieved. 'Chematiri's readings will never fail.'

In order to get some relief from the exhaustion of the journey, Chematiri fanned himself with his folded melmundu.

'Otikkan, have you understood what is happening?'

'Not fully.'

'What can I say? I have brought the ritualist also, as I wasn't sure of the course of action I should take. In such a situation I shouldn't be accused of having acted out of turn.

'Chematiri, you must have heard by now. What a mess it is. The birth of such people spells doom not only for their own families, but for the whole clan.

'Let me explain. That woman from Cheriyedath House! The daughter of Thazhath Namboodiri I hear, has turned wayward. It has changed from rumour to scandal. It has reached a stage where some of us have to meet and decide the future course of action.'

Chematiri Otikkan, bothered by the discomfort of heat and exertion, seemed oblivious to Achan Namboodiri's remarks.

'Why are you so indifferent, Chematiri? As though you are not taking this seriously.'

The appointed hour had come. How long ago had he visualized this moment? He had done whatever he could to prevent it. In the end...at last...he had even tried to murder a child. Still... It was the fault of the times, not the fault of individual action. There was no remedy for this fate. One had to endure it. The whole Namboodiri clan had to suffer. The flag was hoisted, the sacred hour chosen to initiate the purification ceremony of this temple of Parasurama.

'I will join you after a bath.'

Otikkan grew calm as he stepped into the courtyard. To see him so calm stunned the ritualist and Achan.

Chematiri returned bathed and clean, and without any preliminaries, declared: 'Now, this trial of a fallen woman. Please entrust it to a responsible person. Don't delay it because we can inform the King only after that.'

The ritualist nodded on hearing such a well-conceived decision. A solution which ruled out any scope for further discussion. There was nothing more to be said, only action to be initiated. It was a solution suggested by Chematiri Otikkan. Only Akkithar, his own father, was qualified to dispute it.

'I won't be staying long. I am leaving immediately after I see Mother.'

'Why are you in such a hurry?'

'That boy is also with me. At his request I plan to go to a particular place.'

'That low-caste boy?'

'Yes.'

Even though his disciple was insulted by such a reference, Otikkan was not upset.

'I, too, will come with you,' said Achan, rising.

On seeing them, the mother of Thazhamangalam House, seated in the southern section of the inner quarters praying and counting the beads in the tulasi garland,[152] got up.

She asked, 'Anything wrong with your father?'

'No. Nothing in particular. I have come here at Namboodiri's request.'

'I too heard of it. If people indulge in such activities... I have seen her. A very nice Namboodiri girl. Hasn't she stayed at your place too?'

'I have even taught her.'

'Narayana! Narayana!'

'I am leaving, Amme. I wanted to prostrate before you first.' The mother sat on a wooden seat placed in the centre of the room. Otikkan circumambulated her and then prostrated before her. The mother pressed her hands on Otikkan's greying head and wept.

'Everything will turn out well,' breathed the mother.

'Permit me to go.'

'Whatever you do, consult your father. In this matter, if you take a wrong decision, you will be committing a great sin, which will affect your future generations.'

'I will do only what my father asks me to do.'

'Then you can't go wrong. If Akkithar takes a wrong decision, even the great Lord Siva can go wrong.' She paused for a moment and then said, 'My husband was very fond of him. The folly of my sons! Narayana! Narayana! You must come now and then. I am not feeling too well.'

'I shall come.'

∽

---

[152]The basil plant. Garlands made out of the roots of basil are used as rosaries by Namboodiri women while chanting the name of God.

Chami sat in the shaded part of the gatehouse. He had drawn the position of the planets and was calculating. With his eyes closed, engrossed in his calculations, he did not notice the presence of his teacher.

'Chami, what is there to ponder and calculate so much?'

Chami leapt up and shrank guiltily at his lack of propriety. 'I...didn't know that you had returned.'

'Don't worry. I should have known. I shouldn't have made you wait so long by the roadside.'

Chami's eyes filled. There were probably many others endowed with his teacher's knowledge. But that heart! One had to do good deeds and accumulate merit to encounter such a generous heart.[153]

'What were you calculating?'

'That matter which you discussed with me while we were on our way here.'

'What can I do? May I not be fated to declare it with my own tongue. Oh, God!' said Chematiri.

'I calculated and recalculated. That young mistress's fate is sealed. I was miserable when you mentioned it.'

'You were not fully convinced, were you? That is good. Do not accept a verdict, whoever pronounces it. Find out for yourself. That is what is needed,' praised Chematiri.

Indeed! It had never occurred to Chami that his teacher could make a wrong decision. It would be a great sin to think so. Chami had not made his calculations with that intention. The young lady had been his classmate. Even though he used to sit at the gatehouse and they seldom met, they shared the bond of being the students

---

[153] It is a popular belief that by accumulating merit by doing good in the present and previous lives, one can achieve even impossible feats. The low caste Chami has, in this life, the good fortune of having a great Brahmin like Chematiri as his teacher and mentor. Normally this would not have been possible, the caste hierarchy being what it was.

of the same teacher. A special bond. The feeling of being Chematiri Otikkan's students brought them together. Even closer than children born to the same parents, though they belonged to different castes. Chami knew what it was to be Chematiri's disciple. He had visited a certain house to make astrological calculations. They were an aristocratic Ezhava family, rather high in the hierarchy of their caste. For generations they had enjoyed the position of wealthy overlords; proprietors of large trading houses in the main market, they did not like the sight of Chami! To them he was a young upstart. They wanted to pay him a paltry sum and send him off. Chami had given a great deal of thought to the whole exercise. He calculated and predicted the fate of seven generations before and after. He had elaborated on the section that dealt with the results of fate and pinpointed the remedies. But all these efforts had not opened the eyes of that overlord. Let this boy go, the overlord had said. After that he could consult someone with greater skill. He felt that it was indeed a mistake to have brought this youngster. It was at that time that the summons for Chami came from the famous astrologer of the palace, Uzhutra Variar.[154] A messenger was sent with a request to send Chami to Variar's house after he had concluded his business at the trader's house. Chami was not to be troubled in any way; he was to be accompanied by one or two attendants.

The palace astrologer asking for this finger-sized boy! There must have been a mistake. Still, the overlord had to obey. What a privileged position Chami had enjoyed after that moment, all because of barukrupa, the blessings of his teacher. When one had the

---

[154] One of many subcastes; as half-Brahmin, their function is to assist the temple priest in the rituals of worship—in collecting flowers, making garlands, cleaning the vessels used for worship. They are not allowed to perform the actual worship, but are given only the tasks in preparation of it.

honour of being Chematiri's student, one did not require any other certificate of eligibility, degree or title. The great palace astrologer, who was happy with the Ezhava boy, had presented the ceremonial cloth[155] in recognition of his talents; how many such experiences had he had!

'Where did you study?'

'With the great Master.'

'Where, where did you say?'

'At the gates of the greatest Namboodiri, the greatest of all ritualists.'

'Siva, Siva, at the Otikkan House?'

After that the welcome and the feasting would start.

Oh, God! To think that such a teacher could go wrong in his calculations! Yet, the young Paptikutty had once been his student.

'Chami, why are you so despondent?'

'Lord…'

'I am sadder than you about this whole business. But there is no point. These things are not within our control. Father predicted this. Treat whatever we experience as something gained.'

Born in an Ezhava family—be it so, he was luckier than even the most powerful of Brahmins. Chami's eyes filled with tears as they walked along.

'Where is this place? Are we nearing it?' asked Chematiri.

'We are close by. Another half an hour's walk only.'

༄

---

[155]In Kerala, deeds of valour or exceptional merit or talent were traditionally honoured by the presentation of the ceremonial cloth, usually made of silk or fine cotton with gold embroidery. The presentation was done by kings or men in high position.

For a long time, Chami's grandmother had wanted to see her grandson's master. She was bedridden with arthritis and could not get up from where she lay or sit up. She had only one wish: she must meet the great teacher. Before her death, she wanted to see the teacher who had taught her daughter's son and made him an expert astrologer. She had mentioned this to Chami many times. One day, with great hesitation, Chami conveyed his grandmother's wish to his teacher. 'Oh, that's not a problem. I shall visit her when I am in the vicinity.' But till now that day had not come. Today, when he set off for the House of Thazhamangalam, Chematiri had said, 'Chami, today we will go to your maternal grandmother's.' Having said 'ammathu',[156] a typical Namboodiri term for the mother's house, he smiled at the ironical humour in such a usage.

'Let me go first. Could you please wait for some time at this gate?'

'That is good. I made you wait at the gate of Thazhamangalam! Now you in turn make me wait at the gates of an Ezhava house.' Chematiri stood in the shade of the gate of the Ezhava house and laughed heartily. Laughter from an unblemished heart.

Hearing his teacher's ready wit, Chami felt that his heart would splinter in agony.

With great difficulty, Chami's grandmother was brought to the gate by two persons, who lifted the cot she lay on. Chami stood by her, content.

Choking with emotion, his eyes smarting, Chami said, 'This is my teacher, my great lord,' indicating his master who walked towards his grandmother.

The exhausted old woman looked intently at Chematiri

---

[156] The literal meaning of ammathu is 'mother house', derived from amma (mother) and aathu (house). A usage specific to Namboodiris, forming a part of the dialect known as 'Namboodiri Malayalam'.

Otikkan's face. In his holy presence, the old woman forgot all her earthly pains. The wrinkles wrought by pain disappeared. She wore a serene expression and stammered. 'God will bless you. We have starved a great deal when my grandson was young. But now he has grown up and we have no wants. All this was possible because of you, Sir, and your large heart.' The old woman shut her rheumy eyes respectfully and brought her palms together—palms covered with the wrinkled folds of age. The pain that she had endured for years was not visible any more on her face. She lay there, having gained serenity and an inner peace through a divine force.

'Chami, come, let us not delay.'

When they were within hailing distance, Otikkan stopped. 'You need not come any further with me. Send someone else. Don't you understand what I am saying?'

The student understood what the teacher meant and nodded. Before his mind's eye appeared the figure of Varahamihira, the astrologer of astrologers, clearer than ever.

20

The entire countryside was like a tree uprooted and flung upside down. The prayers within the inner quarters grew louder and louder.

'It seems there is a trial at Cheriyedath.'

The aristocratic elder Namboodiris sat by the sacrificial pit and roared in anger. Ageing virgins and young widows trudged like walking nightmares, blaming themselves for what had happened.

'One doesn't really know what will happen or where. It is the very end.'

Their flabby bodies shook as the ritualists stroked their potbellies and protested.

'Nothing is certain. Who amongst us will be indicted, one can't say.'

The Namboodiris, who regarded their secret liaisons as their seventh karma,[157] were stupefied. Would this woman, this 'Object', turn out to be one of the items they had enjoyed after some temple feast? Then we are in a fix.

The King was informed, according to the customs and regulations. His order arrived.

Cheriyedath Paptikutty was kept in one of the outhouses.

---

[157] The six karmas (functions) performed by Namboodiris are yajanam (performance of sacrifice), yaajanam (supervision of performance of sacrifice), adhyayanam (learning; acquiring knowledge), adhyapanam (teaching), daanam (making offerings and gifts) and pratigraham (receiving gifts). The 'seventh karma' is a sarcastic reference to their illicit relationships, which were so frequent that it seemed like a prescribed karma.

Thazhamangalam himself assumed responsibility for the whole affair. Even relatives shunned Cheriyedath House, which had turned into a graveyard, avoided by all human beings. Everyone waited for the feast after the trial to be over. No meal was cooked at Cheriyedath House and even their servants returned to their own homes. All of Namboodiri Kerala shivered feverishly. They blabbered in delirium. The haunting question lingered: the roll call of names.

Let the King's order arrive.

The trial was about to begin.

In order to make sure that the trial was conducted in an orderly fashion, Thazhamangalam Namboodiri went to see the King.

Paptikutty alone went about her daily routine meticulously, as always, without paying any attention to the earth-shaking events that were taking place around her. Those who saw the shining luminosity which surrounded her were stunned.

'What appalling determination!'

'So unshakeable!'

How could Paptikutty be moved, when she had waited for this hour of trial from the night of her nuptials! She could recall the passion and warmth of a thousand nights. She opened and read the destinies she had written with a blunt pencil point and silently enjoyed the implications. Those great men who had fallen at her feet and begged, one after the other!

Here in her hands lay the horoscope of their future days!

She had wanted to include the name of her own great teacher in that list—Chematiri Otikkan, a man who had the ability to read the future clearly by studying the palm.

A great man of action who was like a father to her!

She had performed her act of seduction and brought him to her. She even saw him alone. But…

Even as she sat in the outhouse, her mind full of vengeful thoughts, Paptikutty's burning eyes filled with tears. For a moment, the fire of revenge was nearly extinguished. The hot tears that spilled dimmed the blaze and burned a path down her soft cheeks. She had tried all the tricks she had practised and perfected. The explicit expressions of the act of love practised on learned men, poets and old men were of no use.

The mantras of seduction had grown stiff and stilted. Finally they had failed and come adrift.

'Paptikutty, I didn't think that you would go so far.' Even now that divine voice echoed in her ears. 'I am going. I didn't realize what you were up to. My folly. Do you wish to proceed any further?'

She had tried to pollute that great man of action, pure as fire, who lived a life close to salvation. But she had failed, and now ashamed, all she could do was to hang her head low.

Only with that man had she failed.

'Child, must you go so far?' Again the voice echoed.

That heavenly voice, which could stimulate the smallest speck of an atom or a giant being, flooded even Paptikutty's revenge-filled mind with compassion. The layers that covered her living self shivered in unison. Together they began to search for the source of their origin. Tomorrow, the trial would begin.

How many Namboodiri houses were about to fall?

Not less than fifty.

Not bad at all.

Besides the Namboodiris, the petty chieftains, eminent men, the King...

No, let it stop there for the time being.

The order of the King who ruled the country. She could take it up later.

An order to the Universal Mother who was born from the sacrificial pit of fire, lit by Time, to perform the great sacrifice before the fulfilment of the act of revenge.

Paptikutty smiled, a smile that reflected all the eight glories.[158] The multitude of stars and divine planets, which contained all the semi-divine beings such as yakshas, kinnaras and apsaras, appeared in that smile. And at the centre of it all was Paptikutty, the Mother of the Universe, who gave birth to all of them.

ෆ

'Trial and casting out—these things shouldn't be done in this fashion. Don't Namboodiri men do what they want? Why victimize women only?' announced Young Otikkan, ablaze with fury. Unable to contain his anger, he was sowing the seeds of illness, like the goddess of smallpox.[159]

His fellow student! That shining example of a good wife, who had given him strength to nurture revolutionary thoughts.

'Even this trial is a kind of brutality.'

Unni Namboodiri, who sat in Otikkan's outhouse scratching and tearing his matted hair, said calmly, 'Such ardour and angry arousal are not good. There can be some difference in the behaviour of men and women, but don't forget the basic difference between the two.'

'In the eyes of God, the Creator, aren't both alike?' asked Young Otikkan.

---

[158] The eight divine glories or special attributes are anima (the ability to reduce one's size), mahima (the ability to increase one's size), garima (the ability to increase one's weight or magnitude), ishitwam (the ability to have supreme power), vasitwam (the ability to control one's senses), prapti (the power to obtain or gain) and prabalyam (the ability to be popular, influential). With these eight glories one becomes almost superhuman.

[159] An attribute of Kali, the Mother Goddess, is her ability to bring pestilence through contagious diseases such as smallpox, chickenpox, etc. All over India, there is a belief that when the goddess is displeased or angry, she causes these diseases to spread and only through appeasement and propitiation can this onslaught be abated.

'Not entirely. The first place goes to the woman—the Mother. The Goddess of the Universe. The figure of strength who bears the burden of creation. Because of that, she should be purer. Creation is not child's play. Nor is it to be used as a means of physical pleasure. It is the greatest form of worship. Haven't you understood that there is no greater form of worship than that? In that hour, one attains divinity.'

'Even so, even so.' Young Otikkan made frenzied movements, unable to contain his rage. Roaring and tearing his tuft of hair, he tried to take the edge off his anger.

All that happened must be on account of higher orders. Paptikutty was incapable of such degradation. None of his father's disciples would go against their chosen vocations and pollute themselves. They who had had glimpses of the path to salvation, would they be lured by mere physical pleasure? All this must be the trickery of the some powerful people.

'Anyway, we should not delay now. It is time for action. The appointed hour is nearing. The day this trial concludes should mark the prelude to our act.'

'Yes. The day the ritualist tears Paptikutty's symbol of protection, the umbrella, the Namboodiri women, who on their own are ready to reject the very same umbrella, should come out of their inner quarters and protest. That should be the beginning of our progressive movement.'

The slim Unni Namboodiri strolled in the courtyard of the Otikkan's house with easy, gentle steps. Young Otikkan, who slowly regained his equanimity, sat on the ground plucking weeds.

'It seems that Father is going to be the chief priest and judge. To quote Sruti and Smriti and give a fair judgement. Indeed, a laudable idea! A first-class punishment both ways! Oh, the fate of casting out and exiling one's own disciple!'

'Such is the King's law. Personal considerations have no place in such a court of law. In such a situation, elder brother will not be moved by such feelings,' said Pachu Otikkan sourly as he sat on the veranda, sunk in thought. After saying what he had to say, he swam along in the flow of his broken thoughts.

'When will your father come here?' asked Unni Namboodiri.

'Along with grandfather. After assuming this responsibility, he has been staying with grandfather, observing strict penance for three days. Must be trying to fortify himself to carry out the King's command.'

'Young Otikkan, if you are being sarcastic, please note that a mind unpurified by penance has no right to give a legal verdict. Tenderness of any kind has to be banished from the mind. He may be your father. But I know him better,' said Unni Namboodiri.

'I...I...'

'Only after seeing him can I show my face to the King. That is why I insisted. Didn't you talk about the nature of this impending trial? Its limitations? Normally, only a woman is tried. That is considered to be sufficient. Such is the one-sided greatness of that trial. But in this case, Chematiri Otikkan is convinced that there should also be a trial for the men involved.'

'Then is there to be a trial of the guilty men also?' asked Young Otikkan.

'Your father sent that Chami to my house.'

As twilight gave way to darkness, Chematiri arrived at the Otikkan's house along with Akkithar. Not a word was spoken. Following his sagely father, the son, a man of action, stepped into the inner quarters; his son, the progressive Young Otikkan, sauntered in the courtyard, making pronouncements like an angry oracle. Occasionally, he glanced at the serene face of Unni Namboodiri, his friend and mentor, and sighed.

The night that descended on the courtyard of the Otikkan's house grew darker, witnessing the chronological changes in the stages of three generations.

21

In the veranda of Thazhamangalam House, Achan Namboodirippad stretched on his cot and coughed. Kesavan groped for the words which fell from his master's mouth, strung them together and prepared an order.

The number of guards watching the outhouse should be doubled. Security measures should begin at the very gate. Someone might try to kill her.

To lose caste!

To kill a woman!

In the southern compound, a bird chattered from the branch of a kanjiram tree. Vayu, the God of Wind, carried the news everywhere.

The King's special messenger came flying. Nothing should happen to the polluted woman, who was referred to as the Object. The responsibility was Thazhamangalam's.

Some of the prominent men of the place may have fallen prey to her wiles. Killing her might have occurred to them. Finish her off! Let the old, unused wells be set up as the stage for another 'accidental' death.

Seated in the veranda of his house, Cheriyedath Tundan dangled his stunted legs and bared his teeth. At times he stared at Neelan and was frightened. He scratched his wrinkled skin in an attempt to divert his thoughts.

The ceremonial black rug and the white cloth on top of it were spread for the King. The traditional hanging lamp was carried in, announcing the royal arrival.

The Smarthan, or the Chief Canonical Investigator, arrived. He prayed to all his ancestral deities and made special offerings to all the temples he knew. The guests who came from neighbouring places were given all comforts due to them. The ritualists were welcomed and seated. The religious heads were greeted respectfully and ushered in.

'You may begin,' the Smarthan declared.

The atmosphere of the western veranda of Thazhamangalam House grew still.

The security had been tightened.

No one could slip inside.

The ritualist, Chematiri Otikkan asked, 'Shall we start?'

'Yes.'

'Call the Object.'

The huge wooden door that led to the veranda of the western outhouse, the temporary jail, groaned open. Everyone held their breath.

'Move over here.'

When confronted with her searing beauty, the people who came to see the trial turned their eyes away or looked down. Unable to watch that face for any length of time, they were silent. Leaning against the door jamb stood Paptikutty, the personification of the patient Mother Earth.

'Shall we begin?' the Smarthan spat the words as he cleared his throat. Only Chematiri Otikkan had the courage to look towards the doorway. Many sheaths of memory unfolded and fell away. He remembered the adorable child who had stood in knee-deep water, waiting to give the initial payment to her teacher with an offering of water.

Dark shadows invaded his usually peaceful face.

'May I say something?' the sound, which emerged from the Object, enlivened the scene.

What would she say?

She could say anything. The audience would not be vengeful or partial. The process of law long established according to Sankara and Manu would be followed. Nothing more.

'I may have committed many mistakes. Even so, please bless me. My teacher is also present. That is good.'

Chematiri Otikkan raised his head and opened those eyes capable of seeing the past, present and future, and gazed at her, blessing his disciple mentally. Time, wet with a hint of tears, lingered hesitantly.

'May I ask something? What is my crime? That of being born in a Namboodiri household? Is it really my fault that I was born a Namboodiri woman?'

The audience who thought they were seated on the sacred heights of Brahminism could not digest her words. A woman who went against the codes of wifely fidelity and became a prostitute dared to question the ethics of Brahminism!

'First of all, summon my legally wedded husband and ask him how I reached this plight.'

The sky descended and nearly touched one's head. Their seats sank into the netherworlds.

Neelan!

Must she blame that poor man also? As though what she did was not enough, now she was accusing her husband!

'All of you know his elder brother did not allow the bridal installation to take place. Why? After all, the marriage was conducted with his approval and he had arranged for the ceremony happily. But he did not allow me to cross the gate. Why? Did anyone ask why? Many persons tried to mediate and talk terms. Some who are present here today said: "Obey what the elder brother says." My father not only advised me so, he insisted. What did the elder brother say? Don't you want to know?' she taunted.

The Object could say anything she wanted. She had the right to do that. It was her last chance to talk; let her talk.

The Smarthan looked the Object in the face.

'What did the elder brother say?'

Otikkan sat with his eyes closed.

'I shall tell you. My days of modesty are over. After all, I am no longer a pure woman. Why, not even a woman! In your language I am just an Object.'

The enraged Object leaned on the door jamb. The heat emanating from her sigh scorched the priests seated in the front room, interrupting their philosophical introspections.

'First, some water.'

Into the vessel kept apart for the polluted Object, water was poured. Having accepted the welcome drink of water, the Mother of the Universe awoke, remembering the purpose of her incarnation. She was ready to recite her Vedas into the ears of the clan of Namboodiris.

Mangazhi Vasu stood next to Achan Namboodiri who had adopted the role of Master of Ceremonies; even his twisted face wore an air of compassion.

'Now, I will tell you. Listen carefully. Do you know what was said? That the elder brother should first enjoy the younger brother's wife.'

The hemispheres clashed and clattered. A single blow smashed the eight directions.[160] The very air trembled when it heard the death rattle of Brahminism, now stretched on the bare floor, breathing its last.

Cheriyedath Tundan bared his teeth and made horrible faces, staring into the eyes of those great Brahmins who had donned priestly

---

[160] These are north, south, east, west, north-east, north-west, south-east and south-west.

garbs to conduct the trial according to the Vedic code of ethics.

'Born a woman, would I not have had some longings? The wedding ceremony was over. I waited for the nuptials in the bedroom. The hopes and desires I cherished at that time cannot be described in mere words. At that moment, into that romantic setting, it was not my wedded husband who entered. What was I to do, hang myself?'

The Smarthan's tongue cleaved to his throat, now parched. These words pierced the inner drum of his ears and entered his soul, burning it like hot charcoal. Blood spurted from the pores of his arms.

Only Chematiri Otikkan sat calmly, his eyes closed. His was a serenity untouched by thunderclouds, rain or other elements.

Paptikutty continued...

'You men, who enjoy reciting the Vedas and twisting its meaning this way or that, will never understand my plight. For you, the routine of attending feasts and visiting prostitutes must be maintained. That is enough. Let me ask you, if this law of being faithful to one's wedded partner were imposed on men also, how many Namboodiris would escape being cast out?'

Enough! That was enough. Do not say anything more. Words to stir and torment even the previous births!

The Namboodiris nostalgically recalled their pleasurable times with prostitutes and writhed under the whiplash of the Master of Time.

'Hear me! That night another man also slept with me—the Namboodiri who married me. By the grace of his brother!'

Siva, Siva!

One has heard enough.

Let us appeal to the King. No more! No more! This trial should not proceed. Let someone else conduct the trial. Let them prostitute their bodies or convert themselves into another religion. This will be the end of the sacred temple built by Parasurama.

'Thereafter, do you know how many others groped and clutched my underclothes? Ask! I shall tell you without omitting a single name. But before that, just think for yourselves, if your minds are still not hardened by Brahminism. Have I reached this position by myself? Answer, all you wise and great men.'

Paptikutty waited earnestly for a reply. The Aryan race, with its tongue tied by time, was silent. Only Mangazhi Vasu, rendered mute by his stroke, produced some inhuman sounds. It was like the sound of a conch marking the Last Deluge.

The Daughter of Earth, aeons ago, at the hour of the second fire test,[161] hid herself in the bosom of Mother Earth. Now, faced with a new fire test by Vedic scholars ready to ignite the flames, she spat. Time, defaced by that spittle, sat huddled, waiting for another incarnation before it could wash its face.

The Namboodiris who had spent their lives cooking and eating their fill at the Thazhamangalam dining hall were, for the first time in their lives, startled. They looked at each other, perplexed. The devas watched silently. Only the Sun commanded, 'Eat.' Eat, eat and die. The Universe, witness to all, declared that nothing else was possible.

'Now... Now what...' the Smarthan asked. No one else had the right to question her. The other ritualists could only drop their melmundu to signify their dissent. They could not interfere directly.

'If you have anything else to say...'

The Object rudely interrupted, pushing aside the Smarthan's concession.

'Yes! I do have more to say. But to whom can I say it? It would

---

[161] The reference is to the Uttara Ramayana, where Sita, after being banished to the forest for several years, is summoned to Rama's court to prove her chastity once again before the assembled people. Tired, she calls out to Mother Earth, her real mother, to give her refuge. The story goes that the earth split asunder and Sita disappeared into its depths.

be better to address this pillar.'

The King, who represented secular power, got up from his seat, startled.

What impertinence!

Let the King who ruled the country hear it. Let him hold the ceremony of immersion in the tears of Namboodiri women, thought Paptikutty.

How long could one tolerate these indignities? The Mother of the Universe was impatient. The children who insulted Motherhood were now caught in the whirl of Time and were at their wits' end.

Who would be the first?

Any proofs?

Any witnesses?

Witnesses for this too?

Maybe there were some.

The younger brother had stood guard for the elder brother.

After that, the elder brother led the younger to the sanctum sanctorum himself, tarrying outside to play the drummer, announcing the act of worship.

Such an event had no precedent.

Now?

Father and son?

Maybe!

Teacher, close relatives.

Paptikutty! Goddess! The great Goddess of Illusion!

Even the stately face of Chematiri Otikkan was wet with tears.

'Why are you delaying the procedure?'

Achan, who sat in the seat of the Master of Ceremonies, roared. And then he trembled, hearing his own voice.

From the bushes surrounding the compounds of Namboodiri houses, several Unikkalis raised their heads. Seated in the middle of the elders, Achan shivered. He shut his eyes, hoping to erase those visions. He shook his head at the vision of bluish corpses of Namboodiri women suffocating to death.

His first wife's madness.

His bosom friend's mute condition.

His brother's renunciation.

What else might he be destined to see? Great God!

'So, two from Cheriyedath House. Let us fix that. What is the proof?'

'You want proof for this?' taunted Paptikutty. 'Ask them. Will they have the courage to deny this act?'

'Write it down. The elder Namboodiri, Cheriyedath Tundan, and the husband, Neelan.'

The writer of the proceedings dipped his quill pen in the ink bottle. He brought his trembling palms together worshipfully to gather enough courage to document the final moments of the Namboodiri clan, breathing its last.

The ritualist dropped his melmundu.

'Is her word not enough, do you need further proof?' queried the Smarthan.

The ritualist took the cloth from the ground and replaced it on his shoulder to signify that further proof was needed.

Proof?

Paptikutty laughed.

A roar of laughter from the Mother Goddess.

'A wart on the foreskin of the penis. Enough?'

The council was shattered.

Seated indoors on the black and white cloth spread in his honour, the King collapsed.

'Do you want to hear more?'

No, no. What they had already heard was enough to last for several lives.

Her heart should not feel any compassion. She must snap the

knot of the sacred thread worn by these Namboodiris. Hit at the most vital and vulnerable spot. Let the first blow be on the head itself. Break the lotus-shaped wheel. She must say what she had to say before she lost her strength. 'Don't be so complacent, Chematiri. Add the names of your two brothers to the list.' Saying it in one breath, Paptikutty waited to see her teacher in a sickly fit.

The King peered through the small opening in the door. The Master of Ceremonies, Achan Namboodiri, shivered in his seat.

A stillness seized the outhouse and its surroundings.

Two from the Otikkan House.

Sons of Akkithar!

The great Chematiri Otikkan's two brothers. Venerable scholars. Chematiri's face showed an inner serenity. The emotional change was reflected only in the atmosphere that surrounded his sagely person.

'Child! Am I also on the list? Do not hesitate... If I am, please say it aloud.'

'Oh, Amme!'

The Object, Cheriyedath Paptikutty, slid down and sat, tired, leaning against the wall. Unable to control the melting soul within, her heaving breasts rose and fell. She felt her chest would split. Bringing her henna-stained hands together, she strove to get up from her seated position. Words clamoured at the tip of her tongue, impatient to be free.

'Do not deny me a place in the next world. Don't make me such a sinner. Oh, God! I did think of abasing Otikkan also to carry out my plan of revenge. Forgive me, forgive me. I was singed and unable to stand in that divine presence. Oh, God!'

Words stuck in her throat and struggled to emerge. The council of Vedic scholars horripilated hearing the words which emerged from the depths of the Object's inner being.

They looked at Paptikutty standing before Otikkan, palms together in a worshipful posture, her heart agonized.

'Child, I visualized this hour more than twenty years ago. I tried my best to prevent it. But, there is a limit to human effort. I was unable to save my own brothers.'

Chematiri Otikkan stood up.

22

The sagely Akkithar returned from the temple at midnoon, breaking a forty-year routine. In the light of the afternoon sun, the well-proportioned body of the eighty-year-old renunciate shone like glowing embers. At this unexpected appearance, Chematiri, who sat in the outhouse, felt a stab of anxiety. What was the matter?

'Hasn't Nambyattan arrived? All of you please come into my bedroom.'

Something had happened. Maybe...

Perhaps, Varahamihiran's science had gone wrong in this instance. But there were no indications, no particular hint of bad times. Who can really fathom the wishes of a great sage?

In the inner quarters, where he used to sleep, Akkithar sat on the bare ground, his legs crossed. Near him lay the family heirloom, the staff. The others stood around him, like small planets surrounding the sun to receive light.

'I will die nine days from today,' Akkithar said in a perfectly normal voice.

The sons looked at each other. Chematiri stared at his father as though he had heard an unbelievable piece of news. His disciple, Nambyattan, stood near him, his arms folded respectfully.

Even though it was midnoon, a cold wave swept in and set everyone shivering. It was a pleasurable chill.

'During the next eight days, I shall not talk. I have already stopped eating. I shall lie right here. You should take turns sitting by me. I do not need anything any more. On the afternoon of the ninth day, I will breathe deeply nine times. After that, you know what you have to do, don't you? Place my body on the ground. Whisper the Vedas in my ear. Do all the rituals in the prescribed manner.'

No one said anything.

The hour was close at hand when that long penance would end. Lying in the arms of death, he gave instructions about conducting the final rites. It was as though he was addressing Death itself. 'I am ready. Come. Here is the water to clean your feet and here are my other offerings of welcome.' Forty years ago, Death had beckoned him. 'No,' he had said, 'the time has not come. I have some work yet. When the time comes I shall tell you.'

'For some time now, I have been aware that my hour of death was nearing. This trial and the stress... Don't hesitate; let Pachu and Vasu go.'

Akkithar gazed intently at his eldest son. Then he looked at his other sons, who having been declared outcastes were standing outside the room. Unable to return that pure gaze, they looked down.

'As it is, the final verdict has not been pronounced declaring you as outcastes. The present verdict is based on the Object's words. Pachu, Vasu, do not be downhearted. I am not unhappy. You won't be able to participate in my cremation. That is not necessary. I am happy. You need not offer the cooked rice according to the rituals. Well, this is the fault of the times.'

'Even so...' the disciple Nambyattan began hesitantly.

'Why, Nambyattan, you can say whatever is on your mind. You have to obey the customs and laws of the land. Pachu and Vasu have been declared outcastes. Let them go. Give them what they need for their livelihood. It is after that that they will have problems. Let them do everything after consulting their elder brother.'

When Paptikutty mentioned his brother's names, Chematiri

had reported the announcement to his father with great hesitation. What would father feel? But, on that day, Akkithar did not say anything.

'Let them stay here for two more weeks. Do not touch them. I shall tell you what to do later.'

Now that time had come. The nectar-sweet voice of Akkithar as he spread his bed in the mouth of death.

'I know all about the activities of the young people in this family. No one can stop them. Let's do something. Send them to Madras or somewhere else and educate them thoroughly. Pachu, after this hubbub, you go along with the younger boys. Talk to that priest of yours, your disciple, and make the necessary arrangements in Madras.'

He never usually talked at such length. Probably these were his last instructions; they were so elaborate.

What next?

Chematiri stood ready to accept his father's last words.

'You may ask me anything. Till twilight. Thereafter I will not talk.'

No one felt the need to ask anything. Everything was conveyed without asking. What need then to raise questions?

'Is it time now?' Chematiri raised a doubt. Understanding his son's doubt, a divine smile spread over the father's face. A glimpse of the Ultimate Being residing in the endless Ocean of Milk.[162]

'Are you not able to see it with your mathematical calculations and drawing of horoscopes? Is that why you are asking? Do you know who taught me astrology? To begin with, my father. After that, haven't I told you about a woman mendicant, who stayed for some time on the temple premises? She went off somewhere. Now...' After a moment's silence, he continued, 'Unni, have you seen her?

---

[162] The reference is to Lord Vishnu.

She told me that astrology will not work in all cases. There may be certain people who have conquered time itself. There...there... in their case the God of Death waits for them.'

A sage, who had lost his way and strayed from the Himalayan ranges, to be born in this house. Those who gathered around him stood perplexed by his charisma—that of a worshipper who spent the entire day praying in the temple. A sage freed of all worldly needs. The astrologer in Chematiri began to calculate his father's lifespan; after some time he gave up and sat with his head bowed in defeat. He had heard that it was not proper to restrict the lives of great people to the limits of astrological signs. But...but... Maybe he could not give up the effort due to his pride in his scholarship, not yet entirely extinguished. Unconsciously his mind did penance in the realms of mathematical calculations.

'Have you understood now? Then do not stop your daily routine. One person may sit just outside this room. Don't step in. Enter only on the ninth day. I will not need anything. I ask you to guard this room only to prevent a stray dog or cat entering it. I won't be able to check that. After twilight today, I will lie down. I shall open my eyes only on the ninth day at midnoon. Then, I will breathe deeply nine times. Do not forget.'

Father was teaching them the different aspects of his own death with the same meticulousness that he had shown in the teaching of the Vedas. Oh, God! If I have another life, let me be born to the same father, Chematiri prayed with a burning intensity.

'I shall sit here. Another person will be needed only to relieve me when I go to the pond to have a bath or when I have my food. Please grant me this privilege,' Thazhamangalam Nambyattan begged for this boon.

The great Akkithar of the Otikkan House thus made his final offering before he undertook the last journey to return to the womb of creation. A sage, who through several sacrifices by fire had earned the right to be a ritualist, who later following the very narrow path of penance, finally climbed up to stand face-to-face with Death.

The wandering mendicant whose feet were cracked and broken stood guard at his teacher's cosmic sleep. Nambyattan, who had been purified in the fire of repentance, concentrated on his teacher's silent figure and prayed. The teacher and the student remained thus, inside and outside the room, each covered by an aura of his own, unaware of the passage of the sun and moon.

The hours came and went in the Otikkan's house with precision.

Knowing that the trial had begun, many people migrated to other places. Their flight from home signified their fear of showing faces marked, they believed, by sin. The verdict would be spelt, whether they went or not. The ceremony symbolizing the breakup of familial ties would be performed. Those who remained, those who were not cast out, would be purified. The last rites would be performed while the outcastes still lived. Those who retained their rights to have the last rites performed in the traditional way with water and cooked rice would break their ties with the outcastes.

Pachu Otikkan and Vasu Otikkan could have run off. But instead, they sat, gazing vacantly at the sky over which twilight crept.

∽

'I perform the water ceremony for Parameswara Sharma.' The thought of the sacred chant recited by those who were not cast out, on the occasion of the breaking of familial ties suffocated Pachu Otikkan. To him, the Smarthan's three claps sounded like the final drumbeats of fate. Water given thrice with the accompanying sacred chant! The Smarthan clapping his hand three times!

'In the clan of Viswamitra...'

'We shouldn't have done it, Vasu. It was a terrible mistake. There is no point talking about it now. It is fate. A father who is a sage, a brother who is a man of action; yet we do not have even the right to perform father's last rites. Society will shun us like diseased dogs, Vasu, let's go somewhere,' Pachu Otikkan's voice broke.

'I am ready. But when father is lying in this condition—I am unwilling to go. Again, leaving our nephews and disciples, unable to see elder brother, or only see him once in a while... What will elder brother's wife think? To me, she is like a mother,' Vasu Otikkan wept.

'We have to live here like outsiders; we cannot touch the well or the pond. After we eat, we have to clear away the leaves ourselves. Was it necessary for us to have done what we did?'

It was not an instance of their minds weakening when Kama awoke for half a moment and played havoc with their senses. Time played a calculated game. The hallowed ground was prepared with decorations after sacred rituals; they were drawn into it to perform the dance of the possessed. The power of that chant of seduction, strengthened through a hundred recitals—the speed of the device! The effectiveness of the object used!

'What is the use of thinking of it now? The innocent flight of an insect enjoying its wings! The fall into the blazing funeral pyre! Why did it happen like this? That Kathakali maestro ran off from the stage, not even waiting to wipe the make-up from his face. Only when he reached her presence did he regain his senses. The power of sorcery! Black magic at its sharpest!'

Pachu Otikkan's mind went back to that dance stage.

His eyes reddened with the juice of the thumba flower, conveying the meaning of words and lines clearly, all the nine emotions obeying his dictates, the Kathakali maestro[163] stood onstage, ready for his slow, firm dance which filled the entire expanse of the stage. There was a complete fusion of divine and demonic accompaniments.[164]

---

[163] The reference is to Kavungal Sankara Panikkar.

[164] The quality of sounds made by an accompanying instrument is considered either

The audience directed their concentrated penance on to the stage. It was then that such an artist who gave form to the Divine saw those eyes that commanded, 'Come to me.' He had to obey. His gestures went awry. That dance teacher who had been trained to make his body his eyes faltered in his rhythm and collapsed. He rose hastily and dashed off to the dressing room. In a semi-conscious state of mind, he searched desperately for those eyes.

Ah! What a story!

Pachu Otikkan sat resting his face on folded arms. 'No, it is not magic, just willpower. A kind of penance. A personification of discipline of mind and body. Didn't she spell it out? Revenge. Plain, undiluted revenge, nurtured by the tears of many Namboodiri women. Our young nephew—elder brother's son—the sacred teacher of all progressive minds—only when he explained it did I understand. Till then I never once thought about these things. I, who am the younger, unmarried brother in the family, never knew of the sorrow that lay in the inner quarters. Now I understand; I have understood the real significance of the story of incarnation.'

But Vasu Otikkan could not agree with his elder brother's thoughts. He wished Paptikutty had not been born, even though it was a birth from the sacrificial fire.

'Come. It is time to eat. Pick up that pot of water.' Their elder brother's voice put an end to their wild thoughts.

In their own house, they were outsiders who had to keep their distance. Both the brothers sat in the outer veranda, careful not to pollute the sacred inner quarters. When the polluted ones accepted the water poured by their elder brother from a great height, they

---

divine or demonic. Accordingly, mridangam (small drum) and ilathalam (cymbals) are considered divine instruments because of their soft and mellifluous sounds. Chenda (big drum) and chengala (gong) are considered to be demonic because of the primaeval, deep, earthy sounds they produce.

took some of it in their left palms, circled it around the plantain leaves and took it to their lips. Tears fell on their palms, making the water salty. Drinking that sacred water with the proper chant, they tasted beforehand the bitterness of the hours to be spent in hell. Their hunger was appeased even before they ate, so they threw the cooked rice into the gutter. After they picked up the plantain leaves on which food was served and cleaned the floor with water, they escaped into the darkness of the outhouse.

23

'From now onwards we cannot hold the trial here. Shift the venue to wherever you want.' Thazhamangalam Achan Namboodirippad stepped down from the seat meant for the Master of Ceremonies.

Two of his brothers indicted! Two members of the prestigious Thazhamangalam House! The lover of cards and the elephant lover.

'I have heard enough. We don't know what else she is planning to say, that senseless, ignoble woman.'

The mother of Thazhamangalam hardly came out of her prayer room.

'I cannot participate in the trial any more either,' said Chematiri, refusing to continue.

The Smarthan could not withdraw. It was a hereditary family position. The whole land was divided into three regions—for each area a Smarthan and a ritualist were prescribed by Sankara, the Vedantin.

'We too have decided. Let there be a trial of men also. In such a situation, we have a duty to our countrymen. We have to listen to their opinion also. Revered Brahmins—my father's clan,' His Excellency, the King commanded. 'Remove the Object to a place near the palace.'

Paptikutty's rage cooled, her mind grew calm. It was time for her to leave the earth and rise heavenwards. She had more or less fulfilled the duty of her incarnation.

'Some kind of obstinacy, what else is it? All of it can't be true; she is bent on total destruction. There is no salvation for her,' the elderly antharjanams inside Namboodiri houses cursed.

The Object smiled the smile that had the power to seduce the whole world. No salvation for her! She had come to that conclusion long ago. She was grazing in pastures frequented by the great Goddess Herself.

The great ascetic Gandhari[165] mourning her dead sons cursed Lord Krishna, 'My curse is that your Yadava clan will be extinguished after thirty-six years.'

She had decided upon this long ago; there should be a trial for men also. The list ran on. A seventy-year-old Namboodiri, reputed to be a scholar, was asked: 'Even you indicted? What a fate! Do you have anything to say?'

'Haven't you heard that one of the four fates: short lifespan, childlessness, poverty or loss of caste awaits all superior human beings? I am seventy years old, I have children and grandchildren and I am not poor. The only fate left for me is to become an outcaste. I have fallen a prey to that. The sages are never wrong.'

The old ritualist placed the kindi[166] upside down and walked out, holding his head high, seeking lands unfamiliar to him. Another Kakkasseri Bhattathiri[167] who believed that there was a life outside home.

How many such Kakkasseris died, their corpses putrefying in alien lands!

'How many names so far?' asked Paptikutty.

'Sixty-four.'

'Must I name more?'

'No. That is enough,' said His Excellency, the King. 'Enough,'

---

[165] The mother of the Kauravas and the wife of Dhritarashtra. After the epic Mahabharata war, in which all her sons were killed, Gandhari cursed Krishna, whom she considered the prime reason for the war.

[166] A vessel with a spout.

[167] A brilliant young Namboodiri, Kakkasseri Bhattathiri defeated Uddanda, a Tamil Brahmin scholar, in open debate and established his intellectual superiority.

the King said, 'that is enough.'

It had begun with the Namboodiris, but the curse was a sword which struck down many prominent people from other castes as well. It turned to ash whatever it touched. When it approached the King's clan—'No more! Let's stop! She is deranged!'

Her growing radiance turned all of creation into a plaything.

'Shall I continue?'

'No, no, that is enough,' said the King.

The subjects had to obey the King's order. Wasn't it his prerogative to give orders and that of the subjects to obey?

So, enough of the trial.

'I am willing to dip my hands in boiling ghee,'[168] a Namboodiri blabbered, his cells alive, his nerves thrilling, his head bursting.

'All this is being done with the intention of extinguishing the Namboodiri clan. That the ruling King too should support such a plan is a sin.'

'Also, the question of losing caste doesn't arise. That is done only if you sleep with a chaste woman. By that rule, only the first man who slept with her needs to lose his caste. After that, the woman is to be treated as a prostitute. There is no loss of caste for sleeping with prostitutes.'

'That is what the *Manusmriti* says, but we, the Namboodiris of this land, follow the *Sankarasmriti*.'

'The trial basically reflects irresponsible behaviour. If a name is uttered by the Object, the priest and others do not question it. That then becomes the last judgement. Sheer uncivilized brutality!'

'I am willing to dip my hands in boiling ghee.'

Rivalry reigned amidst those who occupied the seats of justice and the victims of the Object's vengeful behavior.

---

[168] Dipping one's hands in boiling ghee is one of the tests prescribed in the sacred texts for proving one's innocence when one is wrongly accused of a crime.

'What a combination, where is it all leading us? All the names in the list are those of distinguished people. Not one is a commonplace man. Why? I am not saying anything more.'

'The ghee will not scald my hands. Give me the order.'

The Smarthan was startled. He had the authority to give that order, but...

'Wait, let the King give his final order.'

'Till then, are we to live as polluted people, not touching anything sacred?'

'Be careful. Namboodiris will be stoned and driven out like diseased dogs. Be careful. What I say will come true,' said the slim Namboodiri, scratching his close cropped hair. His all-seeing eye could visualize a future when the five great sins[169] would be rubbed into Namboodiri foreheads, calloused by constant prostration. 'Look at the state of the inner quarters. Even a cowshed would compare well in contrast.'

Those who heard this statement were nauseated, thinking of their own houses. They stroked each other's backs to console themselves.

'Must I go on?' said Unni Namboodiri. 'No society which has insulted Motherhood has survived, I envisage Namboodiris fighting with each other, unable to enter their own houses or the temples, wandering aimlessly. We have to find a remedy. Four or five legal marriages and illegal liaisons all over the place. Namboodiris who make empty boasts about reading and assimilating the Vedas. The Namboodiris who enjoy the breath and the physical company of prostitutes have no salvation. There is no repentance for such a sin, only loss of caste. They forget that. They collected all the dirt

---

[169] The five great sins are brahmahatya (killing of a Brahmin), gauhatya (killing of a cow), sthreehatya (killing of a woman), guruhatya (killing of a teacher) and brunahatya (killing of a foetus).

and threw it into the inner quarters. Never once did they think whether the women would have the strength to bear this burden on their broken shoulders. But wait and watch the power of fidelity. Where the faithful wife's tears fall, that place will be condemned as the netherworld.'

Young Otikkan, Unni Namboodiri and Kunhaniyan were in the habit of speaking to gatherings in various places. They spoke in a spiritually appealing tone which they had acquired naturally from reciting the Vedas. 'Aren't you all ashamed? Resident husbanding and perpetually washed clothes as payment! Worse than stud bulls.'

The King was also upset. These young men's loud protests shook the very foundations of the system of kingship.

His position as ruler had been granted to him by the great British. How pleasantly carefree he had been! No responsibilities at all—all he had to do was to wear freshly laundered clothes every day and remain a symbol of grandeur and prosperity.

The plight of those two young people, his niece and her man, separated so early in life... His face was so tender and attractive. They were well suited for each other. Like Kama and Rati.[170] Kunhaniyan and Ramanikutty. His words as he left the palace—'If you want to be with me, come to my house.'

He had had the courage to say so to a scion of kingly glory, who had never stepped out of her own house without being accompanied by attendants who held swords and shields.

'What crime did I commit?' Ramanikutty's weeping voice reached every nook and corner of the palace.

'I am willing to come. But before that, please come here. I want to see you. I feel impatient. What wrong did I do?' She wrote these words in her unformed hand on a postcard. Those illegible letters, grown hazy like an ancient memory, zigzagged here and

---

[170]The Cupid and Psyche of Indian mythology.

there, like someone's bad fate preventing one from following the right path. The postcard soaked with the postman's perspiration pursued Kunhaniyan, who had joined Young Otikkan's movement.

'There are many things I wish to write about. My education is limited to learning the alphabet practised on the floor. What can I write? My heart is full of desires. I wish to see you. Please come soon. I do not have any peace of mind. I will come with you to your house. Let them cast me out too.'

Amalakkad Kunhaniyan could not even weep.

'Maybe in the next birth, conditions will be better. Then, Ramanikutty, we can be together. Let us not worry about this life. We can live apart and yet be husband and wife. I can understand the sorrow and isolation of living there. But, my sacrificial ground is here. The altar has been sanctified, waiting for the sacrifice. Let's not give future generations an opportunity to blame us. We should not be unfit to accept the water offering given by them when they perform our last rites.'

Kunhaniyan prepared this reply with great effort. He wrote and rewrote it several times, changed and corrected the lines. To him, language seemed inadequate to express true emotions.

He was in a quandary, unable to invoke his heartbeats in dead and stilted words. 'Write whenever you can; that is good therapy. Ramanikutty's Kunhaniyan.'

He felt a pleasure different from that derived from a union arranged by the ruling system. A sense of immense satisfaction as he claimed his treasure, loudly declaring ownership: 'Ramanikutty's Kunhaniyan.' The oath of truth confirming that he belonged to no other.

∽

'We should not delay. Only ten days are left for the final verdict. On that day, we should hold the naming ceremony of our new generation. The recital of the Vedas in one generation's ears, signifying their death, should also be the occasion for the naming ceremony of the next,' said Young Otikkan. 'We should not delay any more. The time has come.'

Unaware of even the sun's movements, these young Namboodiris rushed to reincarnate their society.

'I have arranged for at least one representative from each house,' Young Otikkan's enthusiasm knew no bounds.

'You must take special care to see that no one is put to difficulties. Kunhaniyan, you must take charge.'

'Will we be able to bring a Namboodiri woman to this meeting?'

'Why this hurry! Young Otikkan, you are always in a hurry. Be patient for a year or two and we will see a procession of Namboodiri women flinging aside their protective cover. The young girls attending schools...' said Unni Namboodiri.

'Oh, God! Save us!' Kunhaniyan sighed.

'Hey, look, don't worry, let this programme succeed. After that, we will attend to your problem. We will approach the King and get him to issue a special order. Let the Thampurattis who marry Namboodiris live in their husbands' houses. Otherwise...'

'I said right at the beginning that married men should not be persuaded to become ascetics or involve themselves in revolutionary politics. It will lead to unnecessary discomfort and pain. Even now, a girl is suffering because of Kunhaniyan.'

Young Otikkan did not like Unni Namboodiri's observation. 'Let them be sorry. Huh! The sorrow of the inmates of the palace!'

'Young Otikkan!' said Unni Namboodiri sharply; so far he had never raised his voice at the Otikkan. Young Otikkan instantly regretted what he had said in the heat of the moment. 'Kunhaniyan, don't take it to heart. Ichatha can never restrain himself. He says the first thing that pops into his mouth. In his craze for the cause of the Namboodiri community he has become vengeful towards other communities. That is not a good development. As if we have not wrought our own downfall.'

Amalakkad Kunhaniyan looked down, his youthful, innocent face despondent. The insults one had to suffer! Young Otikkan glanced repentantly at his friend. Silently, he begged pardon.

'Even if he is at times sarcastic, Young Otikkan is passionately fond of his friends,' said Unni Namboodiri.

24

During this terrible fallout, there were many injustices leading to the loss of caste of innocent people and a blackening of names which did not spare even the Smarthan.

Meanwhile the unrelenting procedure of law rolled on, the list of outcastes had not ended. Document after document spelt the end of many social identities and pretensions. The King finally permitted the trial of men.

'In the year…in the month of…on the day of…in the presence of His Highness, the King of Cochin, the ruler of all temples, before the village head, in the village…I, the Smarthan, keeping the ritualists and the King's men in mind, write this order.'

Cherikkat Nambota,[171] who had been branded an outcaste, obtained a special order from the Smarthan and set out for Suchindram.[172] On the way he met the King in person and received another order—that he might thrust his hands into boiling ghee, pick up the idol of a bull immersed in it,[173] wrap his palms in a plantain leaf and circumambulate the temple—the proof of his innocence would be the sight of his smooth, unscalded skin when examined later.

Loss of caste for a crime he hadn't dreamt of! Nambota blamed the keepers of time, those all-seeing bodies.

Absolute nonsense!

After the sixty-fourth name was pronounced by Paptikutty, as

---

[171] A typical Namboodiri name, like Ichatha or Nambyattan.
[172] One of the famous, beautiful temples situated at the southern tip of Kerala.
[173] The bull represents Nandi, Siva's messenger and mount.

though still dissatisfied, she dropped an aimless parting shot, 'The rest the aunt will announce'.[174]

Then began the injustices…because she had not named some. Paptikutty! Great Goddess! Save me. Nambota prayed.

He had never seen her before. Nor had he had any sexual relationships with Paptikutty or any other woman. He was not boasting that it was due to a lack of desire. He had not had a chance. Yet, he was declared an outcaste.

For some it was a cruel drama. The elderly Smarthan agonized over the possible naming of an innocent Namboodiri.

'Don't make a fool of me. It is an extreme step. If you are so sure, I will recommend that you obtain an order from the King and go to Suchindram.'

The Smarthan continued to reflect.

The curse would fall on his house. Generations of his family members would have to suffer. He should not have assumed this responsibility.

Nambota was sure that the 'ghee test' would leave him untouched. Only if he was very sure of himself should he do it. Otherwise he should run away. It could still be arranged!

No one would stop him and he wouldn't be forced to dip his hands in ghee. After worship, he who undertook the penance could enter the sanctum sanctorum. Everything had been clearly explained to Nambota.

> The Sun, the Moon, the Fire and the Wind,
> The netherworld, the Earth and Heaven,
> Both Heart and Death,
> Day and Night and in between twilight
> All know the Dharma of Man.

---

[174] The reference is to the aunt of Tundan and Neelan, who was probably the only inmate and witness in Cheriyedath House to all of Paptikutty's liaisons.

The Smarthan would then recite the Oath of Truth.

Nambota was impatient to face the upholders of justice with his clean, unburnt hands held high.

In recent times no one had undertaken such a trial.

With the onset of Kali Yuga, even the sanctity of the trials was not maintained. There was no purity of heart. Trial by dipping one's hands in boiling oil was going to be scrapped. The British King felt it was all unscientific nonsense.

The ruling King also agreed.

'Why was she so particular that his house should be extinguished? That he should die without any successors?'

'The children too can be included because of the time of their birth. Let them grow up as Chakyars. Enacting verses.'

The order. God help me.

Instead of the protective boon-granting gestures of the Goddess, if all eight divine hands of Kali held murderous weapons, only Siva could bear it. Firm, strong footsteps under which the very earth trembled could only be borne by Siva himself. Out of the drops of her perspiration, she created murderous figures. She was blessed with the boon of immortality. The incarnation shaped from the body of the Godhead itself.[175]

An incarnation born to free the world from the arrogance of demons! A soft feminine body to conquer brute animal force.

But Nambota could not display his hands unburnt. At the temple premises in Suchindram, Thazhamangalam Achan Namboodirippad was waiting for him. He had taken his place in the front row in a manner familiar to wealthy overlords. He had also had a meeting with the King and obtained his blessings.

---

[175] The reference is to Kali, the goddess created out of the drops of Siva's perspiration to specifically kill Darika, a demon. Each of the gods presented her with a weapon.

The King had given his order to Nambota to undergo the test.

Yet, he was asked not to dip his hands in boiling ghee by Achan Namboodirippad, who wanted no further investigations, fearing that they would implicate him as well.

A special messenger came with another order.

'I too was a little perplexed. Later I realized that the Smarthan who had recommended your test of innocence to the King did not have the authority to do it. Apart from that the Smarthan also deserves to be punished,' said Achan Namboodiri.

So the Smarthan had been made a scapegoat!

The Vedic scholars unanimously pronounced that the Smarthan should perform the act of repentance.

The King's order! One had to be conscious of that.

The judgement of Vedic scholars!

Thazhamangalam Achan Namboodirippad went to Suchindram and met Nambota to cloak his own corruption and guilt. He welcomed Nambota with a smile and, pretending to be greatly grieved, said: 'What can we do? Do not be unhappy. He does not have the right to do what is not prescribed by the *Smritis*. He shouldn't.'

Nambota, who was yearning to dip his hands in boiling ghee and take out the idol of the bull, was shattered and seared to the soul. Now, because of him, the elderly Smarthan also had to perform the ritual of repentance.

The King's order had effectively quashed the chance to perform the fiery test of truth.

'I am not going home. I must know the truth. You Namboodiris and your King, you can do anything you want. I am not affected by you flinging me out of my caste. I will enter the temple and go about as usual. Who will prevent me? Let me see. I have some land in Malabar, which is under the British rulers. I am a British subject. A curse on your order!' Nambota leapt at Achan, protesting loudly.

The Smarthan also burst out furiously. 'I am not going to perform the ritual of repentance. Who is to decide? The King? Or the scholars of the scriptures uttering all kinds of meaningless remarks? I too have studied the *Manusmriti* and the *Sankarasmriti*. I know the customs. I am the one who gave the order and I can give you the arguments in support of that act.'

The Smarthan did not have to observe repentance, said the King. But Nambota must be declared an outcaste.

'Thazhamangalam, why are you so insistent?' asked Nambota. 'Two of your brothers have gone away. Another brother has become a mendicant. Aren't you relieved? Why are you trying to harm others?'

'Siva, Siva, me? I never thought of such things. According to the King's instructions, I went to Suchindram, that's all. What is in it for me?' Achan stopped talking, not believing his own words.

Mangazhi, who stood next to him, twisted his face and laughed frightfully.

This man must be sent back to his house. Is there a way? He has become a nuisance, Achan thought. There was nothing Achan could do. That stare was enough to frighten Achan as he walked back and forth in his veranda.

The assistant Kesavan waited for an opportunity to interrupt, approached Achan and bowed.

'You must try. Come here.' Achan walked into a corner of the room for privacy and looked covertly at Mangazhi. No, he wouldn't hear anything.

'You have to make him understand. Let him stay in his house. I will give him whatever he needs.'

Kesavan grasped the cloth which had slipped from his protruding stomach and tightened it again. Then he nodded in tune with Achan's tone and expressed his assent.

'What, what are you saying Nambyattan?' Achan addressed Nambyattan, who had grown his hair and beard and was ready to go on a journey.

'I want to go to Palghat, and from there to the northern parts. I shall stop at our outhouse. Two persons from this house have also been included in the list of outcastes. Let them stay in that outhouse. Let them take whatever dues we get from that principality.'

'But that…that…is our main principality.'

'Yes. I know. Even though they are now outcastes, they too have to live. Let them go this very day.'

'Must we go that far?'

'It is important. Mother is also happy. She was very unhappy when she heard of the trial. I talked to her and comforted her saying that elder brother has given them the Palghat principality. Mother's heart is full now.'

'All right. Let it be as you wish. Tell them to see me before they go. And you? When will I see you again?'

Mother was happy. That was enough. For some time mother had not been on good terms with him. The death of Unikkali. Then this loss of caste for so many. Now…Achan Namboodirippad was envious of his brother Nambyattan.

'I do not know when I will return. I shall return before mother dies. So, brother…'

It had become a routine. Whenever Nambyattan set on a journey he prostrated respectfully before his elder brother.

'May you be blessed. May all your wishes be fulfilled.'

The mendicant lifted his bundle on to his shoulders and set off. The bundle symbolized the burden of the results of his actions in his previous births. He walked towards the evening sun. Seeing two suns greeting each other, Achan's heart filled with a sense of peace.

25

The first quarter of the night had passed.

In a small tin-roofed railway station, a gas lamp shone behind a covering. A torch on the iron fence burned slowly, blowing smoke.

Young Otikkan and Unni Namboodiri sat under a jackfruit tree near the station. Amalakkad Kunhaniyan went in to buy a ticket. They were there to see Young Otikkan off on his journey to Madras to write the matriculation examination.[176]

'We never thought that things would take such a turn, did we, Otikkan? The Namboodiri community is truly shaken, isn't it!'

∽

At midnight, the King sat on the seat of justice in his palace. At his instance the Smarthan read the entire order, written on a folded paper. The names of the outcastes were called out by a Tamil Brahmin, according to custom. After each name was called out, he went out to dip himself in the pond to purify himself.

The Brahmins, who had memorized the entire legal code and who acted like machines, stood in front of the outhouse and ordered her, 'Now you can step outside. Leave the shawl and the umbrella there.'

'Wait. I want to say something more. Why have you stopped the trial so soon? I haven't finished. Tell the King that there are more names,' said Paptikutty.

---

[176]According to the British system of education introduced by Lord Macaulay in India, the first public examination that a student writes at the end of ten years of schooling is the matriculation examination. The successful completion of this examination makes a student eligible for college education.

'What?'

'The aunt will say the names aloud.'

That was indeed a good parting shot.

ꕤ

Let the best of Namboodiris who had heaved a sigh of relief prepare another outhouse. Let them then lead the King to the white sheet and black rug ceremoniously spread in his honour. On another midnight, another young Brahmin would bathe and shiver in his wet clothes. The trial and loss of caste would continue until the ruling powers had banished the entire intelligentsia of the region to a foreign land. After that—bliss. The King could pay the annual dues to his British masters and relax. He was carrying out his revenge on his own countrymen. He fought wars with his own people. But whenever he saw a white man, he tied his melmundu below his waist and bowed before him. He made a voluntary gift of his kingdom to the British. All over the country he erected scaffolds to hang people. A slavery which had lasted for years brought about the tendency to cover one's mouth and wag one's tail. Doing so skilfully was considered glorious.

ꕤ

Paptikutty stepped out, spreading around her a glow attained after purification by fire. She pushed open the door of the outhouse backward and closed it with a bang. She looked as though she had gained her salvation from the dependency suffered during innumerable births. At last, she was able to look at the sun's rays and fulfil her innermost desires. Then she looked at the startled Vedic scholars and smiled her seductive smile. That innocent smile which attracted people and sucked their lives out of them. With every step she took, the earth shuddered.

ꕤ

Unni Namboodiri said, 'Young Otikkan, didn't you hear the fearful sound of Brahminism being uprooted? The cough from the Brahmin as he called out the names? The croak emerged as Brahminism was lifted and placed on the ground, its throat constricted, straining to breathe its last.

'As a result, the next day, didn't you see how enthusiastically the first of our meetings was received? Why are you looking so troubled? Is it because you are going so far away? Go and return soon. Be the first Namboodiri graduate. Your victory will not be yours alone. Remember that Kunhaniyan also has come.'

'Everything has gone well,' said Young Otikkan. 'But—Paptikutty and I are of an age. We studied together for quite some time. Now she must be about twenty-two. What will her future be?'

'I also thought—whither next? The King's concession is a paltry sum—and a hut on the banks of the Alwaye River.'

'How many Namboodiris have disappeared? How many houses destroyed with no successors! Degraded by falling into the clutches of Time. Nothing can be predicted.'

'Isn't that you, young Master?'

Young Otikkan recognized the person who addressed him in the golden glow of the country torch. Chami, his classmate. Father's chief disciple.

'What are you doing here? At this time?'

'What about you, Master?'

'I am leaving for Madras. To write the examination. You?'

'Master. Do you know... Look here. Do you know who this is?'

Young Otikkan saw that blazing face in the brilliance of the torchlight.

'Paptikutty!'

Hearing what Young Otikkan said, the night stumbled and woke up. It increased the power of its own darkness. Unni Namboodiri and Kunhaniyan felt completely exhausted and nervous.

At midnight, alone, with an Ezhava boy, a Namboodiri woman...

She had been declared an outcaste.

Still, a Namboodiri woman.

Fellow student!

'My Master told me, "You must be with her. Do not let her do anything desperate." It was my good fortune that I saw her when she had covered her body completely with strips of cloth. Oh! God! I reached the spot, by my Master's compassion, before her self-immolation.

'He had commanded me, "Be with her." Somehow, I talked to her and consoled her. At last she has agreed to go away to an alien place and live there. In Madurai or in Rameswaram.[177] She has to go by this train. My teacher has provided even for that. He entrusted me with the job. Oh, God! His compassion!'

Father! Father had seen to that, too.

Her face shone with a glow greater than the pure golden light shed by the burning torch.

'Bless us. After this we may never see each other again. Only once have I seen your face. I have tasted the water given by those hands. That sweetness remains in all the five elements of my body,' said Unni Namboodiri, who had by then regained his composure, held his palms together in a worshipful gesture.

'Chami, your life has become meaningful. There is no greater offering to your teacher.' Unni Namboodiri felt a great affection for Chami, and a little envy too.

'My teacher is responsible for my well-being. His commands are God's commands. I am just fulfilling it. That alone is my aim, to accomplish which I am willing to give up my life. This young mistress is my teacher's disciple. That is enough for me to respect

---

[177]Two places of pilgrimage situated in Tamil Nadu.

her, even worship her. To me, anything connected with my Master is worthy of worship. Oh, God! Please bless this hapless being who cannot wait upon his teacher in any other way.'

Chami stood, pressing his palms together.

Young Otikkan alone stood immobile. It was a powerful blow to his mind. He leaned on Kunhaniyan's shoulders to keep from falling.

Paptikutty spoke. 'Young Otikkan, why are you so silent? Maybe I am a sinner. Still—I did not anticipate all of it. Some of it was the overt action of an inner command. The rest lies in my obstinacy. However, we grew up together as children. Say something and permit me to leave. May you study well. Never again in our community should there be another. May I be the first and the last. You have tried to tell me about your progressive movement. Do not forget something: the foundation lies in the inner quarters. Please pay special attention to that section: Do not be indifferent to Mother.[178] She won't tolerate it,' Paptikutty said all this in a halting clear voice. Her words were like a chant, touching the hearts of those who heard her.

'Amme! Paptikutty!' Young Otikkan addressed her worshipfully.

Amalakkad Kunhaniyan gazed at that unparalleled beauty and prostrated before her. This must be the Goddess herself, Mother of the Universe.

'What are you doing? Do not buy hell for yourself by worshipping a fallen woman!' cried Paptikutty trying to prevent him, holding out her hands to help him rise.

Then she stopped herself.

'I, I touch you?...touch you... No...no...' she withdrew her hand hastily.

'No, that touch is like a blessing to us. In it lies a divine feeling. The caress of motherhood which has reached its fullness

---

[178]This verse refers to womenkind in general.

will destroy all our sins.'

They were awoken from their reverie by the cold, sharp whistle of the train which seemed to have been flown in by the midnight wind from some unknown world. Once again they became aware of their surroundings. The relationships wrought by karma brought them together; later the same karma separated them; yet before they moved away from each other, they met once more, unintentionally, on that day. All of them stood immobile, silent. As they understood each other without having to speak, language became redundant.

'We may never see one another again in this world. Even if we do, we may not recognize one another. My second birth—let me go. To all of you, goodbye. Chami, you may go now. Do not come any further with me,' Paptikutty said.

'The torch light.'

'No, I like the dark. Darkness will protect me.'

Preparing to go to a life unknown, Cheriyedath Paptikutty plunged into that darkness.

The sound of the train chugging, in its rush to connect one place to another, came nearer and nearer. Inside this ever-moving fire cart, with a single open eye on its forehead which crossed the stations of endless movement of life and death, human beings slumbered forgetful of their real selves.

'We too have to go. It is time,' Unni Namboodiri reminded them. Young Otikkan moved without feeling the weight of his own body. The other three attended to him. Time accepted the offering made on the occasion of the journey, blessing it.

Oh, Paptikutty, Mother of the Universe! Bless us mortals!

Afterword
The Many Incarnations of Kuriyedathu Thatri

Dr J. Devika

A Lasting Memory

More than a century after the sensational excommunication of Kuriyedathu Thatri and a very large number of men whom she allegedly reported to be her paramours shook the aristocracy of the Hindu kingdom of Kochi, the story continues to haunt the imagination of Malayalis. Her story of revenge has invited many interpretations. These interpretations take place in both high literary forums as well as in popular culture. Lalithambika Antharjanam, one of the earliest women to gain recognition in the field of Malayalam literature, retold Thatri's story, hailing her as the Goddess of Retribution who struck at the roots of the rot that had beset traditional Malayali Brahmin life. There have been prurient retellings that exploited the pornographic possibilities of the tale, turning it into a series of sexcapades of a cloistered, high-caste woman. Modernist retellings, which include *Outcaste*, have cast Thatri as the embodiment of cosmic female energy sweeping away the decadence of the Brahmins and preparing the ground for new beginnings, or as the embodiment of aesthetic refinement whose lust was for art, not the male body.

But these appropriations have not really tamed the fear that the story unleashed in this society. As I have said at the outset, the reverberations of Thatri's story continue to be felt in Kerala even in the twenty-first century. This was apparent in the explosion of the number of sexual violence cases in Kerala brought against powerful men—particularly the infamous Suryanelli serial rape case. Both the lurid and sensationalist press reports and the more political accounts focused on the survivor's story evoked Thatri and how she brought about the destruction of many scions of the most powerful Brahmin families of Kochi.

In other words, *Outcaste* is not merely a widely-read novel in Malayalam; it reflects two aspects of contemporary society—the transformation of the Malayali Brahmin community in the twentieth century and the changing nature of women and their agency in traditional communities.

The Event of 1905

As we know, the event that inspired the novel was the smarthavicharam, or trial, of the high-born Namboodiri Brahmin woman or antharjanam named Thatri (Savitri) of the illam (a Namboodiri homestead) called Kuriyedathu, in 1905. In the course of the trial, Thatri named sixty-four paramours, including scions of the most esteemed and powerful families of the Malayali Brahmin aristocracy besides Nair and other Sudra men, in her testimony. The extraordinary nature of the case prompted the Raja of Kochi to allow a purushavicharam in which the accused men were allowed to cross-examine Thatri. But no one escaped. All sixty-four, along with Thatri, were excommunicated. The *Malayala Manorama* (henceforth *M. M.*) covered the case in detail in a series of reports from June 1905 until mid-1906. The case severely jolted the idea of the antharjanam (literally 'indoor-people', a reference to their extreme confinement to the interiors of the illam) as meek and pious and with no connections whatsoever to the world outside. According to reports in the *M. M.*, this woman appeared unrepentantly 'sinful', calculating, ruthlessly bold and outspoken, someone who could argue 'like a barrister' and defeat her opponents.[179] The *M. M.* felt obliged to explain:

> In earlier times, human beings were much less crooked and false. In those times if antharjanams happened to commit some folly out of foolishness or innocence, they would readily confess...they had no intention of deliberately defiling anyone. The antharjanams subjected to smarthavicharam these days must be smooth operators.[180]

The rumour was that she collected information about the moles, discolouration, warts and scars on her paramours' genitalia as incontrovertible evidence that they had had sex with her. After the trial, she was excommunicated along with the men she named and was reportedly sent to Coimbatore, and was never heard of after. There have been other rumours that claimed that a popular Malayalam actor of the mid-twentieth century was her granddaughter, a claim which she has denied.

The excommunication of Nair and other Sudra men led to a flurry of protests against the Malayali Brahmin orthodoxy and the active encouragement of it by the ruler of Kochi from the progressive sections of Kerala society.

The orthodox Namboodiri Brahmin community interpreted smarthavicharam quite differently. For them, the smarthavicharam was a procedure that restored to the illam an 'original purity' lost in the sexual misconduct of its members. This purity could only be regained by either punishing the transgressors or acquitting the antharjanam. Far from signifying a lack, a failing or a state of

---

[179]'Report on smarthavicharam', *Malayala Manorama,* 22 July 1906, p. 1.
[180]Ibid.

decadence (as it did to the newspapers), the successful conclusion of existing smarthavicharam could only signify the continuing efficacy of the mechanisms to regulate sexual conduct among Malayali Brahmins. It was an extraordinary ritualized 'anti-trial', the aims of which were not so much justice for all parties as a confession of guilt from the accused woman. It suspended the human stature of the accused antharjanam until proven innocent. In the period of the vicharam, she was referred to as 'sadhanam', translated here as the Object, but in strict terms, 'instrument', or 'means to an end'. Confined to a special chamber, she was subjected to questioning by the authorities—the smarthans and representatives of the community and the King—until she confessed. The confession was the only way a conviction could be obtained and the trial would continue till then. Reformers in the community pointed out that since the trial involved feasting every day, it could ruin the family if the accused woman did not confess soon. And so, they alleged, the accused woman was subjected to violence to make her confess early. Once the confession was obtained, the woman and the men she named would be excommunicated through a series of very dramatic rituals and she would be considered dead. Any excommunicated Namboodiri, however, could seek a chance to prove his innocence through getting a pampu—a 'letter' from the relevant authority granting such an opportunity—but the woman was cast away permanently.

In the Thatri incident, few men escaped. Though excommunicated, some did manage to secure a share of property from their families and so did not suffer penury, but the prestige of the Brahmin aristocracy was definitely dented. Soon after, in 1908, the reform movement that sought to modernize the Namboodiris, the Namboodiri Yogakshema Sabha, was formed.

Traditional Life in the Illams[181]

The Malayali Brahmins held considerable political and cultural authority and material dominance through their grip over the brahmaswam and devaswam lands (granted to Brahmins and temples respectively) until the twentieth century. Despite the rise of powerful rulers like Marthanda Varma and Saktan Tampuran in the eighteenth century, and unsettling events like Tipu Sultan's invasion of Malabar, they managed to preserve much of their authority in Malayali society well into the heyday of British power.

As the established elite, the Malayali Brahmins did not take kindly to the coming of colonial ideas and institutions; indeed, this appeared as a formidable threat. Perhaps this is a partial explanation of their early reluctance to relate to ideas, institutions and practices that accompanied colonial dominance, documented in both popular 'Namboodiri' stories and accounts by colonial administrators and other contemporary observers. The Brahmins of Kerala were uniquely different from Brahmins elsewhere in other respects as well. This was especially true of the anacharams—observances unique to Malayali Brahmins, sanctioned by a text attributed to Sankara, the *Sankarasmriti*. Over a millennium, there developed in Kerala an elaborate and sophisticated set of social arrangements that preserved their exclusivity and authority and simultaneously allowed them to relate differently with different groups—closely interact with some and maintain their distance from others, extracting different sorts of material gain and services from each. Thus in the traditional illam or mana (the Malayali Brahmin joint-family homestead and also the lineage that was normally coterminous

---

[181] This and subsequent sections draw heavily on my earlier research on reformism among the Malayali Brahmins, published in my book *En-Gendering Individuals: The Language of Re-forming in Early Twentieth Century Keralam*, Hyderabad: Orient BlackSwan, 2007, pp. 111–71.

with it), everyday life was inconceivable without the services of the Nair adiyar (the servant-class), yet strict rules were laid down which regulated the interaction of the Malayali Brahmins with them. Their unique system of primogeniture in joint families allowed only the eldest son—called the moos—to marry within his own caste, and allowed younger males to seek marital alliances with women of the matrilineal Kshatriya castes or Sudra castes, like the Nairs or the Ambalavasis, known as sambandham. Sambandham alliances were considered by Malayali Brahmins to be beyond the domain of kinship and children of such unions were members of their mother's families, with no formal claims upon their father's. As for the jatis lower down, strict and complicated rules of untouchability and unapproachability preserved the exclusivity of Malayali Brahmins. Within their fold, too, relations were regulated to maintain strict hierarchies. Such a complicated system of hierarchies served to regulate a great deal of diversity, much of which set the Malayali Brahmins apart from their counterparts elsewhere—they ranged from royal families such as those of the Rajas of Edappally and Chempakaserry to impoverished temple priests.

One of the major axes of internal regulation among the Malayali Brahmins was undoubtedly sex. Within the illam, relations between men and women and their everyday routines were carefully delineated. Women had to observe elaborate seclusion and they travelled fully covered, virtually invisible, wearing the cloak (putappu) and holding the large cadjan umbrella (kuda). Many male reformers have remarked that a naked and brutal sort of patriarchy operated in the illam, and that a powerful if subtle network of reminders worked tirelessly to instil in women a sense of inferiority right from their infancy. Polygamy was permitted to the eldest son of the illam, who as we have seen, was alone allowed to marry from his caste, as a male heir was indispensable. Widow remarriage was proscribed; indeed, the plight of young widows and antharjanams married off to men on their deathbeds (who, the reformers often pointed out, married these young girls sometimes to facilitate the marriages of their daughters!) was to be frequently evoked in defence of radical Namboodiri reformism. Women could not inherit land, and so their dowry was given as moveable property.

Yet one must remain cautious about attributing to the antharjanams the sort of passivity and meekness that twentieth-century observers and reformers saw. Antharjanams, especially among the Malayali Brahmin aristocracy, often obtained some knowledge of letters; pre-pubertal marriages were uncommon and were not sanctioned by custom. Everyday life in illams was organized through a highly complex set of rules of conduct upholding various hierarchies. Sex difference was certainly important, but not the sole basis upon which this structure of regulation rested; considerations of age, position in the kin network and intra-jati hierarchy, marital status and other factors were also crucial. The very structure of regulation itself permitted the existence of potentially subversive spaces. The antharjanams' extreme seclusion, the practice of their travelling without husbands escorted by servants, the extreme difficulties—material and otherwise—in conducting the smarthavicharam, all left spaces in which the rules ordering everyday life could be potentially upturned. To modern observers, the presence of such spaces indicated the 'decay' of the community. Indeed, in the early twentieth century, in the wake of the Kuriyedathu Thatri case, the *M. M.* was raising the alarm that the women and the servant-class in the illams were colluding against the men, and that breaches of chastity were on the rise among antharjanams, pleading that the patriarchy among the Malayali Brahmins should be reinstated on more modern, stronger foundations.[182]

---

[182] *Malayala Manorama*, 12 July 1905.

Smarthavicharam and the Suffering Antharjanams

During my research into the modern language of binary gender in the early twentieth-century Namboodiri reform movement, I collected news reports of several smarthavicharams that were conducted at that time, and also documented memories of Malayali Brahmin women and men who recalled the stories of such incidents that circulated in their kin circles. Interestingly, I found that they did not always conform to the figure that dominant Namboodiri reformists upheld of the passive and suffering antharjanam who lacked all individuation; rather, the figures that emerged from these sources were closer to the fictional antharjanams who appear in the early short stories of the first-generation Malayali feminist author, Lalithambika Antharjanam, stories of women who suffer within the illam but are neither passive nor incapable of strategizing.

In one instance, for example, the accused woman confessed that she put poison in her husband's milk, and confessed only because her daughter had consumed it. In another, a young woman had a lover who regularly visited her in secret. The local community tried several times to catch him but could not find him anywhere in the illam even after repeated inspections. Each time the men from the community entered the inner quarters of her illam to check, she would stand in a dark corner of a room behind her large cadjan umbrella, hidden from the view of 'alien' men, as was expected of her. But after many such inspections, one of the inspectors noticed that there were four feet under the umbrella, instead of the expected two, and the culprit was caught. The woman left with him after excommunication. In a third account, a woman sought to send money and valuables to a non-Brahmin lover with the active help of Nair maidservants. There were even love stories—for example, in Kottayam, a young girl of an illam fell in love with a Nair student at CMS College. He was a lodger in their outhouse. Her father conducted the smarthavicharam, but immediately thereafter arranged her marriage with the young man, endowing her with a handsome dowry, finding her husband a paying job and gifting the couple a house to start their new life in.

But the most intriguing account I heard was from a younger brother to some men who were excommunicated after Thatri named them, which seemed to strip the event of its mystery, but appeared quite realistic to me. According to him, the entire event was stage-managed by the King of Kochi, a known diehard conservative, and many senior Namboodiris of the leading aristocratic houses who wanted to eliminate the younger men who were starting to demand modernization and question their authority. Thatri, who was apparently known to have several lovers and was on the brink of being ejected from the community anyway, was persuaded to be the centre of a trial and supplied with details of sixty-four men (the number sixty-four being endowed with special significance in the Brahminical traditions was apparently chosen for effect), maybe even more, and asked to recite them during the trial. Since she was being supplied with information through the agents of the state, she was undefeated in the purushavicharam as well. In other words, Thatri's fabled memory, which recalled intimate details of encounters and physical marks, was not even real, according to this account. My informant claimed that this is the reason why so many younger males from leading Brahmin families were on her list. Thatri was sent away immediately and handsomely rewarded to stay untraceable. Even though they may have engineered the response to the trial, it was a wake-up call for the more conservative elements of the community: the effort to modernize the community began in right earnest precisely after to stall any further disorderly moves by those who were chafing under hidebound conventions and restrictions.

Now, I cannot say if this is the 'true story' of Kuriyedathu

Thatri although it provides a better explanation for some of the more mystifying aspects of the incident such as about her memory; there is no way one can really prove it to be true. All one can say is the story keeps growing, and as a tale of revenge and of the fall of an oppressive order, it will be retold as long as patriarchy continues to structure our lives in Kerala and elsewhere.

Translator's Note to the Current Edition Twenty Years Later

I consider it a great privilege to have been entrusted with the English translation of Matampu Kunhukuttan's *Brushte* (*Outcaste*). Various reasons prompted me to take on this task. Foremost among them is my ancestry. My father was a Nair and my grandfather a Namboodiri. So I had a fairly good understanding of the lifestyle of the Namboodiris and the practices that prevailed among them and the Nairs. Secondly, I was struck by the literary merit of the book. Written in Sanskritized Malayalam, encapsulating the grandeur of the former, it is also laced with the acerbic wit of the Namboodiris. I dared to plunge into this effort only because I had Matampu's blessings.

Little did I realize how difficult the task would be. However with the assistance of my able editor Mini Krishnan, I was able to do it.

I think the value of *Brushte* (*Outcaste*) lies in the fact that, apart from portraying the social, political and cultural events of that time faithfully, it also underlines the courage of a woman who not only dared to stand up to humiliation and sexual abuse but also used the system to turn the tables on her oppressors.

It should strike a particular chord with readers today when the Me Too, Time's Up and other movements for women's empowerment around the world are gaining strength, as women (and men!) fight back against centuries of male oppression and the power of patriarchy everywhere.

There are many examples of women wreaking revenge to be found in literature, myth and history. The Greek heroine, Medea, killed her sons to register her protest against her husband. Draupadi, the heroine of the Mahabharata, untied her hair and took an oath to bind it up again only when Dushasana was killed by Bhima and her hair smeared with his blood. Kannagi, whose husband was unjustly hanged by the Pandya king, burnt the city of Madurai to avenge her husband's death. However, all these acts of revenge were personal in nature. But Thatri's (or Paptikutty's) revenge was different. Although it began as an act of personal revenge, by the end it affected the whole community of men who were treating their women badly. It is worth remembering that all the reforms in the Namboodiri community began after this milestone event in the history of the women of Kerala.

Most of Matampu's women characters are strong, supportive, compassionate beings. They make a difference in the lives of the people who surround them and depend on them. Thazhamangalam Achan Namboodiri's mother; Mathukutty, born into a family of courtesans; Ramanikutty, the ruling king's niece who was used to the idea of more than one resident husband, are all good examples. They all belong to the class of traditional, subjugated and oppressed women. But through their courage they chose to be different and redeemed themselves and the men around them.

Matampu, through his book, shows the world that when they have the courage to face the odds, women become leaders and heroines of society. It is the author's clarion call to all women to break their shackles and emerge as independent human beings.

Vasanthi Sankaranarayanan
Chennai 2018

Translator's Introduction to the First Edition

Brushte (social excommunication) was a common practice among Namboodiris (upper-class Brahmins) of Kerala in the nineteenth and early twentieth centuries. The excommunication was done after a trial of caste offence conducted according to the canons prescribed in the *Smritis* (that part of the Vedas where the canonical laws are codified). The trial was called smarthavicharam (trial according to the laws of Smritis). A detailed description is available in W. Logan's *Manual on the Malabar District*, which is given as an appendix to this text. It may not be possible for all readers to consult it before starting the novel but it carries a clear picture of the customary trial proceedings and the various rituals connected with it. Logan describes in it that when a woman is suspected by her own kinsmen or by neighbouring Brahmins of having been guilty of light conduct, she is under pain of excommunication and all 'her kinsmen placed under restraint'. The local chieftain's sanction for the trial of caste offence is necessary. There are special Namboodiri families known as Bhattathiris who are privileged to furnish the president (smarthan) and the number of members (mimamsakas) required to form a tribunal. The author Matampu Kunhukuttan's grandfather was a smarthan for such trials.

It is clear that the trials mainly affected the Namboodiri women. While the code of restrictions on their moral behaviour was severe, it was relaxed in the case of Namboodiri men. As a result, the latter were allowed to have illicit liaisons, provided these affairs were restricted to women of castes other than their own. The virtue of the Namboodiri women was protected and preserved to prevent them from illicit affairs with men of their own or other castes. These women had to remain untouched to avoid any dilution of the Namboodiri lineage. However, this system had an oppressive effect on Namboodiri women. From puberty, they were confined to their houses, known as nalukettus,[183] to avoid any contact with men. The very architecture of these houses, with the four-wall enclosure and the inner courtyard which comprised the women's world, signified this state of seemingly voluntary imprisonment of women. After marriage, they were not even allowed to visit their parents. The only occasion when they came out of their houses was to visit the temples. On such occasions too, they were escorted by maidservants and covered at least partially and symbolically by the protecting palm-leaf umbrellas. The words 'antharjanam' (those who remained inside) and 'asooryampasyakal' (people unseen even by the sun's rays) denote the extent of their house arrest. Any slight deviation from this routine was considered a sin and those women were ostracized and eventually excommunicated.

There was another custom among the Namboodiris that added to the frustration and suffering of their women. Says T. K. Gopal Panikkar in his book *Malabar and Its Folk*:

> ...the laws strictly ordained that only the eldest member of a household shall be left free to enter into a lawful wedlock with a woman of their own caste, the younger members being left to shift for themselves in this matter. In ancient times the only asylum which the latter could find in the existing social circumstances was in the Nair families which settled round about them.[184]

---

[183]From 'nalu' (four) and 'kettu' (walled structure).
[184]T. K. Gopal Panikkar, *Malabar and its Folk*, Madras: G. A. Natesan and Co., 1900, p. 36.

This practice had a dual effect. The younger Namboodiris, prohibited from legal marriages within their own caste, had a number of liaisons with women from other castes. The ratio of eligible Namboodiri men to Namboodiri women waiting to get married was appallingly low. Another unfortunate aspect was that a single Namboodiri man could marry as many as four Namboodiri women. As a result, young girls were married off to old men—either widowers or men marrying for the second, third or even a fourth time. Widowhood or sharing of a husband (with his other wives) were the cruel fates which awaited them. All these restrictions, the consequent sexual frustration and the insecurity of widowhood, had their own effect on the psyche of Namboodiri women. Most of them preferred to suffer in silence rather than face the consequences of illicit liaisons and trials for caste offences. Although there must have been many cases of women who had affairs with men from their own or other castes, few such cases came to light or were announced for fear of being branded an outcaste.

The significance of brushte or the trial described in this novel is that it resulted in not only the loss of caste of the woman in question, but of sixty-four men—Namboodiris, Nairs and Thampurans (upper classes). It is based on an actual event which took place in 1905. Kuriyedathu Thatri, a Namboodiri woman who was frustrated by the innumerable restrictions placed on her by the conventions of the Namboodiri clan and her husband's neglect and indifference, deliberately conducted secret liaisons with prominent men of several upper caste families. She kept proofs of these liaisons either by way of mementos given by her lovers or through recording intimate physical details such as birthmarks on the genitals. At the time of her trial, she produced these proofs and argued that if she were to be pronounced an outcaste, so too should all the men who had had liaisons with her. The logic of her argument was infallible and the Brahmin judges as well as the King were forced to declare as outcastes sixty-four outstanding men from prominent families.

This event rocked the whole social system of Kerala and resulted in various social reforms among the Namboodiris, initiated by a few young revolutionary Namboodiris who formed a society called Yogakshema. Illicit liaisons with other caste women and the prohibition of the younger men in a Namboodiri household from marrying into their own caste were abolished. Therefore, this event was an important landmark in the social, political and economic history of Kerala. It must be pointed out that we do not know the exact nature of the humiliation suffered by the young lady, Thatri, which forced her into this scheme of vendetta, and whether the method she adopted was correct is debatable. But the question one has to ask at this juncture is: did she have any other option? Would those elders, steeped in their traditions and corrupt practices, have listened to her, a woman in agony, alone without support and protection? Thatri is reported to have moved to Tamil Nadu and is said to have lived up to the age of eighty.

There are two other works in Malayalam which deal with the same theme, from two different perspectives—Lalithambika Antharjanam's short story, *Pratikaradevata* (*The Goddess of Revenge*) and K. B. Sreedevi's novel, *Yagnam* (*Sacrifice*).

It is indeed remarkable that a theme which reveals the corrupt practices of Namboodiris and the ill-treatment meted out to their women and resulted in an event which rocked the very foundations of their clan has been tackled artistically only by Namboodiris—two women and a man. Therefore, the three works have a poignancy of their own that reflects a mixture of pathos and revolutionary courage. Though all the three literary pieces are noted for their sensitive portrayal of an event which touched the lives of generations of Namboodiris, Matampu Kunhukuttan's work assumes a greater significance, in that he, a man, is apparently able to view the woman's pivotal role in this revolution in the social structure of Kerala, and of the Namboodiri community in particular. Thatri's act of revenge is justified and praised (in fact, elevated from an act of common vendetta to one of social reform) by Matampu whereas the two women authors have their own reservations about the method adopted to wreak revenge and affect radical social change.

The structure of the novel is very interesting. While the narrative element is preserved, the linear structure is broken by simultaneous introductions of distinct strands of subplots in the story. While the central story takes its own course, the five subplots also flow alongside to their own conclusions. While the heroine Paptikutty's story is the major theme, the five subplots also are important, in that they provide the social and political fabric which led to Paptikutty's story. Thazhamangalam Achan Namboodirippad's family story gives us glimpses into the lives and activities of powerful Namboodiri households that existed in the earlier part of the twentieth century. The feudal system of land ownership, the joint family system, caste hierarchy, the religious as well as secular superiority of these Namboodiri families over the entire land, the corrupt and pleasure-loving practices indulged in by the men of the family, harassment and oppression of the women of the family, all these form a general background for the story which gives credence to the turn of events narrated therein.

The second strand, Chematiri Otikkan's story, with his saintly father, Akkithar, his revolutionary son, Ichatha and his two weak brothers, Pachu and Vasu, forms a counterpoint to the Thazhamangalam episodes. This family represents the virtues of the Namboodiris—strength of character, detachment through spirituality, intellectuality, self-actualization through true knowledge and, above all, tolerance and compassion towards other human beings.

One gets a glimpse of another powerful upper-caste community of Kerala—the Thampurans or the ruling caste. The corrupt and excessive practices followed by them are well described in the episodes of Chinnammu Thampuran, Ramanikutty and Kunhaniyan. Nambyattan's relationship with Mathukutty and the revolutionary activities of Young Otikkan and his mentor Unni Namboodiri form the other strands of the story. Matampu adopts a style of pursuing these six different strands in the plot simultaneously. At times they merge into one another, but in general, they give the impression of tributaries of a river which have a path and flow of their own while being a part of the larger confluence. The shift in emphasis from one subplot to another gives the whole text a lateral density which elevates it to being a novel of a particular era rather than the linear narration of a particular event. The diffused thematic concentration on the custom of brushte, the brutality and injustice heaped on victims through a narration of the social and political milieu they existed in, becomes, in a way, the cause of it. The novel avoids sensationalization of an event which has all the elements of a sensation.

In the end, the different strands of the story are not neatly tied and do not have a definite conclusion. Matampu adopts a different technique where these characters are all left independent, each to pursue his or her individual predilection. Paptikutty and Young Otikkan get into trains and go their way. Chami, Unni Namboodiri and Kunhaniyan watch them go; they do not know when they will meet again. Nambyattan bids farewell to his brother and sets out on his pilgrimage. Akkithar dies grandly and almost ritualistically, so far is he from the universal fear of death. So we are left with a feeling that life is an eternal flow and that it moves on to different spaces and realms, without ending abruptly. Like life, the novel, too, does not really end where it ends. The end is left open, with space for further developments and new avenues.

The cyclical pattern of life, which goes through periods of

elevation, degradation, redemption and regeneration, is effectively captured. The isolated individual's spiritual attainment, and its ineffectiveness against the tidal wave of a whole society's moral corruption, is touched upon. Echoes of kaladosham (the evils of time) are constantly heard. When time overtakes human action, a sage like Akkithar advises that the only remedy is the constant recital of the Gayatri Mantra, which is an invocation not to a special deity, but a plea for eternal and everlasting knowledge and wisdom. Faith in true knowledge is emphasized. Another haunting fact is that in any patriarchal society, the victims are invariably women. Therefore, it logically concludes that woman-power alone can rise and redeem itself from bondage, oppression, humiliation and subjection. Many a time this power has been motivated by revenge, for revenge alone can rise above the feminine qualities of forgiveness, love and tolerance, which at times lead women to submissiveness and domination and subjugation by men. Revenge, the main theme, thus moves away from personally motivated vendetta to social revolution and redeems itself from petty and narrow implications.

Though revenge is the central leitmotif of this book, there are two others—one of the journey and the other of repentance and redemption—that are constantly used. The idea of revenge itself is very different from the Sicilian concept of vendetta or the Western notion of ritualistic annihilation of an enemy. While Paptikutty's initial motive of revenge was born out of personal humiliation and rape, it took on wider dimensions as she continued her unaided, single-minded crusade against her community. On many occasions, the author evokes the image of an incarnation of Kali, the Mother Goddess, the annihilator of demons and evil spirits. The novel begins with a mention of sixty-four arts and takes on the form of an invocatory chant. It brings to mind the well-known religious poem 'Lalita Sahasranamam', where Durga, the divine Mother Goddess, is invoked as 'Chatusastikalamayi', which roughly translated means that she is the source of the sixty-four arts. Again, throughout the book, the constant reference to Paptikutty's self-awareness about the kind of sacrifice she had to perform is also a reminder of another aspect of the Mother Goddess as described in the above mentioned poem—'Cidagnikunda sambhuta' (born from the pit of the fire of consciousness). Throughout, there is a hint that this is not an ordinary revenge, but a spiritual act of cleansing. Paptikutty becomes an instrument of this divine act and is imbued with the aura of an incarnation. Even as she recognizes her avatararahasya (the secret of her incarnation), the reader is also initiated into the need for such an avatara at such a time.

The Namboodiris, the guardians of knowledge and spiritual attainments, intoxicated by their power and ceaseless pursuit of physical pleasure, ignored their womenfolk and subjected them to persecution directly through assault and indirectly through indifference and ritualistic obligations. There was no authority to question them because their caste and their position as lawgivers gave them the power they needed, even to misinterpret religious texts to suit their convenience. There was only one way by which to wake them from their drugged stupor and this was through a rude shock administered by one of their own kind. A woman's revenge took on the dimension of a revolution for social reform, a universal act. Paptikutty saw herself as an instrument of this far-reaching reform. Once she achieved her objective she planned to kill herself through self-immolation. Otikkan, through his disciple, Chami, prevented this and sent her away from Kerala to start life anew.

The other leitmotif of the journey has been used throughout in a physical, metamorphical and metaphysical sense. Akkithar saw his life as an onward journey towards spiritual release. Nambyattan became a pilgrim, a wandering mendicant who sought redemption for his sins. Paptikutty actually gets into a train and moves on towards new lands, new beginnings. Young Otikkan, who initiated a reform movement, also boards a train to go to a new place in search of knowledge and a new life for himself and others in his community. The book ends on a note of continuous, ceaseless journey to new worlds, new beginnings.

The last leitmotif I wish to discuss is the one of redemption through repentance. Here, it is possible that the author uses the Christian idea of repentance. Mathukutty reminds one of Mary of Magdalene and Nambyattan himself becomes a great example of a Christian soul in search of repentance and redemption. The idea of 'sin' itself is of Christian origin. In the Hindu way of life, purification through rituals, even through good thoughts and good deeds and self-immolation, is advocated. This idea of the recognition of one's own sins, active repentance for them, confessing them in public and seeking forgiveness and redemption is rather more Christian than Hindu. Admission of guilt and repentance can become instruments of redemption. Compassion towards the guilty, a typical Christ-like trait, has also been vividly shown in the meeting between Nambyattan and his teacher, Akkithar, whom he had insulted and dismissed in his adolescence. Whether the author was actively influenced by the image of Christ and Christian principles of charity and compassion is debatable. However, his appreciation of certain Western ideas such as English education to widen one's outlook, a less restrictive society which allows freedom of movement, expression and thought, the advantages of a casteless society, all come through clearly in this book. Coupled with his revolutionary ideas and keen sense of reform and change in society, there is also a respect for the highly valued principles of a traditional Hindu society—the learning of the Vedas and the Sanskrit language, the faith in the Gayatri Mantra which is an invocation to knowledge, the faith in karma, regard and respect for mother and family and tolerance towards all. It is therefore a balanced mixture of Eastern and Western thought that is reflected in the text. But the author is far ahead in his times in his appreciation of the revolutionary spirit of the woman, who remained ignored and humiliated. The virtue of the method chosen by Paptikutty to avenge the injustice done to her may not be wholly accepted. But Matampu elevates the act of revenge itself by sublimating it from the whim of a sexually wronged woman to an act of reckoning which the Namboodiris of the time richly deserved. His descriptions of the seductions are poetic and sensitive rather than explicit and vulgar. The bitterness of Paptikutty's revenge is counterbalanced by the heroine's humane expressions and the selfless motivation of her act.

Brushte (*Outcaste*) is a period novel and the author a Namboodiri. The language used by Matampu in this text is a mixture of Sanskritized Malayalam and the colloquial conversational dialect which is special to the Namboodiri community. The wit and humour for which the Namboodiris are famous also comes through well. At times, Matampu uses sheer poetic prose which can be quoted as good examples of the magical power of words when aptly used. His sarcasm and irony are sharp and powerful, but throughout the book these traits are counterbalanced by compassion. The interspersion of a short, pithy word or two with sentences of normal length add variety to the descriptions. It also lends an air of crisp suspense to the whole tone of the narration. Apart from all this is the lavish use of Sanskrit verses.

In order to overcome the difficulties in translation presented by a combination of these factors, I have used approximations wherever possible and have changed the construction of the sentences so that they made sense in English. Detailed notes have been included in order to help the reader understand the references and allusions in the novel without marring the flow of the language. Emphasis has been on not losing the spirit of the novel while simplifying it for a reader unaware of historical and cultural contexts, and keeping the flow of the language creative, instead of turning it into a literal rendering.

The novel is rich in character studies. With his inimitable poetic prose and emotional awareness, Matampu has drawn a world of men and women who are combinations of character traits—strong and weak, vibrant and vicious, sinful and saintly, victimized and vanquished, ritualistic and rebellious. Thus we have a rich and varied range of character traits—the repentance of the profligate Nambyattan and the prostitute Mathukutty; the caring, nurturing mother of Thazhamangalam House; reverence to the teacher shown by Chami; the saintliness of the detached and the action-oriented Akkithar and Chematiri; the cowardice of Neelan and several others; the amorality of the powerful Achan Namboodiri and the slavishness of a whole middle class of Nairs to the upper castes and the British king. It is a virtual panorama of binary oppositions—victims and dictators, slaves and revolutionaries, the traditional and the progressive, love and lust. But these oppositions or polarizations are not representative of a clear-cut, black and white, right and wrong, or good and evil syndrome. There is no overt recrimination or praise, only a suggestion of it. Matampu explores these character traits with such finesse that they come alive and are etched in the reader's memory forever.

The book offers a glimpse of the socio-cultural and political setup in the Kerala of the late nineteenth and early twentieth centuries. The repression of the caste and class system, the oppressive feudal land-owning system, the subjugation of women, the restrictions wrought by extremely ritualistic, religious practices, the self-indulgence and profligacy of the upper-caste males and its effects on the lower castes, the native ruler's submissive attitude to the British and the indifference to the fate of his subjects, are all subtly pointed out. It is a keen study of the life, character, architecture, customs, rituals and relationships of the Namboodiris at the turn of century.

Finally, it is a book which explores the profound emotional depths of relationships—relationships between father and son, mother and son, brother and brother, brother and sister, husband and wife, teacher and student, master and slave, ruler and ruled, young and young, young and old. One almost wonders how one person could have had such a deep, insightful understanding into relationships, having led a restricted, enclosed existence.

It is not merely a novel, but a detailed portrayal of the times it represents. As a literary document, it excels in a mixture of poetic prose, imagery, metaphor, use of sarcasm, irony, various layers of humour and epic structure. Above all, it is a moving piece on the human predicament—tragedy and comedy, pleasure and pain, strength and weakness, love and detachment.

In this attempt, I have relied heavily on the editorial expertise of Mini Krishnan and would like to acknowledge my heartfelt thanks and gratitude for the time she has spent with me in going over difficult passages and rephrasing and rewriting them. We have gone over the Malayalam as well as English versions several times while refining the final text. I have no hesitation in calling this a collaborative effort between me and Mini and dedicating the work to her and my ancestors, the Namboodiris of Kerala, whose wisdom, humour and zest for life have always been a source of inspiration.

Vasanthi Sankaranarayanan

Appendix

[Excerpt from *Malabar* Vol. 1, William Logan, 1897, appearing in the section on 'Caste and Occupations'.]

The episodes in the *trial of a caste offence* among *Nambutiris* are so curious, and throw such light on their ways of thinking and acting, that it is worthwhile to go into the matter in some detail.

The local chieftain's sanction for the trial of the offence was, as already said, first of all necessary. The *Nambutiri* family (*Bhattattiri*) which has the privilege of furnishing the president (*Smartha*), and the number of members (*Mimamsakas*) required to form a tribunal, are different in different parts of the country.

When a woman is suspected by her own kinsmen or by neighbouring Brahmans of having been guilty of light conduct, she is under pain of ex-communication of all her kinsmen, placed under restraint. The maid-servant (*dasi* or *Vrshali*), who is indispensable to every *Nambutiri* family, if not to every individual female thereof, is then interrogated, and if she should criminate her mistress, the latter is forthwith segregated and a watch set upon her. When the family can find a suitable house[185] for the purpose, the *sadhanam* (the *thing* or *article* or *subject*, as the suspected

---

[185]It is called the 'fifth house', i.e., the building next to the usual 'four houses' or northern (*Vadakkini*), southern (*Tekkini*), eastern (*Kilakkini*), and western (*Padinyyattini*) rooms or houses.

person is called) is removed to it; otherwise she is kept in the family house, the other members finding temporary accommodation elsewhere.

The examination of the servant-maid is conducted by the *Nambutiris* of the *Gramam*, who, in the event of the servant accusing her mistress, proceed without delay to the local chieftain who has the power to order a trial. And authority is granted in writing to the local *Smartha*, who in turn calls together the usual number of *Mimamsakas* (persons skilled in the law).

They assemble at some convenient spot, generally in a temple not far from the place where the accused may be. All who are interested in the proceedings are permitted to be present. Order is preserved by an officer deputed by the chief for the purpose, and he stands sword in hand near the *Smartha*, and members of the tribunal. The only other member of the court is a *Nambutiri* called the *Agakkoyma*, whose duties will be described presently.

When all is ready the chief's warrant is first read out and the accused's whereabouts ascertained.

The *Smartha*, accompanied by the officer on guard and the *AgakkoymaNambutiri*, next proceeds to the accused's house: the officer on guard remains outside while the others enter. At the entrance, however, they are met by the maid-servant, who up to this time has never lost sight of the accused and who prevents the men from entering. In feigned ignorance of the cause for thus being stopped, the *Smartha* demands an explanation, and is told that a certain person is in the room. The *Smartha* demands more information, and is told that the person is no other than such and such a lady, the daughter or sister or mother (as the case may be) of such and such a *Nambutiri* of such and such an illam. The

Smartha professes profound surprise at the idea of the lady being where she is and again demands an explanation.

Here begins the trial proper. The accused, who is still strictly *gosha*, is questioned through the medium of the maid, and she is made to admit that there is a charge against her. This is the first point to be gained, for nothing further can be done in the matter until the accused herself has made this admission.

This point, however, is not very easily gained at times, and the *Smartha* has often to appeal to her own feelings and knowledge of the world and asks her to recollect how unlikely it would be that a *Nambutiri* female of her position should be turned out of her parent's house and placed where she then was unless there was some cause for it.

In the majority of cases this preliminary stage is got over with little trouble, and is considered a fair day's work for the first day.

The *Smartha* and his colleagues then return to the assembly and the former relates in minute detail all that has happened since he left the conclave. The *Agakkoyma's* task is to see that the version is faithful. He is not at liberty to speak, but whenever he thinks the *Smartha* has made a mistake as to what happened, he removes from his shoulders and lays on the ground a piece of cloth as a sign for the *Smartha* to brush up his memory. The latter takes the hint and tries to correct himself. If he succeeds, the *Agakkoyma's* cloth is replaced on his shoulders, but if not the *Smartha* is obliged to go back to the accused and obtain what information is required.

When the day's proceedings are finished, the members of the tribunal are sumptuously entertained by the accused's kinsmen, and this continues to be done as long as the enquiry lasts. A trial sometimes lasts several years, the tribunal meeting occasionally and the accused's kinsmen being obliged to entertain the members and any other *Nambutiris* present on each occasion, while the kinsmen themselves are temporarily cut off from intercourse with other Brahmans pending the result of the trial, and all *sraddhas* (sacrifices to benefit the souls of deceased ancestors) are stopped. The reason for this is that, until the woman is found guilty or not, and until it is ascertained when the sin was committed, they cannot, owing to the probability that they have unwittingly associated with her after her disgrace, be admitted into society until they have performed the expiatory ceremony (*Prayaschittam*).

The tribunal continues its sittings as long as may be necessary, that is, until either the accused confesses and is convicted, or her innocence is established. No verdict of guilty can be given against her except on her own confession. No amount of evidence is sufficient.

In former days, when the servant accused her mistress and there was other evidence forthcoming, but the accused did not confess, various modes of torture were had recourse to in order to extort a confession, such as rolling up the accused in a piece of matting and letting the bundle fall from the roof to the courtyard below. This was done by women, and the mat supplied the place of the *purdah*. At other times live rat-snakes and other vermin were turned into the room beside her, and even in certain cases cobras, and it is said that if after having been with the cobra a certain length of time and unhurt, the fact was accepted as conclusive evidence of her innocence.

In cases when the accused offers to confess, she is examined, cross-examined, and re-examined very minutely as to time, place, person, circumstances, etc., etc., but the name of the adulterer is withheld (though it may be known to all) to the very last. Sometimes a long list of persons is given and similarly treated.

Innocent persons are sometimes named and have to purchase impunity at great expense. In one case a woman who had indicated several persons was so nettled by the continual 'who else?' 'who else?' of the zealous scribe who was taking down the details, that she at last, to his intense astonishment, pointed to himself as one of them, and backed it up by sundry alleged facts.

The persons accused by the woman are never permitted to disprove the charges against them, but the woman herself is closely cross-examined and the probabilities are carefully weighed. And every co-defendant, except the one who, according to the woman's statement, was the first to lead her astray, has a right to be admitted to the boiling-oil ordeal as administered at the temple of *Suchindram* in Travancore. If his hand is burnt, he is guilty; if it comes out clean he is judged as innocent. The ordeal by weighment in scales is also at times resorted to. The order for submission to these ordeals is called a *pampu* and is granted by the president (*Smartha*) of the tribunal. Money goes a long way towards a favourable verdict or towards a favourable issue in the ordeals.

The tribunal meets at the accused's temporary house in the *Pumukhan* (drawing-room) after the accused has admitted that she is where she is because there is a charge against her. She remains in a room, or behind a big umbrella, unseen by the members of the tribunal and other inhabitants of the desam who are present, and the examination is conducted by the *Smartha*. A profound silence is observed by all present except by the *Smartha*, and he alone puts such questions as have been arranged beforehand by the members of the tribunal. The solemnity of the proceedings is enhanced to the utmost degree by the demeanour of those present. If the accused is present in the room, she stands behind her maid-servant and whispers her replies into her ear to be repeated to the assembly.

Sometimes the greatest difficulty is experienced in getting her to confess, but this is usually brought about by the novelty of the situation, the scanty food, the protracted and fatiguing examination, and the entreaties of her relatives, who are being ruined, and by the expostulations and promises of the *Smartha*, who tells her it is best to confess and repent, and promises to get the chief to take care of her and comfortably house her on the bank of some sacred stream where she may end her days in prayer and repentance. The solemnity of the proceedings too has its effect. And the family often comes forward, offering her a large share of the family property if she will only confess and allow the trial to end.

When by these means the woman has once been induced to make a confession of her weakness everything becomes easy. Hitherto strictly *gosha*, she is now asked to come out of her room or lay aside her umbrella and to be seated before the *Smartha* and the tribunal. She sometimes even takes betel and nut in their presence.

When the trial is finished, a night (night-time seems to be essential for this part of the trial) is set apart for pronouncing sentence, or, as it is called, for 'declaring the true figure, frame, or aspect' of the matter. It takes place in the presence of the local chieftain who ordered the trial. A faithful and most minutely detailed account of all the circumstances and of the trial is given by the *Smartha*, who winds up with the statement that his 'child' or 'boy' (a term[186] applied by *Nambutiris* to their east coast *Pattar* servants) will name the adulterer or adulterers. Thereupon the servant comes forward, steps on to a low stool, and proclaims the name or names.

This duty is invariably performed by a man of the *pattar* caste. It is essential that the man who does it should himself be a Brahman, and as no *Nambutiri* or *Embrantiri* (Canarese Brahman) would do it for love or money, a needy *pattar* is found and paid handsomely for doing it. Directly he has performed the duty, he proceeds to the nearest piece of water, there to immerse his whole body and so wash away the sin he has contracted.

The next proceeding, which formally deprives the accused woman of all her caste privileges, is called the '*Keikkottal*' or hand-clapping ceremony. The large palmyra leaf umbrella with which all *Nambutiri* females conceal themselves from prying eyes in their walks abroad is usually styled the 'mask umbrella' and is with them the outward sign of chastity. The sentence of ex-communication is passed by the *Smartha* in the woman's presence, and thereupon the accused's umbrella is formally taken from her hands by a Nayar of a certain caste, the pollution-remover of the desam. With much clapping of hands from the assembly the woman is then instantly driven forth from her temporary quarters and all her family ties are broken. Her kinsmen perform certain rites and formally cut her off from relationship. She becomes in future to them even less than if she had died. Indeed, if she happens to die in the course of the enquiry, the proceedings go on as if she were still alive, and they are formally brought to a conclusion in the usual manner by a

---

[186] *Kutti*—child or boy. The phrase *Kutti Pattar* is sometimes used.

verdict of guilty or of acquittal against the men implicated.

The woman thus driven out goes where she likes. Some are recognized by their seducers; some become prostitutes; not a few are taken as wives by the Chettis of Calicut. A few find homes in institutions specially endowed to receive them.

These last-named institutions are of a peculiar character. Perhaps the best known, because it has formed the subject of judicial proceedings, is that of the Muttedatta Aramanakal in the Chirakkal Taluk with extensive jungly land endowments. The members of this institution are respectively styled as *Mannanar* or *Machchiyar*, according as they are men or women. They have baronial powers and keep up a sort of baronial state, for which purpose two hundred Nayars of the Edavakutti *Kulam* (or clan) were in former days bound to follow the *Mannanars* when out of active service. The members of the institution are recognized as of the *Tiyan* (or toddy-drawer) caste, and the sons of *Machchiyars* become in turn *Mannanars* (or barons). The women take husbands from the *Tiyan* community. The women who are sent to this institution are those convicted of illicit intercourse with men of the *Tiyan* or of superior castes. If the connection has been with men of lower caste than the *Tiyan* (toddy-drawer), the women are sent on to another institution called *Kutira Mala*, still deeper in the jungles of the Western Ghats.

Following on the *Keikkottal* (hand-clapping) ceremony comes the feast of purification (*prayaschittam*) given by the accused's people, at which for the first time since the trial commenced the relatives of the accused woman are permitted to eat in company with their caste fellows, and with this feast, which is partaken of by every *Nambutiri*[187] who cares

---

[187] *Nambutiri* and *pad*—authority

to attend, the troubles of the family come to an end.

Apart altogether from the scandals which are thus dragged into the light, it is a very serious matter to a family to have to incur the expenses of such an enquiry, for the cost rarely comes to less than one thousand rupees and has been known to amount to as much as twelve thousand rupees.

Nothing but the dread of being deprived of their caste privileges by the general body of their community would induce a family to incur the odium and expense of such a trial, and this feeling prompts them unhesitatingly to cast out their erring members.